"You can't tell me you weren't hoping to see me tonight."

A corner of his mouth rose in a sexy, confident swagger.

Mari thought of the tattoo on her arm that contained a drop of attraction oil in the ink and recalled her witch friend's words. *Just in case…* She looked at him with narrowing eyes, afraid to give away the truth that yes, she had hoped.

He touched her hand. The contact was instant and went straight through her. It took every ounce of willpower she could gather not to snatch it back.

"Potions?" he asked, looking at her open book. "Hoping to make a love spell?"

"A protection spell."

He laughed. "Darling, witches' spells won't protect you from me."

A tremor of fear zipped through Mari. "Why not?"

His eyes locked on hers. "Because you don't want protecting…."

****

Don't miss the bonus short story included in this book! Two stories for the price of one!
His Magic Touch *by Cynthia Cooke*
Originally published by Silhouette Nocturne Bites eBooks!

Books by Cynthia Cooke

Harlequin Nocturne

Rising Darkness #23
Black Magic Lover #96
The Vampire's Seduction #122

CYNTHIA COOKE

Many years ago, Cynthia Cooke lived a quiet, idyllic life caring for her beautiful eighteen-month-old daughter. Then peace gave way to chaos with the birth of her boy/girl twins. She kept her sanity by reading romance novels and dreaming of someday writing one. With the help of Romance Writers of America and wonderfully supportive friends, she fulfilled her dreams. Now, many moons later, Cynthia is an award-winning author who has published books with Harlequin, Silhouette and Steeple Hill Books.

THE VAMPIRE'S SEDUCTION

CYNTHIA COOKE

TORONTO NEW YORK LONDON
AMSTERDAM PARIS SYDNEY HAMBURG
STOCKHOLM ATHENS TOKYO MILAN MADRID
PRAGUE WARSAW BUDAPEST AUCKLAND

Recycling programs
for this product may
not exist in your area.

ISBN-13: 978-0-373-61869-9

THE VAMPIRE'S SEDUCTION

Copyright © 2011 by Cynthia D. Cooke

HIS MAGIC TOUCH
First published in ebook form by Silhouette Nocturne Bites

Copyright © 2009 by Cynthia D. Cooke

Dear Reader,

Welcome to the world of Vindecare, a school for witches steeped with secrets and intrigue. In this story, I've merged a hot, unbearably sexy vampire with a powerful opponent—a witch. With two adversaries so equally matched, who will be the victor in this seductive game of wills?

Will it be Nicholai, who, after relocating his clan to New York, found they were slowly disappearing and eventually tracked them to Vindecare?

Or will it be Mari? She has no idea that she's a witch; no idea how powerful she really is. The only thing she is certain of is that she can't stop thinking about Nicholai, the man who enticed her to break all the rules.

Witches and vampires—it doesn't get much hotter than that! Grab yourself a fan and enjoy the heat.

Happy reading,

Cynthia Cooke

www.cynthiacooke.com

This book is dedicated to Judy Mills and Sally Winn.
Thanks for the laughter and the long lunches!
I miss you both!

Chapter 1

The black-clad lead singer of Asylum screamed into a microphone, his red-rimmed eyes wide and dilated. The crowd bounced up and down, pulsating in time with the raucous whine of guitars. Blood raced. Adrenaline pumped. Sweat rolled off their foreheads and down the back of their necks. Nicholai inhaled deeply. He loved it all.

For a second, as he lost himself in the heady scents of humanity, in the hunger rising within him, in the energy throbbing at his core, he could almost forget why he came to The Chamber, New York City's premier Goth bar.

Almost.

He circled the dance floor, his attention focused on a beautiful woman with long dark curls. Her lips curved with the promise of seduction as she raised her arms high above her head and gyrated her hips, moving in rhythm to the pounding drums.

Nicholai's gaze traveled down the length of her slim,

tanned throat to her exquisite bare shoulders. She dipped her head and a vein pulsed in the narrow channel along her neck. Hunger stirred within him—rising, demanding release. He pushed it down.

Not yet.

She shot him a slanted look; her shining emerald-green eyes held his gaze. Her bright red lips a slash of blood across the paleness of her face. Fire blazed through him. She smiled—a come-hither twist to her lips that had his feet moving toward her. Even as his mind said…*no*.

Not yet.

This wasn't why he was here. No matter how badly he wanted—

"You're in luck." Darby's voice stopped his progression toward the floor. She rubbed her taut stomach against his backside, her hot breath whispering in his ear.

Her heat, her smell, moved through him, stoking the fire already stirring in his blood. Yes, luck would be with him tonight, he thought, as his gaze locked on the emerald-green eyes of the woman across the floor.

Darby clutched his shoulders, her nails digging in as she ground her hips against him in time to the throbbing music. She leaned close and whispered behind his ear. "There are at least three of them here."

Nicholai clamped his teeth together and sucked in a deep breath. Three witches to choose from. Three witches to bring to their knees. *Excellent*.

He pivoted and faced her, grabbing her around the waist. She wound her arms around his neck. He caught a subtle hint of gardenias and pulled her close as his hunger sharpened. The roar of her blood rushing through her veins tormented him.

Soon. Until the witch threat was eliminated, he would be completely dependent on her. And while Darby was scrumptious, he couldn't help longing for something a little…different.

Over her shoulder, he sought eyes of emerald-green, but she wasn't there. Darby would have to do. He guided her across the dance floor and beyond the curtains behind the stage. Enveloped by heavy black fabric, they were alone. His fangs dropped, sharpening. "Tell me what you've learned."

"I will," she crooned. "But you can't feed. The witches will sense you and we can't let them know you're here. Not until we know how strong they are."

Her sweet, ripe skin, so warm and moist, beckoned him. He reached with his tongue and took a small taste. *Damn.* Irritated, he pulled away, pushing his hunger down once more.

"Have you learned how they've taken out my clan?" he barked, then clenched his fists in a feeble attempt to rein in his mounting rage. "Have you found where they are holding Marcos?"

"Let's go," Darby insisted. "You need to feed. We can come back."

"I'm not going anywhere." Impatient, he pushed aside the curtains, his vampire's gaze searching the room for the aura of a witch, but he saw nothing. "You said the witches are here."

She peeked around him. "They are."

"Then they're shielding themselves."

Darby stepped back into the shadows. "We need to stay on guard." A slight tremble shook her lips. "They're very powerful."

She was afraid. What was wrong with her? He'd lived over two hundred years facing down torch-wielding mobs, hunters, demons and slayers. Did she think he would cower before a trio of girls?

"Not more powerful than me." He grabbed her by the arms

and pulled her up against him. "No one has ever been able to penetrate my shields."

He buried his head beneath her thick mane of black hair and pierced her soft olive skin. Her surprised cry quickly turned to a desire-laden moan. Warm blood filled his mouth and sluiced down his throat. Renewed strength surged through him and he focused on shielding them not only from prying eyes, but from any extraordinary senses in the room.

As he drank, he swept his hands up and down Darby's body, caressing the softness of her breasts, the firm roundness of her ass. He coaxed her closer and closer to the edge of ecstasy. He could hear it in the racing of her heartbeat, smell it in the subtle shift of her scent. He pushed his hand against the juncture between her thighs and within seconds sent her hurdling over the edge.

Her blood, warm and sweet, chased the tension from his body. His senses dimmed. The roar of the music all but disappeared. The smell of sweat, smoke and Darby's passion ebbed and all he was left with was a thick cottony cloud of nothingness.

No!

He fought against the void, reaching for the noise, the warmth, for Darby, but his fingers grasped only darkness, emptiness…nothing. Fear enveloped him within its cold grasp. He knew what was coming. He'd experienced the cloud before, mostly during his daytime rest, during his most unguarded moments. He tried to block it, to stop what was coming. But couldn't.

Nicholai. Help me! Marcos's voice seared through his mind, reminding him of his failure. Reminding him of all he'd lost. *Hurry before the bitch comes back!*

Nicholai wrenched back from Darby, shaking the fog from his mind. Noise from the club came rushing back, knocking him off balance. Pain pierced his temples. The shrill ping of steel strings, the hammering of the drums, the roar of the crowd, overloaded and overwhelmed his senses. Hissing in torment, he pressed his palms against his ears, bending forward until his equilibrium stabilized.

This had to stop. He had to find Marcos.

As the nausea passed, he wiped the remnants of Darby's sweet drink from his mouth and his fangs receded into his gums. Darby swayed toward him, pale. Too pale. Damn! He'd taken more than he should have. It wasn't that long ago, he would have been strong enough to sever Marcos's connection. He would have been able to keep in control. But now...

He pulled Darby out from beyond the curtains and helped her to a table. Pushing through the crowd, he went to the bar and ordered her a tall glass of orange juice. He brought her the drink and sat close to her, resting his palm on the inside of her thigh, monitoring her heartbeat, making sure she was going to be okay. He couldn't lose anyone else. Especially not her.

"You okay?" he asked.

She glanced at him, her eyes wide and vulnerable, and nodded. But he could see he had frightened her.

He was an ass. He couldn't continue like this. He'd promised Marcos, he'd promised all of them, he'd never go back to the essence. Not after what had happened before. But he couldn't continue like this. He had to have the strength to do what needed to be done. He had to find Marcos and the rest of his missing brethren.

"That's them," Darby said under her breath.

Nicholai's senses spiked to razor-sharp intensity as the woman with the emerald-green eyes sashayed onto the floor with her friends. Why was he surprised? Of all the beautiful women in the room, she was the one he'd been drawn to. Had she planned it that way? Was she powerful enough to overtake even him?

Without demon essence in his system, he could no longer be sure.

Though they'd tried in the past, there had never been a witch strong enough to overpower a vampire, let alone capture damn near an entire clan. Whatever weapon they had, he would find it. He would stop them.

Nicholai watched the witch with the emerald eyes, the way her body moved, the laughter flashing across her features and once more felt lust heating his blood. He loathed her. Her kind disgusted him, and yet, he couldn't stop wanting her. Was that how she'd captured Marcos? By using her tight curvy body as a snare?

The women laughed and danced as if the room revolved around them. And to some extent it did. People parted, making room for them. Every eye, male and female, was riveted on their shapely forms. Bitterness burned in his throat.

"I followed them here from the institute," Darby said, finishing her juice.

Color was back in her face. Relief flickered through him. He lightly touched her cheek with a pang of guilt. He had to regain control before he lost everyone.

"Are you sure you want to go after the witches?" she asked, fear lingering in the depths of her black eyes, though now her fear was for him. She was no longer sure of him. She was losing faith.

He leaned forward and looked her square in the eyes. "I won't leave Marcos and the others. I will get them back no matter what I have to do. Now, tell me what you've learned."

"The Institute of Vindecare was formed to hide witches from persecution during the days when witches were being burned at the stake."

"As they deserved to be," Nicholai gritted. "Demon's whores. All of them."

"Nevertheless, now its sole purpose seems to be to train them, to broaden their skills."

"And to kill vampires." He growled deep in his throat as he watched the women leave the dance floor and settle at a table near the far end of the bar. Each one was young and beautiful, but the one with the long, dark brown curls and wide green eyes was the witch he couldn't tear his gaze from.

"We don't know how they're doing this. We should leave. Start over somewhere else." The anguish in Darby's eyes implored him even as Marcos's tortured cries still echoed through his head. Not only would he find and rescue his brethren, he would find the weapon the witches were using against them, and make sure they could never do this again.

"My clan is my family. They depend on me. I won't let them down."

"But going after the witches alone? We don't know how they're doing it. We should wait. Watch." She reached for him, begging with her outstretched hand, angering him further.

He didn't have time nor use for fear. Rage seethed inside him. He stood and turned toward the arrogant bitches that had taken so much from him. The urge to destroy surged through him. He took a step toward them then forced himself to stop. To wait. To be smart. Be patient. Plan their downfall.

"Nicholai." Darby touched his hand.

He stiffened, wrestling his emotions under control. "I won't go without my clan. I wouldn't leave you, I won't leave them."

She clutched his hand for a long moment then nodded, released him and gestured toward the women. "Sheila Johnson, the tall blonde, is the one who's been at the institute the longest. She's your best bet to find out what they're up to. The redhead, Ally McNair, is strong and ambitious but undisciplined."

"And the brunette?"

"I don't have anything on her. She must be new."

He looked back at Darby, one eyebrow raised.

"My sources are good but they can't know everything."

"She's the one I want."

"But—"

"Bring the car out front, then come back in and wait for me."

She rose and squeezed his shoulder. "Be safe."

He didn't say anything as she left. He returned to the bar and ordered himself a drink, standing as close to the witch's table as he dared. Darby had her ways of getting information, and he had his. These women held the answers he needed to what was happening to his clan. He *would* find out the truth of where their power came from, and he *would* rescue his brethren.

No matter what he had to do.

And if he had to take out a few witches in the process? All the better. He hated witches with their muttered chanting and intense eyes. He especially hated eyes of emerald-green.

Once he found his brethren, he'd pluck those gems right out of her pretty head and keep them as souvenirs.

The witch turned toward him and a cold calm settled through his bones. He stared into her deep green eyes and gave her his sexiest, drop-'em-dead smile then leaned back against the bar and waited.

I'm coming, Marcos.

Mari Saguna stared into the man's dark eyes and a shiver tore up her spine. She'd been playing with him, practicing the new persuasion techniques she'd been learning all month at the institute. And it had worked! She was actually able to get people to notice her, to *want* her. But maybe she'd gone too far with this man. Something about the way his gaze followed her every move… Her heart kicked up a beat. Sweat dampened her palms.

"Now, there's a hottie," Sheila whispered into her ear. "And he can't take his eyes off you. What do you feel from him?"

Mari's eyes swept over the man, her gaze taking in dark eyes and chiseled cheekbones, a strong square jaw and inviting mouth. His lips lifted, twisting slightly as he noticed her perusal. Those lips would be more than she could handle. Just looking at them, at his strong, thick neck, wide shoulders and the bad-boy sweep of long, dark hair, sapped the strength right out of her.

"Focus on your impressions down here." Sheila tapped her stomach. "What's your gut say about him?"

Right now, it was fluttering up a storm. Mari tried to ignore the wanton need forming in her belly and dug deeper, refocusing on the man's deep brown, almost black eyes. "Power."

"Good. What else? Concentrate on more than those bulging pecs."

Mari took a deep breath, relaxed her center and concentrated. Blocking out the raucous sounds around her, she focused her energy on the man standing by the bar.

"Determination. Excitement. Anger. And…" She crinkled her forehead and tried to grasp hold of the final elusive emotion. "Pain."

Sheila looked perplexed. "Sounds like he has a few issues. Try probing for more. Is he dangerous?"

Mari did as she asked, thinking back to her lessons at the institute. She bent her head, closed her eyes and cleared her mind of everything except him. No pounding music, no laughing, chattering people. Everything faded to black as a vision formed, and it was just the two of them, the man and her, standing on opposite ends of the dance floor. Their eyes locked as they studied each other.

He moved toward her, pantherlike, each step filled with purpose. As he stopped in front of her, he reached out and with a gentle touch beneath her chin, guided her to him. Leaning forward, he tenderly pressed his mouth against hers.

His soft lips were skilled and inviting. They moved expertly against hers, stealing the strength from her limbs. His tongue swept across her bottom lip. She opened her mouth, inviting him in.

He entered, deepening the kiss, taking control, sweeping the inside of her mouth, cherishing her tongue. The tension in her tummy contracted into a tight ball of need. Her knees weak, she clutched his shoulders, pulling herself closer to him.

Close enough that she could feel every part of him, his thick muscular thighs, his warm hard chest, his strong wide shoulders. She held tight to him as his mouth released hers then gasped a deep breath as he rained fiery kisses down the column of her throat.

His skilled touch moved across her body, the curve of her breast, the gentle slope of her waist and hips, around her bottom then beneath her leather skirt. A shiver of excitement shot through her, bringing her up on her toes as long determined fingers played with the lace edging her panties, moving....

Mari's eyes shot open.

Shit! Slightly confused and completely off balance, she realized she was still sitting next to Sheila on a bar stool and the room was once again teeming with people. She shook her head but couldn't shake the craving, the overwhelming need for that man's touch, his kiss. She licked her lips and imagined she could still taste his mouth.

"Wow, girl, you're flushed," Sheila said, laughing.

Mari fanned herself as a wave of heat rolled over her, then placed a trembling hand to her racing heart. "Definitely dangerous."

"Whoo hoo!"

Mari let out a small laugh. "I feel like I've just been ravished."

"Honey, you look like you've just been ravished."

Mari tilted her head and glanced at the man beneath her long dark curls. He couldn't know what she'd seen and felt, and yet the cocky twist of his lips implied he did, that he knew exactly how much she wanted him and was more than willing to oblige.

Sheila nudged her. "Sounds like you're in for a hot night. Lucky girl! Just make sure your brother doesn't find out. Remember we're supposed to be practicing our craft at Java Blue."

Mari's eyes widened with shock. "Nothing is going to happen. Trust me. I don't even *know* this guy. I do not sleep with strangers." She let out a wistful sigh. "No matter how hot and sexy they are."

"Don't be such a wuss, Mari. Remember what we came here for. Practice what you learned in class today. Go on! See what you can get him to do. You're the one in control, not him. You have the power to make him do or not do whatever *you* want. Use it. I plan to." Sheila's lips lifted into a wicked smile as she sauntered onto the dance floor right up under the chin of a hot Latino.

Sheila was right. It was time to jump in with both feet and take control of her life. To take chances. She had to if she was going to find out the truth about what was really going on at Vindecare, what had brought her mother there and if it had anything to do with her death.

Mari took a deep fortifying breath then turned back to the dark, dangerous and exceptionally hot man by the bar and approached him. "*You have the power to get him to do whatever you want. Use it!*"

"You've been staring," she challenged, stepping a little closer than she normally would to someone she didn't know.

"Have I?" His voice was deep and carried a hint of an accent she couldn't place. "Perhaps you've been staring at me."

"Perhaps." Her gaze fell to his lips. She recalled their taste and the powerful feel of them as they took complete possession of her. But it hadn't been real. It had been a fantasy. *Her* fantasy.

Ask me to dance. Focusing her energy, she pushed the silent command toward him. Nothing happened.

Frustrated and slightly confused, she stepped closer. "Perhaps I've been waiting for you to ask me to dance."

One corner of his mouth twitched and tipped up in an arrogant smirk. His gaze traveled down her body in a slow sexy perusal, lingering on her breasts, giving her heart a jolt.

Without warning, she recalled the feel of his hands on her breasts and her nipples tightened, tingling in response. She shifted from one foot to the other, waiting to see what he'd do next.

He oozed confidence, standing as still as a statue of some ancient god, one haughty eyebrow lifted, mocking her.

Who was this guy?

He held out his hand. "Dance?"

His voice was warm, deep and slightly raspy. The sound of it grated through her, leaving a path of shivers in its wake. For a split second, she wondered if she'd bitten off more than she could chew. Would he be too much for her to handle?

Of course he would. She should start on someone who wasn't so strong willed. Wasn't so *sexy*. Someone who didn't turn her insides to mush with one melting glance. If she was smart, she would turn and walk away. Now. But then he took her hand and like a lemming with no will of her own, she followed him onto the dance floor.

He snaked an arm around her back and held her close, intoxicatingly close. Suddenly she knew she wanted someone like him tonight. Someone who would challenge her, someone *dangerous*. If she could maneuver someone like him into doing exactly what she wanted, she would deserve an A on the night's assignment. But even better, she'd definitely be on her way to becoming a powerful witch.

Mari entwined her fingers around his neck. She took a deep steadying breath but it did nothing to soothe her racing heart or salve the ache burning at her core.

Her insides were quivering, liquefying into a molten, lusty need. Each nerve ending felt exposed as every part of her rubbed up against him. Her thighs against his thighs, her breasts pressed against his rock-solid chest, her belly against his hard, massive sex. And then he began to move; rocking and swaying, they danced in time to the music as if they were one.

The room darkened and multicolored strobe lights circled around them. Excitement flooded through her and her heart dropped as if in a free fall. Was she ready for this? For him?

He slipped his muscular thigh between her legs. Erotic shudders pulsed through her. She held him tighter, and looked up into his eyes, probing, penetrating. Suddenly she couldn't breathe.

His eyes were fathomless, a deep well filled with emotion—pain, torment, love, desire—that overflowed and crashed over her. She held on tight as wave after wave rippled through her, making her want to cry out. Until finally the sound of his voice pulled her back from the yawning abyss.

"What is your name?" he asked, and she grasped on to the sound, the question, wondering what in the hell had just happened? What kind of connection had she formed with this incredibly sexy and powerful man?

"Mari Saguna," she muttered.

Surprise flickered in his eyes. He leaned down close to her ear. "Mariana Saguna," he said, rolling the name off his tongue, "is the name of a beautiful Romanian gypsy. And yet, you have the green eyes of a Celt. You bewitch me, Mari."

His tongue flicked across her earlobe. Shooting tingles almost lifted her off the ground. He guided her back and forth across his thigh, the seductive movements stealing her breath and what was left of rational thought.

The stiff cotton of his shirt rasping across the thin silk covering her breasts added to the clenching need pulsing through her. Large hands swept up and down her back. Teasing, massaging, captivating.

What was she doing? He was a stranger, and yet he danced as if he knew her...*intimately*. And she was letting him. Worse, she *wanted him*.

His hands moved lower, cupping her buttocks outside her leather skirt. He shifted and she could feel him, all of him, hard and large beneath his jeans. She bit her lip and ground her pelvis against him, feeling her need rising with each thrust.

The wine, it's gone straight to my head. She should stop. And yet she couldn't.

She wanted what he was offering.

His lips brushed against hers and her eyelids fluttered closed. He kissed her, his mouth possessing hers. She pressed her tongue against his, taking his warmth, wanting more.

He pulled back from her and she almost cried out. What was wrong with her? She didn't even know this man's name.

"Nicholai," he said, his voice washing over her. "My name is Nicholai."

Stunned, she stared up at him. *Surely he hadn't read her mind?*

"Sounds like a Romanian gypsy name, too," she said, and he laughed, a rich, husky chuckle that started deep in his chest and rumbled through her.

The song ended and they stood in the middle of the floor,

not moving, his fingers barely resting on her ribs and yet fire rippled through her at his slight touch. She stared into his eyes. She wanted to be with him, wanted to feel his skin against hers, his lips on her body, his hands on her breasts.

She stepped once more into his embrace and knew she would leave with him tonight. And in the morning, when her brother caught sight of her, when he discovered what she'd done, there would be hell to pay.

But at this moment, she knew with certainty it was a risk she was willing to take, and a price she was more than willing to pay.

Chapter 2

Mari followed Nicholai off the dance floor and into the crowd by the bar, her hand grasped tightly in his. His skin was cool to the touch, even though she was burning up. She turned, looking for Sheila and finally spotted her standing in the arms of the Latino. Sheila smiled at her and gave her the A-OK sign.

Mari hoped it was okay. She was considering leaving with a man she hadn't said more than a few words to and knew nothing about. But even as fear needled her with warnings, Nicholai's grasp on her hand loosened. He scraped his index finger along her palm sending shivers up her arm. Warmth spread through her.

How could his touch have such a strong affect on her? So strong she didn't care about anything but being alone with this tall handsome stranger. Never had she been so reckless, so—

Someone tugged on her arm, pulling her to a stop. She

turned to find Ally standing behind her, a look of disapproval darkening her expression. "What are you doing?" Ally asked.

"Is there a problem?" Mari didn't get on that well with Ally, but still she was surprised the woman would confront her like this.

Nicholai leaned down and whispered into Mari's ear. "I'm going to the bar. Would you like another glass of wine?"

She looked up at him, smiled and nodded.

"You've bitten off more than you can chew with that one," Ally warned as he walked away.

"We're just getting to know one another. It's okay."

"Is it?" Ally's tone was sharp and suddenly Mari had to wonder. *Was it?*

Was there more to Ally's interference than mere dislike?

"There's something off with that one," she continued. "Do yourself a favor, and stay far away from him." She turned and walked to the bar where she stood next to a dark-haired woman Mari had noticed earlier talking to Nicholai.

Did they know each other? Did Ally know Nicholai? Unease twisted in Mari's stomach.

"I'm sorry about that." She gestured toward Ally as Nicholai returned and handed her the wine.

"It's good to have friends who care about you, even if they are misguided."

She hoped he was right. Though she wasn't sure she considered Ally a friend. At Vindecare, Mari lived with her brother and a lot of other people studying witchcraft and yet she'd never felt more alone.

He smiled as he took her hand and her heart lurched. She wished it would stop doing that.

"There's an empty table in the back," he suggested.

As they walked toward it, a wave of negative energy hit Mari so hard, she faltered. Nicholai caught her by the arm. She leaned into him, as anger—no, it was more than that—

as jealousy rolled over her like a dark cloud, seeping into her pores and churning her stomach. She turned toward the source and saw Ally and the dark-haired woman both watching her.

Shaken, she turned away. Was Ally jealous of her?

Still light-headed, she let Nicholai help her to a table in the corner, hidden in the shadows away from the crowds and the bar.

"Are you all right?" he asked.

"Yes, thank you. I just got…dizzy."

He brushed the hair off her face, running the pad of his finger along the side of her head, outlining her cheekbone, her jaw. "You are very beautiful."

She smiled and tilted her face into his hand.

Nicholai continued his gentle caresses, running his hand down her shoulder, her arm, taking her hand in his. With his slight touch he ignited a fire that lit up her skin and turned her on, making her want and need more than any man ever had before. It scared yet excited her at the same time.

"Any place in particular you'd like to go?" he asked, leaning close, his warm breath tickling her cheek.

Yes. No. Maybe Ally was right. She should at least try to get to know him better before being alone with him. She was about to suggest coffee when suddenly his fingers were dancing up the inside of her thigh, sending fire shooting straight through her.

Her eyes widened as they caught his, but he just moved closer, the corner of his oh-so-kissable lips lifting in a smile. Her gaze darted around the room, but the crowd was thick and loud and no one seemed to be paying attention to them.

Under the table, hidden by darkness, his fingers rose even higher, flitting beneath her skirt. She caught her breath, but didn't move away. Nor did she try to stop him. Up and down, circling round, his touch was soft and teasing.

Her tongue slid out and moistened her suddenly dry lips.

He scooted his chair next to hers and dipped his head to nuzzle her ear.

"Anything in particular you're craving?" he asked.

His finger flitted over the silky fabric of her panties, skimming her sensitive spot and bringing her up in her seat.

"Coffee?" he purred against the skin just below her ear.

Her breath expelled in a shudder as a low moan caught in her throat. His lips slid down the column of her neck and he pulled her skin into his mouth sucking on it, gently nibbling.

"Wine?" he asked, his voice rumbling low in his chest.

She arched her back as desire washed through her. He slipped his finger beneath her thong, and she was lost. At this moment, she'd go anywhere with him.

His finger slid inside her, inflaming the ache within her. She swallowed hard, no longer wanting to leave. No longer wanting anything but him, right then and right there.

He withdrew his hand. "Perhaps you desire something a little more substantial?"

She bit her lip to keep from crying out, from grabbing him and pulling him back. Her heart was pounding. Damn it all, but she had never wanted anyone so badly in all her life. She shifted in her chair.

"Something." His mouth brushed against the corner of hers. "Like this." He kissed her, thrusting his tongue inside her mouth, sweeping, sparring, demanding.

Yes. More. Now.

She moaned and shifted again. Her hand fell into his lap. His erection was massive. He wanted this as badly as she did. So give it to her. Now. *Here.*

A giddy rush of excitement filled her at the thought of having sex with him right there with a clamor of people surrounding them, yet all too drunk to notice or care, each searching for their own release, their own moment of pleasure.

She kissed him, hard and wet, trying to show him exactly how she felt, exactly what she wanted. She envisioned him pressing her up against the wall hidden in the shadows behind them and burying himself deep within her. She pushed the vision toward him, making him see it, feel it…want it.

Wasn't that why she was there tonight? To practice her persuasion techniques on strangers? To get them to bend to her will? And this was her will right now. He wanted her, too. She could feel it in his burgeoning erection grasped tightly in her hand. She squeezed him as well as she could through the stiff denim, wanting desperately to feel more of him, all of him. To bring him as close to the edge as he seemed determined to take her.

She moved her finger along his zipper, found the clasp and pulled it slowly open. He gasped, pulling her tighter as she slipped her hand inside his pants, inside his boxers and grabbed hold of his smooth skin. A triumphant smile widened her lips. She leaned forward and whispered in his ear, "I want you."

Nicholai couldn't get over how hot the little witch was. Her touch and the salty taste of her skin almost had his fangs descending. He caught the eye of one of the patrons at the nearest table and mentally suggested he go dance. Immediately the couple rose.

Completely alone, Nicholai pulled Mari on top of his lap, positioning her to straddle him. Beneath her short skirt, the tip of his erection pushed against her thin silk panties, reaching for her heat.

He longed to rip the fragile fabric away, to drive himself deep within her soft, warm core, but he couldn't. Not yet. Instead he kissed her once more, tasting every part of her. He gently suckled the tender skin of her neck while probing her mind, but once again came up empty. Whatever information he was going to pull from her, he was going to have to get it the hard way. By talking.

By getting her to trust him.

He'd take her out to the yacht, open up a bottle of Dom Pérignon, ask her about her life and her family while giving her a slow seductive massage. He'd get her to open up about Vindecare. Find out exactly what they did there, who's in charge and what the hell they'd done with Marcos and the rest of his clan.

She broke free from his kiss, her hair mussed, her lips swollen, her green eyes hooded and heavy. *Mercy.*

His cock jumped, and she shifted, rocking in his lap, her smile wide and mischievous.

"Why don't we—" Before he could finish, she shifted again, her hand dipping between them. Yanking her thong to the side, she descended, taking him deep inside her in one swift thrust.

"Bloody hell," he gasped as her warmth encased him, her slick heat sending fire shooting to his core.

She grabbed his shoulders and started to rock in time to the music, slowly at first then harder, faster. How had she gotten the upper hand? How had the little witch taken control from him and turned this into what she wanted?

He grabbed her hips to lift her off him, just as her orgasm began to build. She tightened around him, pulsating, pulling him deep within her. Unrestrained pleasure swept through him. He ground himself against her, his mind nearly gone with it. What kind of power did she have, he wondered, barely able to hold on to coherent thought. How was she able to weave her web and ensnare him so quickly?

The tempo in the room increased, the drumbeat quickening to a hair-raising rhythm. Her body moved over his, bucking, tightening. Blood pulsed through his veins, rising, building... his fangs descended.

He turned his face into her hair, tasted her skin, smelled the musky scent of her passion and it pushed him closer to the edge, to the precipice where he'd be lost and completely vulnerable for that endless second.

Her heart pounded, the blood raced through her veins, and he wanted it. He had to have it. He clamped down on her neck once more, sucking her skin into his mouth, wanting so badly to take a small luscious bite.

"You can't taste. Don't let them know you're here."

Darby's voice echoed through his mind, but he couldn't stop. He had to have her. Just a taste. A small bite. He opened wide. The witch arched her back, her head rolling backward, pulling away from his mouth.

Damn!

Her core tightened, throbbing powerfully around his erection, drawing him toward the edge, closer and closer until…he lost all thought, all control and fell with her. Pleasure pulsed through him as his release filled her.

Nicholai, help me! Get me out of here!

Mari's head snapped up, her eyes narrowing with confusion.

Through the haze of his fading orgasm his gaze met hers and a connection formed. Had she heard Marcos's tortured pleas?

Then the connection was gone. She gasped a deep breath and fell forward, burying her face in Nicholai's neck. Slowly, after a long moment, her heartbeat and breathing returned to normal.

He'd lost control and she had taken charge. It was unthinkable and it would never have happened if he hadn't been in such a weakened state. He couldn't continue like this.

Yes, he promised Marcos he wouldn't take demon essence again, but he wouldn't be able to save them like this. He needed the essence to regain his strength.

He ignored the languid warmth from their lovemaking and eased the witch off him. Making sure no one's eyes were on them, Nicholai settled her into the chair next to him then fixed his clothing and stood. He still had a job to do, information to gather. This night would not be a loss. "You ready to go?"

She nodded, smiling, and with his arm around her and her head buried on his shoulder he walked her out of the club and toward the limousine waiting for them at the curb.

"Where are we going?" Mari asked as he helped her into the back of the limousine.

He climbed in next to her. "Where would you like to go?"

"I'm not sure." She glanced around her, her gaze falling on Darby up front in the driver's seat. She stiffened and her wariness thickened the air around them. "Maybe I should wait for my friends."

Nicholai leaned forward and closed the privacy window separating them from Darby. "We can wait for your friends here if you want. Or I can take you home and you can wait for them outside your gates. Either way, I'd like to spend more time with you. Alone."

Surprise widened her eyes before they shifted, becoming guarded. "How do you know there are gates where I live?"

Without skipping a beat, he took her hand into his. "I came to The Chamber tonight to find you. I sought you out, because I need your help."

She moved away from him, shifting to the edge of her seat. He was losing her.

"When my assistant sent me to the club to find a witch, I certainly never expected you to be so beautiful, nor had I planned for what happened between us." He leaned forward and looked her right in the eyes. "You must believe that."

Her cheeks colored and guilt flashed bright within her eyes. She blamed herself. *Perfect.*

"Although I can't say I'm sorry for what happened." He leaned forward to nuzzle her neck, but she pulled away.

"You know I'm a witch?" she asked, her voice high and tight. She was afraid. The subtle scent of her fear permeated the air.

"I should have told you right from the start," he said, and shrugged. "I don't know what came over me."

Certainly not her feeble attempt at using magic to seduce him, though that's exactly what he hoped she would think.

Her hands twisted in her lap before she shoved them between her legs. "Why were you looking for me?" she asked, walking right into his net.

"You are a witch, are you not?"

She pressed her lips together and stared at her hands. "I'm not sure exactly. I am very new to all this."

"But you live at Vindecare?"

She nodded, her big green eyes meeting his. He could see the wariness hovering within, the doubt, and the vulnerability. "Yes," she murmured.

"Then you are just the person I need."

"Why are you interested in Vindecare?"

"A friend of mine was last seen going into the estate. He hasn't been seen or heard from since."

Her forehead crinkled with confusion a second before caution filled her eyes. Yes. She knew something. Or at least she suspected something.

"I'm trying to find out what happened to him. Can you help me?" he pressed.

"Is your friend a witch? Is he learning the arts?"

"No."

"Then why would he have been at Vindecare?"

Nicholai hesitated. "I'm not sure. I thought maybe…" He

brushed her hair back from her face, his fingertips lightly grazing her skin. This time she didn't pull away. "Maybe he met a woman he couldn't stop thinking about."

She relaxed, her lips almost softening into a smile. "You miss your friend."

Her statement surprised him.

"I've felt your pain," she added.

Their brief connection in the bar. He suspected as much, but had hoped he'd been wrong. Having this little witch inside his head couldn't be good.

"I'm sorry." She leaned back into the seat once more. "I can usually control it, block other people's feelings. But while we were...um, while we were in the bar, my guard was down and I felt something from you. I felt...pain."

He cleared his throat. He'd have to tread carefully around her. She saw and felt too much. "Yes. I miss him. Sometimes I fear he needs my help and yet, I don't know what I can do." He shook his head. "It's very frustrating."

"Do you have a picture of him?"

Nicholai almost laughed. The only picture he had of Marcos was a portrait over two hundred years old. "His name is Marcos," he said, avoiding her question.

"Sorry, I haven't met anyone by that name. I haven't met everyone at the estate, though."

"How long have you been there?"

"Only three months." She stilled. "I came looking for someone, too."

"Did you find them?"

"Yes. And no." She titled her head back and stared up at the tall buildings through the car's large moonroof. Grief rolled off her in waves.

"I'm sorry."

She turned her head and gazed at him, the limo's interior lights glimmering in her eyes. "What for?"

"Losing people can be hard."

She nodded and they sat in silence for a moment, both staring out the moonroof.

"New York is so different from the country estate in New England where I grew up. I've only been living here for a short while, and yet it seems like I left my old life a long time ago."

He placed his arm around her shoulders and pulled her close to him.

"Do you miss your country estate?"

"Yes." She looked tired for a moment, and then mustered a smile. As he stared at her, he thought of the taste of her lips and the fire in her touch. He'd like to feel that fire again, but this time under his terms. This time he wanted to be the one to set the blaze.

He kissed her gently.

She kissed him back, a purr lingering deep in her throat.

"I can't help thinking…"

"What?" she pressed.

"That my friend, Marcos, needs my help. That he's in trouble."

"At Vindecare?" Skepticism twisted her lips. "The house is teeming with people."

"Do you know who is in charge there, who owns this place?"

"Yes. My brother, Sebastian."

"Your brother?" Was she involved?

He probed inside her mind once more, desperate for a sense of her intentions, for an indication of how much she knew but, once again, he came up empty.

Frustration squeezed his middle. Was she leading him into a trap? Would he be next? Was that why he couldn't read her?

Her jugular pulsed in her neck, taunting him…calling to him. One small bite and he'd know the truth about her and

Vindecare. One tiny sip and her secrets would finally be revealed. He had no choice. He had to take the chance. His fangs descended and he leaned toward her.

Chapter 3

Mari leaned forward out of his reach. "We're here."

Nicholai pulled back, cursing under his breath as the car rolled to a stop. They were parked in front of a large grey stone mansion tucked among century-old oaks that stood like sentinels behind tall iron gates.

Vindecare.

He took in the towers rising beyond the tall gnarling oaks. The Gothic estate looked like a dark castle that should be perched high on a rambling hill in England rather than set as it was in an exclusive community on the Hudson River in North Manhattan.

"It's incredible, I know. I still can't believe I live there," Mari said. "But if there is anything…wrong going on in there, I will find out. Trust me. I need to know, too."

"I appreciate that," he muttered, as he reined in his frustration.

She took his hand in hers. "I can sense how much your

friend means to you, how much you miss him. I know how that feels."

He leaned forward and kissed her softly on her mouth. "I believe you," he said, and he almost did.

Almost.

"Do you want to wait for your friends to arrive before going in?" he asked Mari, but it was just a formality. A nicety to put her at ease, even as he gently sent a mental suggestion that she decline.

She smiled and leaned into him, her lush body warm and soft. He caught a hint of her perfume mingled with musk from their earlier lovemaking, and inhaled a deep satisfying breath.

"That would give us more time alone together," she said, surprising him. She kissed him, her lips gently grazing his and causing a momentary distraction.

She seemed impervious to his suggestions. Again, he wondered how powerful she was.

"What exactly do you do in there?" he asked, taking in the tall walls flanking the iron gates.

"What do you mean?" She scooted back in the plush leather seats, her expression once more becoming guarded.

Ah, finally. She *was* hiding something. He pushed harder.

"There are a lot of rooms, a lot of places to hide…."

He stared into her sparkling green eyes, trying desperately to read her.

"As I've said, I haven't been here very long, and I haven't explored every part of the house yet."

"If it's anywhere near as fascinating on the inside as it is on the outside…" He filled his mind with open curiosity and gently nudged it toward her. Would she take the bait? *Would she invite him in?*

"I've been busy with my classes and…and getting to know

the other people who live here. I just haven't found the time to fully explore the place." Her gaze dropped to her lap.

A lie. Why?

She twisted her fingers together. Her anxiety was building. Not good.

"I have a lot to learn, a lot of tasks to practice," she said.

"Do you?" He arched his eyebrows in an exaggerated gesture. "Not such a good witch, are we?"

"Stop it!" She laughed and punched him on the arm, her guard and anxiety dropping. "Very funny."

"Which room is yours?" he asked, lowering his voice to a seductive, silky timbre.

She studied the large leaded-glass windows that shone with subdued light from the open foyer. "Up the stairs, four doors down on the left." She counted the windows. "There, that one. Why? Are you going to scale three floors up the stone wall to see me?"

"Would you be surprised?" He leaned over and nibbled on her bare shoulder just below the straps of her silk chemise. "Maybe I'll just throw pebbles at your window."

She smiled. "Like my very own Romeo."

He kissed her once more, soft and sweet. She felt at ease again, open and trusting. "Any way to get in without being noticed? In case I want to sneak up to your bed at night."

She laughed. "I might be able to sneak you up into my room when everyone's asleep, but I'm not sure I'd be able to get you back out in the morning."

He pulled her tender earlobe into his mouth and gently sucked. A soft moan escaped her lips.

"Unless you left real early," she added on a throaty sigh.

He rained kisses down her neck.

"I don't know why my brother doesn't allow outsiders in the house. Stupid rule." She exhaled deeply.

"Not even men who want to date his sister?"

"Especially not men who want to date his sister."

"Then we'll just have to make sure he doesn't find out."

"Yes," she agreed. "No one must find out."

For a moment he lost himself in their kiss. She was sweet and delectable—like fine wine or silky milk chocolate. As the sound of blood rushing through her veins grew louder, filling his head, stealing his thoughts, he knew he had to taste her. To take a small nip. He could think of nothing else but her warm blood trickling down his throat. Only then would he be able to see everything. In a flash he'd know what she was up to, if she was a danger to him, and how involved she was in the plot to annihilate his clan.

And if she wasn't? If she was as fresh and sweet as she seemed...?

His fangs sharpened, descending.

As if once again sensing his intentions, she pulled away from him. "Come on. Let's go. I'm going to show you exactly how to find my room."

Damn.

He covered his teeth with a half smile. "Promise?"

"Absolutely."

"I don't want you to get in trouble."

"We'll just have to make sure Sebastian doesn't find out."

"And my friend Marcos?" He pushed.

She stared at him. "You really think he's in there somewhere?"

"If he could have left or called me, he would have."

"You think he's being held captive? In Vindecare?"

Nicholai nodded, searching her gaze, looking for the truth.

"Well, I must admit I highly doubt it, but I'm willing to look around. It will give me a good excuse to check out the house."

"It is a fascinating house," he prompted.

"Now, if I were going to hide someone in a Gothic castle I'd either choose the basement or the attic. You decide."

An innocent enough question, especially when coming from a woman with a playful grin on her face and excitement dancing in her eyes. "You're enjoying this, aren't you?"

"Just a little. I like to be naughty every now and then, even if it has been a long time." She sighed. "Although I must admit this has definitely been a naughty night."

"I certainly won't argue with that." Nicholai winked, and followed her out of the car.

They walked up to the gate. He watched carefully as she punched a five-digit code into the keypad, then stepped back into the darkness as she spoke into the monitor.

"I'm alone, Johnny. Got tired and came back early."

"All right, sweetie. Glad to hear you're staying out of trouble."

"Always. Hey, is my brother still up?"

"No. Turned in hours ago. You need him?"

Nicholai held his breath. Would she betray him?

"Nothing that can't wait till morning." She flipped off the monitor and the gate opened.

Nicholai let out his breath but didn't drop his guard as they walked along the brick-paved drive up to the front of the house.

"No dogs?" he asked. "Or surveillance system?"

"Nah. Though I wouldn't mind a little poodle." She slipped her hand into his as they walked.

The little minx was enjoying herself. He almost wished he could share her enthusiasm. But this wasn't a game. She might not believe him, but someone in this house was systematically destroying his family. He would find out who and how. And if his little witch was in on it, he'd make sure she was sorry she ever crossed his path.

"The front door?" Anxiety nudged him as they drew closer.

"Don't worry. No one is ever in the front hall." She pushed open the door and walked inside. "This is why I have a hard time believing anyone could be held prisoner here," she whispered. "We barely have any security."

He didn't follow her through the doorway; he couldn't. Would she invite him in?

She stopped and turned back to him, looking confused. "Come in! It's okay, really," she whispered.

All the invitation he needed. The invisible wall forbidding him entrance dropped away and he stepped into an empty hall illuminated by a single dim lamp.

"Well, what will it be, attic or basement?" she whispered.

He closed his eyes and reached out with his senses, feeling for Marcos. Fury coalesced with anguish sucker punched him, bending him over.

"What's wrong?" Concern sharpened Mari's whisper and stole the smile from her face.

"Down." He gasped a breath and stood upright. "In the basement."

Worry lines pinched her forehead. "What's going on?"

Her enthusiasm had disappeared along with her smile and was replaced by fear and uncertainty. For a moment, he wanted to snatch back her excitement, to bring back the lighthearted innocence and easy laughter that had fallen from her lips and warmed his insides. If only he could believe it was real.

"I'm not sure," he whispered. "But I have to find out."

Suddenly Mari wasn't so sure she was doing the right thing. Every now and then a wave of darkness rolled off Nicholai, an endless roar of emptiness that washed over her and filled her with fear and sadness. Something was very wrong. Something he'd buried deeply.

Maybe she shouldn't have brought him here. But he was

so certain his friend was here. And if he was right? If there was even the slightest possibility that he could help her find out what was really going on around here, how could she not take it? There were too many secrets in this house, and so far she hadn't made any progress finding out what had happened to her mother.

She turned away from Nicholai, hoping to put a little distance between them so she could shield herself from his emotions. She opened a door off the main corridor and stepped onto a staircase, following it down to a windowless hall lined with doors on either side.

"Where are we?" he asked, his voice sounding tight and brittle.

"I'm not sure." She knew the staircase led to the basement, but she'd never been down here before. As they moved forward, voices sounded from an opened door at the end of the hall. Mari stopped. "Someone's coming."

She opened the door closest to them. They darted inside and she eased the door shut. With her ear pressed against the wood, she stood in the dark listening as two men deep in conversation passed.

She blew out a relieved breath then suddenly became acutely aware of Nicholai standing next to her. He rested his hand on her lower back. Tingles shot through her, spreading warmth in their wake. She wondered how a simple touch could affect her so strongly. She was tempted to lean into him, but stopped herself. There was something off with him; one moment she could feel his desire for her, and the next... it changed to something else. Something she couldn't quite grasp.

He stepped away from her. She peered through the darkness, but couldn't see him. As she moved forward, she bumped into a piece of furniture. The clinking sound of rattling glass filled the room as a familiar scent swept through her, stirring painful memories.

"What's wrong?" Nicholai asked.

She hadn't made a sound, and yet he'd sensed her emotions once more. Perhaps he hadn't been entirely truthful about his friend not being here to study the arts. Perhaps he'd had some empathy training, too.

She brushed her hand along the wall until she found the switch and flicked it on. As the room filled with light, images assaulted her: a dresser scattered with crystal decanters, a large bed covered with deep red silk, an oil painting of her mother and a tall man in a charcoal-gray suit above it.

The painting caught her, pulling her forward as a small cry filled her throat. She'd never seen her mother looking so young, so beautiful. And her father…she only had one small faded picture of him. No memories, no stories to fill up the emptiness in her heart.

"What is it?" Nicholai was suddenly beside her, his hand on her arm.

"My mother." She stepped toward the dresser she'd bumped into and picked up a perfume decanter—her mother's favorite scent.

"Where is she?" Nicholai asked, curiosity edging his voice.

"Dead." Quiet surprise floated through her. How easily the devastating word fell from her lips. It had been three months and until this moment, whenever she'd spoken of it, her throat closed up and a fist of pain squeezed her chest. She would have to force out a softened version of the truth—her mother had passed, she was no longer with her, she'd had an accident.

Or so her brother, Sebastian, had said.

"I'm sorry," he said, but his eyes remained flat. A platitude, said but not really felt, and one she'd heard too many times before—from the police, from Sebastian.

Mari shook off the ungracious thought and looked around the room once more. A cold unease washed over her. Surely this hadn't been her mother's room?

Icy fear cut through Mari's veins. Had her mother been kept down here in the bowels of this house? Was that why no one had mentioned meeting her? Mari's stomach turned as nausea rolled through her.

"Is that your father?" Nicholai asked, gesturing toward the painting.

Mari glanced up at the man standing beside her mother. "Yes." She walked toward the painting. "I never knew him. He died when I was small. My mother never talked about him or this place. I didn't even know I had a half brother until after…" She couldn't continue.

"A brother is a big secret to keep," Nicholai said.

"My mom was a very private person." Mari repeated the excuse she'd been telling herself since she got there. The only reason she could think of why her mother would keep something so huge from her. But she knew deep in her heart, there had to be another reason. And a damn good one.

She approached the bedside table and opened the drawer. Her mother's recipe book was inside. Tears flooded her eyes. She swiped them away and held the book tight against her chest. "Every day after school I'd meet my mom in the rose garden and we'd sip tea from the herbs she grew herself." A lump filled her throat. She forced it down.

"Even after I'd gone away to college, I'd call her every afternoon and we'd talk. It's those phone calls I miss the most. I still have the herbs and the recipes to make her special teas, but I just don't have the heart to drink it now that's she's gone."

Her heart clenched, and suddenly it was too much—the memories, the loss, the overwhelming emptiness. She was all alone in the world now.

Then Nicholai's arms encircled her. She buried her face into his chest and took a deep breath, grateful that she had someone to hold on to, someone who could help her forget. If only for a moment.

She buried the book in her bag. There must have been a reason her mother had been here. A reason she hadn't told her about this place, about Sebastian, or about the fact that they were both witches. There were too many secrets buried in this house. Mari would unearth them and discover what really happened to her mother, and what could have brought her back to a city she hated so much.

Mari's pain shuddered through Nicholai and, for a moment, he believed she didn't know anything about his missing brethren, this place, or what went on here.

"I'm sorry," he whispered again. And he was. Nicholai knew death. Dealt it. Lived with it. In fact, one could say, death was his constant companion. But there was no death like that of losing one's mother. A mother was the only person in the world who loved you no matter what you'd done.

No matter what you'd become.

He held her close, enjoying her softness, her warmth. "I feel lucky to have met you tonight, Mariana."

She smiled. "My mother used to call me that."

"She was a beautiful woman. Your parents made a striking couple."

She stared up at the painting. "I wish I'd known him. All I was told was that he was in charge of Vindecare. And his name—Count Von Lucieus."

Stunned, Nicholai stiffened. The name hung in the air like the curse it was. Von Lucieus. The man who'd waged war against vampires, killing scores of them until finally the vampires triumphed and he was brought down like the rabid dog he was.

Had the Count survived? Had he been lying low these past two decades, waiting to start up again? Rage burned Nicholai's insides. Was that what had been happening to his clan? Were their disappearances about something bigger? The start of a new war?

He looked down at Mari, beautiful and flushed with innocence. Was she innocent?

Suddenly it all made sense. Her supposed naïveté and innocence was purposefully used to tempt him. To seduce and overwhelm him. She'd lured him here, the leader of his clan— the Count's final prize.

How could he have been so wrong? She'd duped him into trusting her and he'd believed she was naive enough not to know what was going on right beneath her twitchy little nose.

Get out! Every instinct within him shouted.

"Come on," she said, sauntering toward the door, her hips teasing him, swaying with seduction. "Let's go see if your friend is here."

How would she play this game out? He followed her through the door, his senses on high alert. She led him down the hall toward an opened door at the end. If she'd never been there, how did she know where to go?

Was she leading him to Marcos and to a prison of his own?
Run!

She stepped inside the doorway and flicked on a light. He hovered behind her, crossing through the door onto deep red velvet carpet. Large wooden furniture and medieval crossbows filled the room. Rapiers, sabers and axes crisscrossed the walls.

"Wow, it looks like a museum," she muttered, as if she'd never been there.

She walked toward a staircase in the far corner of the room that descended into darkness and beckoned to him. "Come on. This looks like the way."

Warning bells fired off in his mind.

Nicholai.

Marcos! Bloody hell, he was so close.

Mari turned to look at him. Her face pinched into an expression of confusion, her gaze darting from him to something behind him. He turned around and saw the wall of mirrors empty of life, except for Mari.

He cast no reflection.

The game was up.

"Is this how you trapped Marcos? Do you think you'll get away with it? That we won't have our day of vengeance?" he bellowed, as his unleashed fury filled the room.

She faltered, the blood draining from her face and stepped down onto the first darkened step.

Earsplitting sirens filled the air. Lights were extinguished and replaced by a flashing red glow.

Marcos roared, the sound thundering in Nicholai's head.

Nicholai turned and bolted. He'd be back. On his terms, and then everyone in this monstrosity of a house would pay.

Especially the witch with eyes of emerald-green.

Chapter 4

Mari didn't move a muscle. She couldn't. She was frozen in place as sirens blared and red lights pulsed around her. *What just happened?* What did he mean by *vengeance?*

A violent chill shook her as Nicholai's words echoed in her mind. He was so angry. She could still feel the pressure of his anger pushing down on her. But why? *What had she done?*

And where had he gone?

She had to get out of there. She hadn't gone two steps when a panel door in the wall swung open and her brother, Sebastian, hurried into the room.

A hidden elevator? Brain-numbing alarms?

"What in the hell is going on here?" he thundered.

Mari froze, her heart beating painfully in her chest. The hard lines of Sebastian's face formed an expression she'd never seen before. He stopped short, surprise widening his eyes as he saw her. "What are you doing down here?"

* * *

Nicholai ran through the corridors as the sirens blared. He retraced their steps down the long hall and ducked into a side room when he heard two men coming toward him. After they passed, he bounded up the stairs to the main floor and almost made it to the front door when he saw that redheaded bitch from the club come in.

He slipped behind a large potted plant. She walked by but after a few steps, stopped. Without turning, she stood still, listening, her head cocked to one side. He concentrated on shielding himself until, once again, she moved forward. Albeit with reluctant steps. She'd sensed him before he'd had the chance to shield himself, but she wasn't going to push it and search for him. Smart move on her part.

He waited, not moving an inch until she'd disappeared from sight. A very powerful witch, that one, and he'd do well to keep his eyes on her.

Within no time, he was out the front door and into the night. Keeping to the bushes, he started toward the gates and the limo waiting for him when floodlights lit the yard.

Exposed.

Damn!

"What's that awful noise?" Mari yelled, slapping her hands against her ears.

Johnny ran into the room and toward a panel in the wall. He popped it open and hit a switch. Blessed silence filled the room.

"Apparently you triggered the alarm," Sebastian said. "It's pressure sensitive and wired into the stairs leading to the cat-acombs. We keep all our records down there so it's armed at night. Were you looking for something?"

A reasonable question. But there was nothing reasonable

about his expression or the hostility rolling off him. Mari's stomach dropped. What could she possibly say?

"I'm guessing her friend put her up to it," Ally announced as she breezed into the room.

Disbelief rose in Mari's throat as she stared at her coconspirator, who was supposed to keep her secret.

"What friend?" Sebastian's tone sharpened.

"The vampire Mari picked up at that new Goth club downtown."

Mari sucked in a sharp breath.

Shock widened Sebastian's eyes.

Vampire? *What?*

"You brought a vampire into my house?" Sebastian's tone shook with restrained indignation.

Mari stared at them. Had they both lost their minds? But as her thoughts reeled with the insanity of their words, she remembered Nicholai standing in the middle of the room, the wall of mirrors behind him. *He'd had no reflection.*

Ally laughed; her red painted mouth opening wide as the maniacal sound bounced off the walls.

Fear slammed into Mari's chest. She took a deep breath and clenched her fists trying desperately to staunch the panic racing through her.

Ally was insane! They both were. They had to be.

"That will be all, Ally." Sebastian's dark gaze hardened into sharp daggers.

Ally shrugged, tilted her head in a coquettish grin, then turned and sauntered out of the room, her hips swaying in a come-hither motion.

Mari took a step to follow. The quicker she got out of this house, the better.

"You don't believe the man was a vampire?" Sebastian's voice stopped her. His words were calm, but a frenzied sheen lit his eyes. Her gaze fell on her pale reflection in the mirrors behind him.

Nicholai didn't have a reflection.

How was that possible?

A lump caught in her throat.

She must be mistaken. It was a trick, a misperception due to the dim lighting. But the lights weren't that low. Not before the alarms went off.

Mari's stomach twisted into a hard knot. "I'm going to bed."

"I can see you don't believe, but if you did bring a vampire into this house then you are in serious danger. We all are. We need to talk about it."

"Seriously? Think about it, Sebastian. If Ally truly believed the man I was with was a vampire then why on earth would she have let me near him, let alone bring him back here to *her* home? It's absurd." She remembered his lips trailing kisses down her neck and the intimate way they touched, and shivered.

"You're right. I don't know what she was thinking. She should have brought you home immediately, and trust me, I will speak with her about that. There is a lot you need to learn about what we do here at Vindecare, a lot you need to learn about yourself."

Mari stiffened. He was right about that. Especially if she was going to discover what really happened to her mother, because one thing she knew for certain, her mother didn't die in a car accident. "Does that mean you're done keeping secrets from me?"

He paused, his eyes narrowing. "You're right. I have been keeping secrets. And those secrets could have gotten you killed tonight. You, my dear sister, are a true-blood-born witch and the mortal enemy of the vampire. You were very reckless tonight. Had this vampire discovered the truth about you, you wouldn't be standing here right now."

Mari kept her mouth shut, but couldn't help the cynicism she felt crawling across her face. *Nicholai did know she was a witch and yet, here she was.*

Sebastian lifted an eyebrow, mocking her. "You are very special, Mari. You're not just an ordinary witch. Your mother and our father were both very powerful. They were the Von Lucieuses and were known worldwide for their power and for the war on the vampires they sieged." He gestured, his arms wide.

"A war with the vampires?" She thought back to Nicholai's shock and the way he had stiffened when she'd mentioned her father's name. She shook away the insane thoughts. There were no vampires. Nicholai was not a vampire!

"I didn't want to have to do this, but I can see you don't believe me. You've left me no choice." He grabbed her hand and pulled her back toward the stairwell in the floor.

"What are you doing?" she demanded. She tried to tug free, but he was too strong. Terror shot through her as he pulled her down the darkened stairwell. "Sebastian, let me go!"

"It is time you faced the truth."

Shouts sounded from the house and an engine roared to life somewhere behind him. Nicholai ran at full vampire speed— a veritable blur to the naked eye. Even in a vehicle, there was no way the witches could catch him. In three long bounds he was up the wall. He could see the limousine waiting down the street a mere half mile away. But before he could jump to the sidewalk, something struck him. Fire burned through his shoulder. Pain arced down his arm.

"Bloody hell!" he roared, unable to control the furious twist of his features as his inner self surfaced. He yanked the arrow out of his shoulder, howling as a chunk of skin and muscle came out with the sharpened metal tip.

A jeep appeared through the tree line, barreling toward him. A man stood, straddling the backseat and holding on to the jeep's roll cage as he steadied a crossbow, lining it up to take another shot.

Nicholai jumped off the high wall, landing hard on the concrete sidewalk below. In the distance the limo's red taillights wavered, their glow shimmering in the darkness. He tried to run toward it, but he couldn't seem to make his legs move.

He fell to the ground. Crawled. Pushed himself back up. Were the red lights closer? He couldn't tell. The men were coming: he heard the clank of the gate, the roar of the jeep, the squeal of brakes.

Now he knew how the witches overpowered his clan. Fast-acting and completely debilitating poison.

Marcos, I was so close!

Tires screeched. The jeep? The limo?

He squinted through a blurry haze, but couldn't focus. Someone grabbed him, yanking him up.

"Marcos," he muttered, as his world faded to black.

Too quickly Sebastian forced Mari down the darkened staircase. She gripped his arm, terrified she would trip and fall. Then what would he do? Would he fake a car accident to explain it away? Was that what had happened to her mother? A tight ball of dread formed in her stomach as the thought struck home.

As they reached the bottom he led her down a hallway, rooms illuminating and doors opening before they reached them then closing just as swiftly behind them. Some sort of sensors or Sebastian's powers?

What were his abilities? How strong was he? With cold

certainty she realized he was right. She didn't know anything about him or her family.

They finally stopped. She blinked and refocused as the bright lights buzzed to life. She could easily be standing in a hospital room. Everything was too bright, down to the glossy white floors, and pristine counters lined with apothecary jars, cotton balls and boxes of rubber gloves. A stainless-steel box as long as a man sat atop a table in the middle of the room. What looked like a bag of blood hung from an IV stand, its long tube disappearing inside the box.

Alarm seeped through her veins.

"Say hello to our guest, Mari."

Mari forced herself to follow her brother and take a step toward the box. Her stomach lurched. Her throat tightened. She leaned forward and peered in then sucked in a startled and painful breath. A man lay inside, his hands and feet secured by thick plastic tie wraps, the IV pumping blood into his arm.

She stepped closer. He was ghostly pale, with dark smudges staining the skin beneath his eyes. Horrified she watched the labored rise and fall of his emaciated chest.

"This man should be in a hospital, not lying here hidden beneath the house," Mari stated. She recalled the absolute darkness of the room when they entered and felt her knees weaken.

She grasped the side of the box as horror washed through her. What kind of man could do this to another human being? She stared up at her brother in disbelief. What kind of monster?

The man inside the box turned toward her and opened his eyes. Mari gasped in a sharp breath. His eyes were a clear, icy blue unlike any she'd ever seen before. My God! Even this close to death, he was beautiful. She would even say angelic with his translucent pale skin and fine white-blond hair. A tear seeped from the corner of his eye and her heart broke for him.

She glared at her brother. "Why is he locked up down here in the dark and not at a hospital? How could you do this to him?"

"Hospitals don't know how to deal with cases like him." Sebastian's mouth twisted into something ugly. He turned to the counter behind him and pulled open a drawer.

"What are you talking about?" This was crazy—*he* was crazy. She couldn't imagine why she thought she could ever get a straight answer out of him. Was this the friend Nicholai had been searching for? God, she hadn't believed him. She had been so horribly wrong. She tried to recall what Nicholai had said his friend's name was. And then it came to her.

"Marcos," she whispered.

The man's eyes met hers and a small smile lifted the corners of his parched lips.

She had to get help. She had to tell someone. She had to tell Nicholai!

She reached down into the box to grab Marcos's hand. "Don't worry, I—"

Sebastian turned back to them and in a swift arcing motion, swept a sharp knife across Marcos's neck, slicing deep into the skin.

Mari screamed as Marcos howled, the pain-filled sound piercing her ears. Deep crimson blood seeped from his neck and pooled beneath his head.

"How could you?" Mari grabbed a towel off the counter and pressed it against the Marcos's neck. *Please don't die,* she thought, and held the towel tight.

Fire flamed in his eyes, turning the icy blue to inky black. Fear pinched the base of her neck, but she ignored it and pushed harder, applying more pressure even as the white cotton turned red beneath her fingers.

Sebastian leaned down into the box, smiling wide. His chuckling turned Mari's stomach. "Stop," she cried.

Marcos snarled, his beatific face transforming into that of a rabid animal. His mouth opened wide and wickedly sharp teeth gnashed toward her brother.

Horrified, Mari jumped away from the box.

"You see, dear little sister," Sebastian said with triumph gleaming in his eyes. "This is not someone who needs help. This is a vampire who, if given the chance, would rip out your throat and drain you dry. He has no compassion, no love in his heart, no human emotions. He is a beast. A monster who cannot be let loose into the world above."

Mari turned cold with shock. Was it possible? Were vampires real? But if they were, if it was true, then that meant…

The blood drained from her face.

Nicholai?

Chapter 5

Mari stared wide-eyed at the box, still unable to form a coherent enough thought to respond.

Johnny poked his head in the doorway. "He got away. A limousine picked him up before we could reach him."

Mari's gut churned. *Nicholai?*

A muscle in Sebastian's jaw twitched, the only outward sign of the rage seething within him. Rage that engulfed Mari as completely as if she'd been submerged in an arctic pool.

Sebastian's hard gaze locked on hers. "Who is he?"

Mari's throat tightened. She couldn't speak, couldn't swallow.

"Mariana," Sebastian warned, his voice low, his tone deadly. "The man you brought here is an animal. A monster like this one. He will kill you, and he will enjoy doing it."

Mari stepped forward, her head swimming with thoughts and images. She remembered the feel of Nicholai's arms wrapped around her as they made love in the bar, the way he kissed her, his lips nibbling and caressing her neck. She gasped, her hand fluttering to her throat. How close had she come to dying tonight?

"We must know his name."

She'd thought she'd cast a spell on him, that her persuasion techniques had made him want her. But she'd been wrong. He'd targeted her from the very beginning. Hadn't he said as much?

"Nicholai," she whispered.

Marcos, the *monster* lying in the steel box, turned toward her, his cold blue gaze boring into hers. For a second, she thought she saw hope flash within the icy depths. Then she realized the deep cut in his throat was gone with nothing but a smear of blood to prove it had ever been there.

A violent shudder shook her.

"Let's go," Sebastian said, and strode toward the door.

She rubbed her arms and quickly followed, suddenly afraid he might leave her there with *him*.

"It's time you knew the truth about Vindecare and what we do here."

The truth. She wasn't sure she could take much more of the truth. She glanced over her shoulder one last time as she walked out the door, leaving the room with its box to fall into the bleak dark once more.

A sharp sliver of fear sliced through her. Though she wasn't sure if it was because she'd just left him in there, or because he was there—a vampire, suffering alone in the darkness.

A vampire.

How was it possible? She didn't know; she only wished to God it wasn't. She followed Sebastian up the stairs and back into the room with the weapons lining the walls. Johnny and Ally stood in the corner, talking quietly. They stopped as they saw her, reproach filling their eyes.

Mari remembered the wave of hatred that had rolled over

her in the bar. Had Ally wanted Nicholai to hurt her? Had she been surprised to find he hadn't?

Mari took a deep steadying breath and followed Sebastian into a small elevator hidden in the wall. Before the panel door slid shut, she saw Ally descending the stairwell leading down into the catacombs.

What was she up to now?

Mari was about to ask Sebastian, but changed her mind as the elevator stopped. Bed and the seclusion of her room was all she wanted now. She needed to be alone so she could remember every word Nicholai had spoken, every soft touch of his hands and lips. How could he be a vampire and she not have known it?

She followed Sebastian out of the elevator and stepped into a visual nightmare. Numerous large paintings covered the walls, horrific images of vampires and demons feasting on humans, torturing them with wicked triumph gleaming in their smiles. Humans lay strewn across the canvasses. Their bodies slashed, their clothing shredded, agony writhing across their faces.

Mari turned away.

"Hard to look at, I know," Sebastian said. "But we must look. We must remember and make sure it never happens again."

"Again?"

"These paintings aren't the sick renderings of a twisted mind. They are our history. What happened years ago in the old country when our kind was persecuted not only by religious zealots, but also by vampires. They fed off us because they were afraid of our power, afraid of those few who had the gift to stop them."

He believed what he was saying; she could see the fervor in his eyes, hear it in his voice, feel it washing over her—an icy shower of fear that prickled her skin. She looked at the paintings again and wondered, what if Sebastian wasn't insane? What if he was right? Her stomach tightened as she thought of Marcos in his box and the inky black abyss of his eyes. His face had changed into something monstrous. *Something inhuman.*

She shuddered and wondered if she would ever be able to fall asleep again without seeing that face every time she closed her eyes.

Sebastian walked toward one of the paintings, his hands clasped firmly behind him. "What do you know of our father?"

Our father? "He died in a riding accident when I was a baby. Other than that, my mother didn't speak of him."

He turned facing her, his lips drawn into a tight line of disapproval. "She lied to you. He died fighting in the war against the vampires."

Taken aback by his accusation, Mari stilled, waiting for him to continue, her insides twisting into knots as an uncomfortable silence stretched between them. Finally, unable to bear the awkwardness any longer, she lifted her chin and leveled her gaze at him. "If she lied to me, I'm glad for it. I'm having a hard time grasping—" she flung her arm toward the paintings "—everything. Even after what you've shown me. I can't imagine trying to explain to a child that there really are monsters hiding under the bed."

"Children shouldn't be coddled. They can see and understand easier than adults. In their hearts, they already know the truth about the world around them. It's only with age that they learn to rationalize away their fears."

Maybe so, but Mari was thankful she hadn't known. She didn't want to know *now.*

"Why do you suppose your mother never told you about me? Or this place? Or your gifts?" he asked.

"How would I know? Did you ask her?"

"She said she wanted you to lead a normal life. She ignored your talents and treated your heritage like an abomination."

Mari stiffened, bristling at his words. "That's a little harsh."

"You are blessed with a pure bloodline leading all the way back to the old country. You have untapped powers and an incredible potential for greatness. You alone have the unique ability to rid the world of a vicious evil. Together, we can fulfill our father's legacy of destroying the threat of the vampire once and for all. I'm only sorry you weren't old enough to remember him. He was a man of great vision."

Her gaze once more fell onto the paintings. What kind of man surrounds himself with images of torment and death? A man like her brother.

"He had high hopes for you, Mari. Even at a young age, you showed great potential. He suspected you would be a key asset to the cause, but died before he had the chance to test you."

Test her? "What do you mean?"

"Your blood is poison to the vampires. It's the one thing that can defeat them. It's what we've been hoping for. It's what we need."

"My blood?" Bitter apprehension seeped into her bones.

"The longer you stay with us, the stronger you become. The more potent your blood becomes. Once your powers are fully developed, you will be unstoppable."

She shook her head, denial thick in her throat. "I don't know what you're talking about. I haven't become stronger."

"Can't you feel it?"

An insidious whisper of knowledge moved through her. Yes, she'd changed. She could sense things about people now, feel their emotions, their thoughts and intentions. Something she could never have done before. But if she was so powerful, so important in his fight against the vampires, would he ever let her leave? Her gut twisted at the thought.

"You've been testing my blood?" The hard truth dawned on her. "They said I was low on iron, that they were checking my iron."

"A slight mistruth. At the time you were not ready for all this." He gestured his arms wide, taking in the paintings covering the walls. "Three months ago, you were reeling from the death of your mother. You weren't ready to see the beast in the basement."

Marcos.

She hugged her arms as a cold chill swept through her. At this moment, she doubted she would ever be warm again.

"This man you met in the bar tonight—"

Her wary gaze snapped to his.

"—you brought him into our home."

Nicholai. Could it really be true? "I...I don't know."

"A vampire killed our father and tore apart our family. Tonight, it could have been you." He stepped in front of her and took both her hands in his. "I cannot lose you, too. You're the only family I have left. You must be more careful. Promise me, you will never see this...Nicholai again."

Family. She wished she could feel that way about him. Wished she believed he felt that way about her. But there were too many years between them. Too many...*secrets.* Why hadn't he come to New England with them? Why stay in this house alone without them?

"If Nicholai had bit me..." she started, the words trembling on her tongue "...would my blood...?"

"It would have paralyzed him, but perhaps not immediately. He could have had time to realize what was happening, to hurt you. Vampires are very strong, and when incensed, rabid. And you're still not at full strength. Promise me you'll stay away from him."

She nodded. But as she did, images of Nicholai flitted through her mind: his generous smile, his gentle touch, the warm taste in his mouth. She had felt so alive and uninhibited with him. But it had all been a lie. He wasn't even human.

Sebastian pulled her into an awkward embrace. "All we have is each other, now. We need one another. I don't want to lose you."

"You won't," she said, and realized he was right. He was the only family she had left. Her mother was gone, and he was most likely the only person who knew what had happened to her. But why the elaborate ruse of faking a car accident? If he knew anything about her mother, he would have known she didn't drive.

There were too many secrets in this house. Too many lies.

"I'm sorry, Sebastian, but I'm not sure I can stay here."

"You can. I will keep you safe. You can stay as long as you want. You are my sister. This is your home."

Home. Was it?

"Sebastian, I can't stay here without knowing the truth about my mother's death." She stepped back from him. "I know she didn't die in a car accident."

He studied the floor for a moment before finally meeting her gaze. "Why didn't you say something before now?"

"What could I say? I know you're lying to me."

He took a deep breath. "I'm sorry. I didn't want to have to tell you. But after what happened tonight, I can see how wrong it was to keep the truth from you—how easily it could have been you next."

A fist of dread clutched Mari's chest and squeezed so tight she couldn't breathe.

"Your mother also found the room with the stairs and one night followed them down into the catacombs. Down to the vampires. She got too close to the one you saw tonight. He beguiled her with his beauty, with his hopelessness. Sympathy overcame her better judgment and in one swift moment she was lost."

"Marcos killed my mother?" Astonishment broke Mari's voice.

"Marcos? Yes. How is it you know his name?" he demanded, his tone too loud and too sharp.

"From Nicholai," she whispered.

"You must stay away from this Nicholai."

"No worries there. Obviously, Nicholai sought me out specifically to get into this house. Marcos was the reason we went down into the basement."

She thought of her mother, her kindness and generosity. Like her, she would have been horrified by the beautiful man trapped in the box. Like her, she would have wanted to help him. She would have gotten too close.

A violent shudder shook her. What if Mari hadn't tripped the alarm on the stairs? What if she and Nicholai had made it into the catacombs and found Marcos? Would Nicolai have killed her as easily as Marcos had killed her mother? Anguish tore through her.

Finally she had the truth she'd been seeking and, more than anything, she wished she didn't.

Ally headed down the stairs into the lair of the vampires and into the room where they kept Marcos secured in his stainless-steel tomb. She peered down at him and smiled. Of all the vampires they'd captured, she fancied this one the most. She loved staring into his fathomless blue eyes, but more than that, she liked the way he tasted.

His plump lips looked even more inviting than usual. There was something different about him tonight. Or maybe she was just keyed up after her night out.

"Hello, darling," she murmured. A muscle in his jaw twitched but he didn't open those gorgeous eyes and look at her. That's okay. He wouldn't be able to deny her for long. Now that Mari's blood was getting stronger, it was even harder for him to fight her. Although she did enjoy the battle between them—it made him all the sweeter when he finally succumbed.

He despised her but soon he'd be begging for her attention. One can only go so many days with nothing to do and no one to look at or talk to. He only had her to rescue him from the eternal darkness. And as long as he got his weekly dose of the serum that kept him incapacitated, there was nothing he could do to fill the endless empty hours. Yes, it wouldn't be long before he was counting the seconds until he saw her again.

"Did you miss me?" she asked as she stared down at the most breathtaking creature she'd ever seen.

His beautiful blue eyes opened then narrowed.

"I have news," she cooed. "Your good buddy, Nicholai. The one you call to for help? He was here tonight. Not more than fifty feet away. We almost had him, but he got away." She pouted, pushing out her lower lip. "But don't worry, one way or another, he'll be back. I'll make sure of it. And I'll put him in a box right here next to you, so you can be together. Always. For eternity."

She smiled while unclasping his jeans. "You see, Marcos, that's how much I love you. How much I want you to be happy."

She reached inside his pants and took him in her hand, stroking his soft flesh before bending over and taking him into her mouth. He roared in anger or frustration, she didn't know which. She didn't care. Given time, he'd respond to her ministrations.

He always did.

And when she was done taking what she wanted from him, she stood and licked the last of him off her lips. "You always taste so sweet, lover." She took the knife off the nearby counter and slid the sharp blade across the soft skin of his lower belly and watched the crimson blood seep out of the wound.

She leaned down and licked, suckling the tender skin. As his blood flowed into her mouth, she felt his hatred for her, his frustration at being completely powerless.

And it filled her with exaltation.

As the sweet vampire drink rolled down her throat she felt herself growing stronger. She could hear Sebastian at the top of the house speaking with his milquetoast sister, and Johnny in the room above talking with his men about increasing security, as well as the lovers on various floors enjoying each other's touch.

Yes, she could hear it all, feel it all. With just a small sip of Marcos's blood—she was filled with power. All consuming, addicting and not something she would dare tell Sebastian about.

As she finished, she kissed his shallow wound and watched as it healed. Feeling empowered, she leaned down and kissed Marcos on the lips.

He gnashed at her, his sharp teeth nipping her tongue.

She smiled and wiped a drop of blood off her lip. "Thank you, lover. Someday you'll kiss me back. Someday you'll want me as much as I want you. And while you lie here by yourself, think about how much fun that day will be."

She closed his pants, gave him a soft pat and left him. And as she walked away, the room once again slipped into utter darkness.

Chapter 6

Nicholai pried open his eyes, then rubbed the grit out of them as he tried to focus. The ceiling fan above him circled round and round, filling the room with a gentle breeze. Someone stirred next to the bed. He turned his head and saw Darby resting in a deep leather chair, an opened book in her lap.

"Hey," he said through a scratchy throat, his voice sounding garbled.

Darby's sleepy eyes opened and a slow smile spread across her face. She put the book aside and leaned forward, touching his hand. "Hey, back. How are you feeling?"

He tried to sit up in the bed, but a throbbing ache gripped his muscles. He couldn't remember the last time he'd felt pain, especially pain like this. "Like I've been run down then backed up over."

She stood and helped him into a sitting position. "You might as well have been. You've been out for thirty-six hours."

"Thirty-six? What in the hell happened to me?" Images flashed through his mind—shouts, headlights, *pain.*

Her mouth twisted with disgust. "Those witches shot you with a poisoned arrow."

"Poison?" Wolfsbane couldn't do this, he thought through the throbbing in his skull. "What kind of poison?"

"We don't know yet."

"My head is pounding. Can you close the blinds and dim the lights? And turn off that damned fan."

"You still have a lot of the toxin in your system." She stood, pulled down the blinds covering the UV-tinted windows, pushed the button that shut off the lights and fan, and left the room.

He closed his eyes, as blessed darkness fell over him and tried to still the roiling through his stomach. A poison that paralyzes vampires, how could they fight that?

"Here, drink this," Darby said a moment later as she walked back into the room. The subtle scent of gardenias drifted after her. Usually he found it comforting; right now it made him nauseous. She handed him a warm mug of blood.

Greedily, he sucked it down, not realizing how desperately he needed it until it moved through him, warming him and soothing his stomach. He thrust the empty mug at her. "More."

Her eyebrows rose, but she left the room without commenting.

He was dehydrated, achy and sore. Whatever this weapon, this poison, was, he had to find it and he had to stop them. Not only for Marcos, but for all of them.

First, though, he had to find out exactly what he was up against. How much poison did they have? And how many witches were involved?

As he finished the second mug of blood, his strength slowly returned, and with it, his anger. Fury and frustration coalesced and surged through his chest, tightening his fists. Was this how Marcos and the others were feeling? Weak, nauseated, in pain? He flung the mug against the stone fireplace where it shattered into a hundred bloody pieces.

Darby frowned, but was smart enough not to say a word. He stared at her, remembering the taillights of the limo as they wavered in the distance. But he couldn't recall much more than that.

"What happened? How did I get here?"

"Christos helped me get you into the car before the men in the jeep reached us. Luckily, he was there—otherwise, I wouldn't have been able to lift you into the limo on my own."

Nicholai stilled. The head of the NYC clan of vampires? "Christos Poulos? Why would he be there?"

"I called him after you went into the house."

Uneasiness crept through him. Pushing against the leather-covered headboard, he shifted higher on the bed. "Established clans are not always welcoming to newcomers—you know that. As a courtesy, I called him when we arrived. He was less than thrilled. Why would *you* have called him?"

"He's my source. The one who told me about Vindecare in the first place."

Dread dropped to the pit of Nicholai's stomach and it had nothing to do with the poison. "And you didn't tell me this, why?"

"Because I knew you'd react this way. I can tell you're upset, but you're wrong about him. He is kind and helpful, and frankly, we can't fight the witches without him. If I hadn't called him, you'd be dead right now, or at least chained up in that creepy old estate. So remove that annoyed look off your face and be thankful."

He narrowed his eyes, realizing he didn't have the strength nor the energy to fight with her right now, and she knew that, too. "You really are getting too cheeky, Darby."

She smiled. "I know."

Never in a million years would he have doubted Darby's loyalty. But he didn't believe for a minute that Christos Poulos didn't know the history of Vindecare, and who exactly ran that house. So, why send Nicholai there? Was he involved somehow?

"Why don't you tell me how you hooked up with Christos in the first place? And while you're at it, explain why in the hell I should trust him? Vampires are notoriously territorial. There's no damned good reason why he would be helping us. Helping *you!*"

"We have the same goals—find out what's been happening to both our clans. We aren't the only ones who have been hurt by the witches. I met him while gathering information on Vindecare and we've been working together ever since. He's quite charming."

He stared at her, trying to decide just how taken she was with the vampire, and how much danger she was in. "Did he find you? Or the other way around?"

"Kind of a mutual thing. We sort of ran into each other."

Yeah, like he believed that. "You trust him?"

"With your life." She smiled.

He wished she was right, but he knew better. Vampires didn't befriend humans unless they wanted something from them. What the hell did Christos want?

"Christos thinks we should leave."

Ah, now he was getting somewhere. "Really?" he asked dryly. "And why is that?"

"You are weak. Who knows how long it's going to take for you to recover. The witches almost had you. We should go back to Europe. Regroup, find out what we can, and come back when we're stronger in numbers, and in knowledge."

"And in power," he muttered.

"Yes. In power. You've taken a severe hit. We don't know

what the long-term effects of the toxin will be. We don't know if you will ever fully recover."

She was right about that. Unfortunately. But it didn't matter, he wasn't going anywhere.

"Marcos and the others are in that house. I felt them."

"We'll come back for them."

"By then it will be too late. They are enraged and in pain. If they continue to be trapped down there, exposed to the poison and who knows what else, they will be lost to us. I won't leave them."

"Then what do you suggest? Your last plan didn't go all that well, and you're in no shape to have a go at it again."

He picked up the large crystal off his nightstand and stared into the smoke swirling within its depths. "I have all the power I need right here. Summon Helena."

Darby's face turned ashen. "No," she whispered.

"This isn't a debate, Darby."

"You promised."

"Now I'm breaking it."

"Don't do it. You know what happened to you before. People died. You can't do it again, especially not in your weakened condition." She paced back and forth, raking her fingers through her long hair. "I won't let you. I won't stand by and watch you destroy yourself all over again."

She stopped, and with her hands on her hips, confronted him. "You weren't the same, Nicholai. The demon's essence changed you."

She was wearing him out. "I won't discuss this with you. Not now."

"Do you remember what you were like? Demon essence was all you lived for. You were addicted, and you didn't care who you hurt to get it. You couldn't function without it and it nearly destroyed you." She pumped her fists toward the ceiling then sat back down in the chair. "Why would you want to go back to that place again? After everything that happened? You almost killed your own brother trying to steal that demon."

"I didn't, and Damien has never been happier. Now are you going to call Helena or will I?"

Her lips thinned into a straight line of disapproval. "You'll need a witch to transfer the demon into."

"I've got one. A Von Lucieus."

Darby's eyes widened and she sucked in a breath.

"A little detail your new friend, Christos, must not have thought important enough to share with you."

"Are you sure?" she said, her voice a strangled whisper.

"Yes."

"He must not know...."

"Either that or neither one of you did your research very well."

"There is no mention of Von Lucieus associated anywhere with Vindecare."

"Interesting, since he owns it."

"No. It's owned by Sebastian Saguna."

"Then he took Mari's mother's name."

"The witch from the bar?"

"His sister."

Darby leaped out of the chair, cursed under her breath and paced back and forth once again. "You can't do this, Nicholai. If you use his sister as a vessel for the demon just so you can drink the essence, she will die. No one ever survives, and the war will start all over again. Do you really want that?"

He was growing tired of this argument. He needed strength to fight the witches, to rescue Marcos and the others, and the only way to get that strength was through a demon's essence. And if he had to kill a witch to get that essence, then so be it.

Luckily for all of them, he just happened to have a demon in hand. He smiled as he tossed the crystal from one hand to the other, staring into the smoky depths, wondering how badly Asmos wanted out of his crystal prison.

He looked into Darby's troubled eyes. "As far as I'm concerned, the war has already begun. And yes, they almost beat me. But once I'm infused with Asmos's essence, I won't be just another vampire they can poison and capture. I will be much stronger than they could ever imagine. When I'm done with them, those witches won't know what hit them."

Mari sat in the back of her persuasion techniques class staring out the window at the birds flitting through the trees. What was she doing? Why was she still here? She had the answers she'd come for. Her mother had died at the hands of a vampire. But if her mother had been so against Vindecare's teaching, why had she come back here to begin with? Why not stay at home in Vermont?

The questions circled round and round in her mind, stealing her concentration and her ability to sleep. And if she wasn't thinking about her mother, she was thinking about *him.*

What was it about him that had made her forget her inhibitions, forget about everything but his next kiss, his next touch? Even knowing what he was, even knowing she could never see him again, she couldn't stop thinking about him.

"Concentrate on your breathing, Mari." Mr. Hoskins stopped next to her and drummed his pencil on her desk.

Mari instantly closed her eyes.

"Take a deep breath. Feel yourself relax." Her teacher's warm voice washed over her.

She did as he said, not daring to open her eyes and see if he'd moved on. She knew better.

"Surround yourself in bright white light. Can you feel its warmth? Does it hurt your eyes? Concentrate on the light at all points through your day, during each meal, while you brush your teeth and get dressed. Do it at all times until you get to the point where all you have to do is think of the light and it is there, surrounding you. Protecting you. Guiding you. Do you understand?"

Mari nodded and tried to focus. She concentrated on that spot in the center of her forehead, trying to find the zone, the light, but each time she did, all she saw was deep dark eyes.

Damn him!

Nicholai hadn't been interested in her; he'd only wanted access to this house, and she'd been foolish enough to give it to him. She should count herself lucky that the alarms went off and chased him away, or who knows what he would have done to her. He didn't deserve this much thought, this much... power. Why couldn't she stop thinking of him? What kind of spell had he cast on her?

A shiver tore through her.

"Concentrate, Mari." Mr. Hoskins's voice sounded above her head.

She jumped and tried her deep breathing techniques once again.

Nicholai wasn't a witch. She was. Vampires don't cast spells.

"Visualize what it is you're trying to accomplish," Mr. Hoskins continued. "See it in your mind."

Mari pictured the small rodent in the cage in front of her. She focused on making it wake up and climb on its wheel. She pushed her thoughts, her energy toward the sleeping hamster, just like she'd done in the bar with Nicholai.

What she'd felt with him had been magical. They'd formed a connection so strong everything else melted away and it was just the two of them, their power, their energy, their *need*.

But had it been her power that drew them together or his? She had seen him across the bar looking so hot, so danger-ous. She'd focused on him and then suddenly his gaze had locked on hers. Before she knew it, his hands…his lips…he was touching her…*everywhere*.

Heat rolled through her, latent desire…embarrassment.

It had been his powers. *Not hers!*

"Mari, your aura is a jumbled mess. You're not focusing."

She opened her eyes. This was ridiculous. She couldn't do this. The hamster was still sleeping. It was nocturnal and had probably been up running and running on its little wheel all night.

"I'm sorry, Mr. Hoskins."

Nocturnal.

Was Nicholai nocturnal?

"You can do this, Mari. I know you can."

She looked up at him and shook her head. "I can't. Really. I thought I could. I thought I was making progress, but now I know better."

Disappointment filled the instructor's gray eyes. "Of course you can. You just have to believe in yourself. Your mother had problems with this class, too, but eventually she got it. Some people's talents are stronger in other areas. You just haven't found your specialty yet. But, trust me, you will."

At the mention of her mother, a deep ache squeezed Mari's chest. She took in her teacher's salt-and-pepper hair and the lines etched around his eyes. He looked older than her mother. Was it possible?

"My mother?" she asked, the word cracking over her lips.

He smiled, his face gentle and kind. "She was my student, too. Although I've learned a thing or two about teaching since then, so hopefully your learning curve won't be quite as long as hers was."

She couldn't imagine her mother sitting right here in this room.

"She wasn't that much younger than yourself when she came to Vindecare. She was a strong woman. Headstrong, independent, a real fighter. I was very sorry to hear about her accident."

"Thank you." Mari stared at him, probing with her mind, pushing like she'd learned. From what little she was able to sense, he was telling the truth.

"Then you didn't see my mother when she was here recently?"

He looked surprised. "No. I'm sorry to say I didn't." He patted her on the back. "All you need is a little more time and practice. Focus and you'll get it right."

"Thanks, Mr. Hoskins." She smiled at him as he walked away, but she couldn't help wondering why he or anyone else hadn't seen her mother. She must not have been here very long. But why had she been here at all?

And why had she been down in the catacombs with Marcos?

Thinking of the handsome vampire with ice-blue eyes had her thinking of Nicholai all over again. She'd felt his pain. He'd been almost desperate to find his friend. Could someone with that depth of feeling really be a cold-blooded monster?

She shook the thought right out of her head. Nicholai had played her for a fool, and she danced to his song. Never again.

She would learn everything she could about being a witch and do whatever it took to get stronger. No vampire or anyone else would ever get the best of her or her family again.

The doorbell rang, and Darby left the room. Nicholai closed his eyes and hoped she'd leave him in peace.

No such luck.

"Christos is here," she said softly as she returned to his room.

Annoyance surged through him. "Did you call him?"

"She didn't." A tall vampire with black hair and unusual amber-colored eyes walked into the room. He wore cream slacks and a gauzy cream shirt open at the neck. Suave and debonair came to mind and Darby couldn't seem to take her eyes off him.

Displeasure simmered deep in Nicholaï's throat. He swallowed it.

"Christos Poulos." The vampire held out his hand. "I heard you were awake."

How? Nicholaï glanced at Darby. She shifted her gaze away. The traitor. "Sorry, if I don't get up," he said, his voice even.

"How are you feeling?"

"Better. I hear I have you to thank for that." Nicholaï forced an easy smile on his face. Or at least he tried to.

"Glad to help. I happened to be close by when Darby called."

"Lucky for me."

"I've been keeping a watch on Vindecare. Other than the excitement with you, that place has been quiet as a tomb for the last twenty years."

"So, why keep an eye on them?"

"Whenever we have faced trouble in the past, the witches have usually been behind it. Either them or their little hairy pups."

"Weres?"

"There's a monastery full of them close by, but they manage to keep to themselves. Higher calling of guarding the demon portals and all that."

Nicholaï refrained from letting his gaze fall on the crystal. Unfortunately, Darby didn't.

"Tell me about the poison," Christos asked, sitting in the leather chair Darby had left by the bed, draping his large hands on his knees.

"It was intense and fast-acting. The burning was extreme.

In less than a minute, I had no control over my muscles. The missing vampires of my clan hadn't stood a chance."

Christos's face hardened.

He knew something.

"What is this poison?" Nicholai insisted. "What do you know?

"Not anything I can share. Yet."

Chapter 7

Mari looked up as the door to the classroom swung open and Ally breezed in. She inhaled a quick breath. She still hadn't talked to Ally since the other night, and hoped she wouldn't have to now. Without looking in Mari's direction, Ally handed Mr. Hoskins a folded piece of paper, then turned and left the room.

Mr. Hoskins opened it, read it and then slipped the note onto Mari's desk as he continued making his rounds to the other students. Mari stared at the piece of paper, ignored it then opened her notebook again, trying to go back to her focusing.

Whatever it was, she didn't want to know. She stared at the hamster again, willing it to wake up and run on its little wheel, all the while squashing the urge to give the cage a violent shake. She blew out a frustrated sigh and leaned back in her chair, her gaze once more falling on the folded piece of paper sitting on her desk. Relenting, she shut her notebook and snatched up the note.

Jacob from the infirmary wanted to see her. She frowned. What could he possibly want? She packed up her things, nodded to Mr. Hoskins and left the room.

As most of the classrooms were on the second floor, Mari took the staircase down to the main floor, then walked past the atrium to the infirmary in the back of the building.

"Hello, Mari," Jacob said, looking up from his microscope as she walked through the door.

Jacob was just a few years older than she, though he'd been at Vindecare for years. And apparently, he spent most of his time in the lab since she never saw him at any of the social functions the school offered.

"How are you feeling today?" he asked, as he stepped away from a microscope. He made a final notation on his chart then set the clipboard on the counter.

"Fine. A little tired. I haven't been sleeping well."

His forehead furrowed as he studied her. He gestured for her to sit in the chair against the wall so he could take her blood pressure. He slipped the cuff around her arm and pumped the little rubber ball until the cuff tightened.

"Looks good," he said, when he took the reading.

"Good to hear."

She studied him as he looked over her chart, flipping through the pages. "I understand you talked to Sebastian," he said finally as he set down her chart.

"Yes."

"And you're okay with everything?" He sounded a little skeptical.

As he should.

"If you mean, am I okay that you lied to me about having an iron deficiency? Not really."

He rolled back on his heels and nodded his head. "I totally get that. But you know I had no choice."

"We always have choices, Jacob."

He was nodding again. "That we do."

"So? Why am I here?" she asked, refusing to let him off the hook.

"I just wanted to make sure we are okay."

"What do you mean?"

"That you aren't too upset with me."

"Would it matter if I were?"

He hesitated, his eyes searching hers for a long moment. "Well, yes, it would."

"Okay, then. I want the truth."

"About?"

"What exactly are you using my blood for?"

"I thought Sebastian told you."

"I want to hear it from you."

"We are trying to develop a poison that will protect us from the vampires."

"Do we need protecting from vampires? Up until two nights ago, I didn't even know they existed."

He paused. "Vampires will always be a threat to us. When we least expect it, one of our families is slaughtered. No reason. No justification or provocation. Just ask your friend, Ally, about that sometime."

"Ally?"

He stepped back. "Better yet, maybe you shouldn't. Forget I said anything."

She stood. "You've got to be kidding. How can I forget something like that?"

He pressed his lips together, as if he knew he'd already said too much.

"Ally and I aren't friends. I won't say anything. I, too, can keep secrets. And besides, you owe me," she pressed.

He took a deep relenting breath. "All right. But only because you need to know what we're up against, and how important the success of this program is."

"All right." She sat again, leaning forward on the edge of her chair.

"Ally came to us when she was twelve. She was a wisp of a girl, shaken and suffering from post-traumatic stress syndrome. Her whole family, including both her sisters, had been tortured and massacred by the local vampire clan in Manhattan while she watched."

Mari cringed, trying to reconcile the strong, confident, take-charge witch with the scared little girl he was describing. "Why did they do it?"

"Who knows? They're animals, targeting witches and wiping out entire families. That night, Ally had hidden in a cupboard. The poor girl witnessed the whole thing and still managed to stay quiet enough to survive. She's got guts. You've got to give her that."

Mari took a deep breath. It was hard to hate someone who had been through something so horrible. "I guess that explains a few things."

Jacob grinned. "I know she can be a little difficult at times, but once she has your back, she'll never let you down."

"That's good to know."

"Do you mind?" he asked, as he came toward her with a tray.

"Didn't we just do this last week?" Somewhere in the back of her mind, she remembered that she should wait three weeks before giving blood again.

"Yes. Don't worry. I'm not taking very much, just enough to test the strength and numbers of your spiral cells."

Spiral cells? There was a term she wasn't familiar with. "What are those?"

"Spiral cells contain the abnormal hemoglobin that is toxic to the vamps."

"Do you take blood from all the witches?"

"They've all been tested, but you're the only one that has the anomaly."

"Really?"

"Yep. Now, do you mind?" He gestured toward the tray.

She nodded her consent and he wrapped a tourniquet around her upper arm.

"Make a fist."

She did and he swabbed her skin with alcohol, patted her veins until they swelled, then stuck in the needle.

"So, why am I the only one? How did I get so lucky?" she asked, though she had to admit, she didn't feel very lucky.

"Legend has it that long ago all witches were born with the spiral gene pattern that rendered their blood poisonous to vampires. But as witches married humans, their offspring lost that special chromosome factor. It's only the true-blood witches who carry the spiral cell gene."

"So you're saying I inherited it? That all of my ancestors married witches?"

"Yep. Both of your parents had to have a copy of the spiral cell gene in order for you to have two copies, which makes you very special, and very powerful."

Mari laughed. She couldn't help it. For a "very powerful" witch, she sure was having a hard time grasping her so-called powers.

"So, tell me," she asked, casually, hoping he wouldn't notice how fast her heart was beating. "If my mom also had this spiral gene, did she give you blood, too?"

He nodded. "Absolutely. I'm very sorry about her accident." His sympathy washed over her, taking her by surprise. Though, she was getting used to the sudden onslaught of people's emotions and at least she could tell he was being truthful about that.

"Thank you. I miss her a lot."

"Is it true she never told you that you were a witch?"

"Uh-huh. Up until three months ago, I was one of those boring normal people."

He smiled. "I find that hard to imagine."

"Trust me. My mom kept me very sheltered. Although, I am glad she never told me about the vampires. That was one bit of all this I'd prefer not knowing anything about."

"Don't worry. They aren't a threat to you. One bite, and those little spiral cells of yours would travel straight to their brains, attaching to their synapses, blocking them and rendering them useless. Nothing better than zombies." He stiffened, tilting back and forth on his feet, mimicking zombies from low-budget TV horror movies.

She laughed. "Stop!"

"It's true."

"But surely you aren't able to get enough blood from me to stop all the vampires."

"That's why we're doing everything we can to figure out how it works, so we can synthesize our own."

"Yeah?"

"Yeah." He smiled. "It's really cool."

"So, are you close?"

He sighed. "No. We haven't had enough time. When you first got here, the number of spiral cells in your blood was significantly lower than it is now. Your powers as a witch have been growing stronger every day."

A shadow crept into her mind at his words. "Why? What was so different now?"

"We aren't sure."

"And my mom's cells?"

"Hers were in normal ranges. Unfortunately, she wasn't with us long enough for me to make any real progress."

"I see."

But why had she come here in the first place?

She could feel sorrow rolling off him. And yet, she also felt fear. He was also frightened. But from what? *What was he hiding?*

"Well, that should do it," he said, withdrawing the needle and taping some gauze over the wound.

She nodded and stood, but as she turned to go, he stopped her with a hand on her arm.

"Would…would you like to go out for a cup of coffee some-time?"

She stared at him, wondering what he wanted from her, and what he could be hiding. Did it have something to do with her mother and what she'd been doing there? "Sure, anytime." She forced a bright smile. "I'll see you later."

"Sounds good."

She walked out the door and instead of returning to class, headed toward the atrium where she made herself a cup of coffee and sat in the corner trying to absorb everything she'd just heard and felt.

A powerful witch. She was powerful enough to sense when someone was hiding something from her, but not powerful enough to know what that something was.

Yet.

But as Jacob said, she was growing stronger every day. She looked out the large windows at the marble statues adorn-ing the garden surrounded by twelve-foot-high walls. As she gazed at the stone faces that kept Vindecare's secrets, she couldn't help wondering if the walls were meant to keep people out, or to hold the witches in.

* * *

That evening, Nicholai felt well enough to get out of bed and walk downstairs. Helena would be arriving any moment. He needed an Adept of her skill level who would be strong enough to handle the transfer of a primal demon like Asmos into Mari.

That Helena was able to drop everything at a moment's notice and fly out to see him was a testament to their deep friendship. That she was in the States at all meant his luck might finally be starting to turn.

"Dear God, Nicholai, what have those demented witches done to you?" Helena asked as she swept into the room, her silk wrap swishing around her, the overpowering scent of Chanel swimming in his head.

"It was a close one, but I'll recover," he said and kissed both her cheeks. "It's Marcos and the others I'm not too sure about."

"Don't you worry yourself about that. I'm here now. When Darby sent the emergency signal, how could I not jump on the nearest flight and get here as soon as I could?"

"I do appreciate that." He smiled widely, but it faltered as she suddenly wavered in front of him.

"I know you do, sweetheart. Here, let's have a seat so you can tell me everything. You don't look like your normal handsome self."

Relieved, he dropped to the sofa. "Helena, I need you to transfer a demon trapped in one of the Cadre's crystals into a witch for me."

Her eyes widened. "You have one of the Cadre's crystals?"

He smiled and shrugged. "Shh. Don't tell anyone. I'm afraid this one just happened to get lost."

The Cadre, an organization in England that devoted itself to capturing demons in crystals, would move heaven and earth to get the crystal back *if* they knew he had it. Luckily for him, they didn't.

Helena laughed long and loud. "And you just so happened to find it, did you? No wonder you hightailed it across the Pond as fast as you did. I've had occasion to wonder about that."

"That was just one of the reasons."

"And the other?"

He needed to detox. Too much demon essence had him coming apart. Darby had every right to be concerned, but that no longer mattered. Nothing mattered except getting his strength back.

"I wanted a change. And not just of scenery."

She shrugged her shoulders. "Those Cadre Adepts were always too snobbish in my book with all their rituals and ceremonies. My gypsy training wasn't good enough for them, but I can run rings around their Adept powers any day of the week. Well, except maybe one. How is Damien? I'd heard you and your brother reconnected. True? Is the hatchet buried?" Her eyes twinkled with the unanswered questions of wagging tongues.

He supposed that could have something to do with her timely arrival. "It is not the right time for my brother and I to fix all the damage that has been done. Maybe some other day."

"If you can survive the witches, eh?"

He couldn't help but chuckle. "You're right about that one."

"I bet she was a looker, this witch who got the best of you."

"Her eyes could rival the greenest of gemstones."

"You always were a sucker for the beauties."

He smiled. "I suppose it's my cross to bear."

Darby stepped back into the room with the tea. She poured Helena a cup, adding a healthy amount of sugar and cream then handed Nicholai a mug of warm blood.

He'd tripled what he normally drank in a day, and was slowly starting to feel the effects of the poison wearing off. But the burning ache in his shoulder just wouldn't stop. He feared it never would.

He couldn't fathom what kind of poison these witches had. He only hoped what he was about to do would be enough to stop them.

"All right, Nicholai. Fetch me the stone and let me see what you've got."

Nicholai gestured to Darby and she left the room to retrieve the crystal.

"I take it you're going to use your green-eyed beauty as the vessel for the demon?"

Nicholai's insides grew warm at the thought of her hot blood infused with the demon sliding down his throat. "Absolutely."

"I must say, Nicholai, I wish there was a different way. For a while there, you were becoming too much like the demons you'd absorbed—full of rage and diabolical. I worry a part of them might be in you still."

"The only thing I have in me is a witch's poison. If Darby hadn't been there to collect me, we wouldn't be having this conversation right now."

She tsked. "I understand. I just want you to be aware what you're getting into. You made it back from the brink of darkness once before. There is a good chance that you won't be able to break free this time."

"I understand. And truth be told, a part of me wishes I didn't have to do this." He recalled vividly the pain of withdrawal, the shakes, the nightmares and the feeling that if he didn't get more demon essence into him, he would crawl right out of his skin. It took a long time to recover from that. And he'd had to move halfway across the world to do it.

Darby walked back into the room and placed a large crystal on the table in front of Helena. The Adept picked it up and held it up to the light, gazing into the swirling mist inside. "Who is the demon?"

"Asmos."

Helena's skin paled beneath the heavy makeup. She dropped the crystal onto the table, where it landed with a loud thud.

"Asmos?" She shook her head. "No, Nicholai. He is primal. He's too powerful a demon. It must have been a very strong Adept to capture such a demon."

"He was. Is."

"Damien?"

Nicholai nodded, knowing he hadn't given his brother a choice. It had taken everything he'd had to capture Asmos into the crystal in order to save the woman he loved. And now it would take everything Nicholai had to make sure he finished what he started. He would have Asmos's essence, no matter what he had to do to get it.

"Asmos is older and stronger than any demon you've ever absorbed before."

"I know."

"You realize there will be no coming back from this one, Nicholai. You and Asmos will be joined for eternity. You understand that? He's stronger than you. He might even..."

"Overpower me?"

"Yes. Have you considered that? Especially now that you're in such a weakened state."

He had to admit, he hadn't believed it was possible. And perhaps before it wasn't. But now?

"Please, Nicholai. Listen to her. Don't do this." Darby's eyes filled with tears.

Impatience made him tense as he looked at her. "Do me a favor. Make yourself useful and go find out where our pretty little witch is keeping herself, eh?"

In a huff, Darby grabbed her bag off the table. "Talk some sense into him, Helena," she pleaded, then hurried out of the room.

"I'm afraid I have to agree with her," Helena said, as the front door slammed shut.

"The witches have taken them all, Helena. I'm the only one left of our clan. The only one left to save them from their torment. And it is torment. Trust me. I have felt the effects of the poison." He sucked in a deep breath before the anger and frustration could grab hold of him once more. He would not let that happen. He was in control. He had to be.

"I brought them here because *I* had to get out of England. I had to get away from the Cadre, and I had to recover from my addiction. Because of my weakness and my insistence on going after Asmos in the first place, I have made enemies. Now I have lost everything and everyone. I will not abandon my clan. I will do whatever it takes to rescue them."

Helena nodded. "All right, Nicholai. I will help you. But I insist you wait a few more days until you're stronger, otherwise neither you nor the witch will survive the transfer. And I'd like to make sure I come out of this in one piece, too."

He let out a relieved breath and leaned back into the sofa, exhausted. "Thanks, Helena. I owe you big-time for this one."

"Yes, you do. And don't worry your handsome little head about it." She smiled, and leaned forward to kiss his cheek. "I'll collect. I always do."

Chapter 8

After dinner, Mari sat in the corner of her room, watching TV, trying to think about anything but the soaring walls surrounding the estate. Her gaze kept drifting out the window, toward the front of the house and the tall iron gates blocking the drive.

Were they to protect the witches, or to lock them in? There was still so much about Vindecare that she didn't trust or understand. Why would a school be conducting experiments to create a synthetic poison? Were the vampires as much of a threat as Jacob said?

And if they were, how was it that no one knew about them? Except for Ally. Was she the only one?

Mari stood and grabbed her bag, turned off the TV and pulled on her sweater. She had to get out of here, if only for a little fresh air and to still the questions circling around in her mind. She hurried down the stairs and, without telling anyone where she was going, slipped out the front door.

She inhaled a deep breath of night air as she rushed down the long drive and out the estate gates without notice. Almost breathless, she hailed a cab halfway down the street. "Java Blue, please."

It was really ridiculous that she should feel so free, so rebellious, sneaking out of the house for a cup of coffee, but that was how restrictive her life had become. Especially since *that* night. It seemed someone always needed to know where she was going and what she was doing. If they even let her leave at all.

She hated it.

A few minutes later, she walked into the Java Blue coffee shop. She placed her order then stepped back, glancing over her shoulder to make certain she hadn't been followed. Foolish thoughts, especially since it wouldn't take much effort for someone to find her. Everyone knew she was addicted to caramel lattes.

Though every now and then, she did miss her mom's Valetude tea. Her heart swelled with sadness as she thought of her mom. The pain, like a tender bruise that refused to heal, tugged at her. Along with the questions that wouldn't stop: Why had her mother come? Why hadn't she told Mari about her heritage? Better yet, why hadn't she told her about Sebastian?

"A brother is a big secret to keep." Nicholai's words replayed in her mind. As they did, the skin on the back of her neck tingled. She glanced around her. He wasn't here.

She sighed. Another person she just couldn't keep out of her thoughts for long, no matter how much she wanted to.

"Whipped cream?" the guy from behind the counter asked with a wide, more-than-friendly grin.

She'd noticed him before, his cute dimples and wind-tunnel hair that somehow always managed to look great.

"You bet," she said and smiled in return as he added a

dollop of extra cream then drizzled caramel sauce all over the top of it.

"Very decadent choice," a deep voice whispered from behind her, his warm breath fanning her cheek sent goose bumps cascading down her arms.

She gasped, her hand fluttering to her cheek as fear shot through her, kicking up her heartbeat and stealing her breath.

Nicholai.

No! It couldn't be.

"Here you go," the guy with great hair said. He was still smiling at her, his eyes twinkling with interest. Why couldn't she have met someone like him at the bar that night? Someone nice, someone…*safe.*

She forced herself to smile as she stepped forward to claim her coffee, then squared her shoulders, took a deep breath and turned.

No sign of Nicholai.

If he had even been there.

She blew out a relieved breath. She wanted to collapse into the nearest chair, but stayed standing on shaky knees.

Only one man had ever been able to make her heart beat that fast and send her temperature soaring. No reason to hang around just in case her senses had been right and it had been Nicholai standing over her shoulder, whispering in her ear.

But she wasn't ready to go back to Vindecare, either. She stood at the door gazing out onto the street. Searching.

Cautiously, she stepped out the door and into the throngs of people walking by. She glanced around her for any sign of the tall handsome vampire who, with one touch, turned her inside out, but saw no sign of him.

She moved through the crowds sipping her coffee that had suddenly lost its flavor and turned toward the bookstore up the street. Hopefully a good book would give her the distraction she needed.

She wandered through the store, perusing the shelves, drinking her coffee, and found herself staring at book covers with sexy vampires, shirtless and oozing promises of passion through dark, sardonic eyes. She had to stop torturing herself. He wasn't here. She could never have anything to do with him again. He was dangerous. Strike that. He was *lethal*.

She started toward the front of the store when she felt that same strange tingling on the back of her neck. Her pulse quickened. She rubbed her neck and without turning, quickly moved toward the front of the store. As she passed a table full of giggling teens, she glanced over her shoulder, fully expecting to see Nicholai behind her.

Again, no one was there.

She was jumping at shadows. She considered calling Sebastian to send a car, but then thought better of it. She didn't want to have to explain why she needed it, or why she'd left the house without telling anyone in the first place.

Better to deal with this on her own. It wasn't like she was alone in a dark alley. She was in a brightly lit store surrounded by people.

She turned down a row of shelves, looking back once more, and stopped as black leather teased the corner of her eye. She searched behind her, but saw no one. With a trembling hand resting against her thudding heart, she spun back around.

Nicholai stood in front of her. "Hello, love."

She choked on a startled gasp.

"You knew I was here. You felt me." He smiled, one corner of his mouth lifting into a wicked grin.

She shook her head. "No. I didn't. Not for sure."

He leaned toward her. "Why do you have no faith in yourself? Your abilities are much stronger than you give yourself credit for."

She took a step back. "No…uh…how would you know?"

"I can sense them. I can sense you."

A shiver tore down her spine. *What did that mean, exactly?* "What do you want from me?"

"I just wanted to see you. How are you?"

"How am I?" She stared at him, confused, and frantically tried to sort out what he was up to. "Why would you care?"

"Why wouldn't I care?" His voice dropped an octave, its warm timbre scraping across her nerves as he stepped closer to her.

She moved backward until she bumped up against a shelf. *Trapped.*

"You…disappeared," she stammered.

"I couldn't stay." He stepped closer, so close if she took a deep breath, her chest would touch his.

"Couldn't? Why not?"

Say it. Admit the truth.

"You know why."

"Do I?" Did she? Could it possibly be true? *Was he a vampire?* Even now, as she stared at him, she couldn't be sure. How could anyone be sure of something so unbelievable?

Her gaze raked over his face. He looked different than he had that night. Still drop-dead gorgeous enough to steal her breath, but he also looked…sick. His face was so pale it was almost translucent and dark veins streaked the thin skin beneath his eyes.

"It's the lingering effects of the poison," he said, softly.

"Poison?" The words stuck in her throat as ice water pulsed through her veins.

"One of the guards at Vindecare shot me with an arrow." Gingerly, he touched his shoulder, and pulled down his collar so she could see the ugly purple bruise and ragged scar where the skin had begun to heal. "It was carrying some kind of toxin."

She gasped a deep breath, her eyes widening.

"You didn't know?" he asked.

"No." She shook her head as anxiety laced with guilt sliced through her chest. Had her blood done that to him?

His eyes studied her.

He knew she knew something. She could see it in his face, in the way he stared at her. A large lump caught in the back of her throat. She coughed. "Will you be all right?" she asked, once she caught her breath.

"Yes, though I'm sure you wish otherwise."

"No." The denial came out more forcefully than she'd intended. She lowered her voice. "That's not true."

"Ah," he smiled. "The first truthful thing you've said tonight."

"I'm glad you're okay," she murmured, and brushed past him, hoping he'd let her walk away.

He didn't. He rested a hand on her arm, stopping her. She looked down at his long fingers lying in the crook of her arm and wondered how it was possible, knowing what he was, knowing how he must hate her, that her heart could still quicken at his touch?

"I'm not evil," he said softly.

She looked up and met his eyes, wishing he were telling the truth. That he wasn't just trying to trick her into taking him back to Vindecare.

"Nor am I a monster who wants to hurt you."

He caressed her cheek, his fingers smooth and gentle.

She wanted to believe him. She wished she could read him as easily as he seemed to be able to read her. But he was a blank slate.

"You were only interested in Vindecare. Not me," she said. "Why should I believe anything you have to say?"

His sensuous lips lifted in a gentle smile and his eyes filled with longing. "Yes, I knew you lived at Vindecare, and that drew me to you in the bar. But everything that happened after that first dance…well, that was an unexpected surprise. *You* were a surprise."

"Really?" She couldn't believe him, wouldn't. Even though the fear rushing through her veins was fading, and changing into curiosity. She wanted to know the truth.

"I hadn't planned what happened between us. We are good together. Connected in an unexpected, yet incredible way. I must admit, I haven't felt like that in a long time."

She stared into his eyes, mesmerized by their melted rich dark chocolate color. They locked onto hers as he tried to make her understand, make her believe.

Could she? Better yet, should she?

"Like what?" she asked, knowing she shouldn't. Knowing she should run as fast and as far from him as she could.

His lips parted, but he hesitated, apparently searching for the words to explain how he'd felt. "It was like I wasn't quite in charge. Like I was lost in that gray zone where the mind knows what is happening, but the body is running the show and refuses to relinquish control."

Mari sucked in a quick breath. Yes, that was exactly how it had felt for her, too.

"Though I must admit, I wasn't entirely comfortable with it," he added.

She smiled. "Now that, I believe."

He laughed then, the sound bubbling up from deep inside him as an easy smile crossed his face.

"I really had no intention of hurting you. I promise. Maybe under different circumstances…perhaps once my friends are free—"

Marcos's image flashed through her mind. Along with the absolute realization that she was responsible for what was happening to his friends. It was her blood causing all this pain. If Nicholai ever discovered the truth…

She stiffened and pulled away from him. There could never be different circumstances, not for them. "No."

"What?"

"Your game of seduction is not going to work on me. Not again."

"Is that what I'm doing?"

"I'm not a fool. I know full well you were only using me to find Marcos, and had we found him…well, I try not to think about that. It interferes with my ability to sleep at night."

"Have you seen Marcos?" He straightened, his tone deepening and suddenly becoming serious.

Unbidden, his hope washed through her, flowing through every part of her, drowning her in the oncoming waves until she could no longer feel anything but his wish that Marcos was okay. There was no anger, no malice or intent to harm. Only hope and fear for his friend.

Overwhelmed by his emotions, tears rushed to her eyes. "Yes. I've seen him." *And I'm so sorry.*

"Is he…?"

She pictured Marcos lying in the dark in his stainless-steel coffin. "He's alive."

Relief filled Nicholai's eyes, and the connection between them was severed. "Thank you. I needed to hear that," he said. "I haven't been able to hear him…. The poison… I was too weak. At least I hoped that was the reason."

Mari's heart ached for him. For Marcos. It was just so… cruel. So evil.

She shook it off. He'd killed her mother. She mustn't forget that.

"He has no compassion, no love in his heart, no human emotions. He is a beast." Sebastian's words pounded in her mind.

But she felt Nicholai's compassion and his love for his friend. Could her brother be wrong?

Nicholai grabbed her hand and pulled it to him, placing it against his chest. "Help me stop them. Help me rescue my friends," he pleaded with her, his eyes wide with intensity and desperation.

"I can't," she whispered. Though she had to admit, a part of her wanted to. But then she remembered what Marcos had done, how much he'd taken from her.

"You can. You're stronger than you think."

Anger blossomed and filled her voice. She yanked her hand back. "Marcos killed my mother." Pain rushed through her heart and chased away the tenderness his vulnerability stirred in her.

"Did he?" Skepticism filled Nicholai's eyes.

She reminded herself that he would do anything, say anything to get her help.

"While he was poisoned and locked up as a prisoner? How did he manage that?" Nicholai asked.

Doubt seeped into her mind. "I'm not quite sure."

"So you're taking someone's word for it? Without any details?"

"Her neck was broken."

He nodded. "I see."

But he didn't see. She could tell that. "She had very little blood in her," she continued, trying to recall the scant details from the police's accident report.

"Puncture wounds?"

"I don't know."

"That would be a telltale sign that it was a vampire who killed her."

"Would he have bit her?"

"If he was that close, that hungry, why wouldn't he have?"

But he couldn't have drunk from her. Her mother's blood was toxic. Like Mari's. Her eyes snapped up to his. "I'll have to read over the report again when I get back home."

"You should do that. In fact, I'd also be very interested in what they say."

He was messing with her. "Why?"

"Because it's important that you realize we're not the evil ones here. My friends and I are the victims."

She shook her head, trying to stop it from spinning. But *before* she could answer, he pushed her into the shelf, blocking her body with his own, his lips mere inches from hers.

"Shh," he urged as she opened her mouth to protest.

She bit her lip, her hands splayed against his rock-hard chest.

"Stay still," he whispered, his warm breath heating her cheek. "It's your redheaded friend from the bar."

"Ally?" Oh, God. "She can't see me with you. She'll tell my brother."

"I gathered as much."

Mari closed her eyes and held her breath, hoping Ally would keep walking by and disappear. But the longer Mari stood there, the more aware of Nicholai she became. His strength beneath her fingertips, his scent—earth, spice, heat—and the tickle of his hair next to her cheek. If she just turned her head a little bit...

She stiffened and tried to put some space between them, but it didn't help. Every part of him was touching her. He was so big, so full of power. And, God help her, at that moment she wished she didn't know the truth. She wished for just an endless second, he would wrap her in his arms and kiss her senseless.

Because he didn't look like a vampire and he certainly didn't feel like a vampire. He felt like a man.

A man she couldn't seem to forget.

Chapter 9

Nicholai stood hidden in the doorway of a shop closed for the night, watching until the cab with Mari inside pulled away.

"What do you want from her?" Ally asked, stepping into the shadows next to him.

"What makes you think I want anything?" He turned to her, impressed by her gumption. It wasn't very often he ran across a witch who was brave enough to approach him alone in the dark.

"I don't know. Maybe it's the stalkerish vibe I'm getting off you."

He smiled. "Is that what you're doing with me?"

"Actually, I'm surprised she still trusts you, even after everything she knows," she said, ignoring his question.

"She doesn't."

"Maybe. Maybe not. But she wants to."

Does she? Good. That would certainly make his seduction easier. He only had two more days to convince her to be alone with him.

But what was this witch's game? "Jealous?" he asked, stepping closer to her.

A smile quirked her lips while a sparkle lit her eyes. Her gaze raked slowly over his body. "That must be it."

"Sorry, but I'm a one witch kind of guy."

"Really? Now, why don't I believe you?" She stepped up next to him, resting her hand on his chest.

Marcos's scent reached him. Shocked, he stilled and inhaled deeply. Yes. She'd seen him.

She's been with him.

He slipped his hands around her waist and pulled her hips against his, grinding. "You like to play dangerous games?"

"Only with bad boys I know I can handle."

"And what makes you think you can handle me?"

She leaned forward and sucked his neck, drawing the skin into her mouth, teasing it with her teeth. "What makes you think I can't?"

She swept her hand down his abdomen, grazing her fingers across the defined ridges, then lower, scraping against denim. He stiffened beneath her sure touch.

She smiled as she kissed him. "Want to come out and play?"

He'd picked the wrong witch in the bar that night. It wasn't Mari who knew about Marcos, who smelled of him, who was actively hunting down his clan. It was this one.

As her hand moved, he brushed it away from him and grabbed hold of her wrist. "What is this?"

She clutched a penlike device topped with a sharp needle.

The poison?

Fury swept through him. His fangs descended, and it took tremendous willpower not to snap the delicate bones in her wrist.

For the first time, fear filled her eyes. A small group of women came out of the bookstore, laughing, their heads together in some shared joke.

"Sheila, wait for me!" Ally called.

The group stopped and turned toward them. "Ally?" a tall blonde answered, stepping away from the others and toward them.

Ally tried to pull away, but Nicholai tightened his grip.

"Let me go," she growled.

"Ally? What's up?"

One witch he could handle, but a group? That would be foolish. He leaned down close to the redhead's ear. "Go ahead, little girl. But you can never escape me. I've got your scent now."

She shuddered. He released her then laughed softly as she ran to catch up with her friends.

He turned and walked down the street. Painfully aware that once again, he'd narrowly escaped the witches' clutches. Another second and she would have shoved that pen into his skin, easily delivering the poison.

He wouldn't have stood a chance.

Mari could have also administered the poison with that little pen at any time that night. But she hadn't. Why?

Because she didn't have one? Because she wasn't involved? It surprised Nicholai how much he wanted to believe that. Somehow her scent had gotten under his skin and he couldn't stop thinking about it. About *her*. About how much he still wanted to be with her.

But he wasn't a fool. How much she knew, and when she knew it, didn't matter. What mattered was rescuing Marcos. He climbed into the back of the limousine waiting for him. His desire for Mari would make what he needed to do all the sweeter.

Just a couple more days and she'd be his.

* * *

The next morning, Mari hit her alarm for the third time. Just five more minutes, she thought as she drifted back to sleep again. When she woke forty minutes later, she bolted from the bed.

"Damn." She'd overslept again. She'd been plagued most of the night with restlessness. Why couldn't she sleep? That guy at the coffee shop must have made her latte caffeinated, that's the only thing she could think of.

No more lattes for her.

She jumped into the shower for a quick soap down, brushed her teeth, pulled her hair back into a ponytail then threw on some jeans and a sweatshirt. She practically ran to her Potions class.

"Good morning, Miss Saguna," Professor Whalen said, looking down her long thin nose as Mari hurried into the class five minutes after it had started. "Glad you could join us."

Mari gave her an apologetic smile, then rushed to her seat.

"Girl, you look like something the cat dragged in. What happened to you?" Sheila asked.

"Nothing. I haven't been sleeping well."

"Well, you're in the right place. Let's whip you up something for that."

Mari laughed. "Uh…no. Thanks, though."

"What? You don't trust my conjuring abilities?"

"Sheila, you have many fine abilities, but conjuring isn't one of them."

Sheila's blue eyes twinkled as she stuck out her bottom lip in an exaggerated pout.

But she did have a point. Potions were the one thing Mari should excel at. Her mother had taught her how to grow herbs, what they were used for and the best way to use them to retain their potency. In fact, she could say she'd had a life's worth of lessons in potions. What they were learning in class now was no different than what she already knew, except that when combined the herbs and oils could become so much more than she'd imagined.

So why not make something to help her sleep? Perhaps her mother already had a recipe in her book of herbs. She would have to remember to look after class.

Mari pulled out her notebook and practiced combining the assortment of scented oils for a vial of attraction potion. As she wrote down the formula, she once again thought of Nicholai.

Was he really attracted to her? Did he feel some sort of connection like he'd said or was he just playing with her? Trying to manipulate her into sneaking him back into Vindecare again? That was more like it, and there was no way she'd be stupid enough to fall for that trick again.

Though she had to admit a small part of her wanted to be with him. For the first time since her mother's death, she'd felt alive—her nerve endings on fire, her blood pulsing through her just for the sheer joy of it.

He added excitement to her otherwise dull life of classes and note taking and following the rules. She never had been very good at doing what she was supposed to do. Surely, being a witch had to have some perks? Some fun?

Yes, but not fun with an incredibly hot and sexy vampire.

She sighed and thought again about the wild-haired guy in the coffee shop. He was more her speed. But every time she tried to recall what his eyes looked like, or the shape and color of his mouth, she pictured eyes of dark chocolate and a sardonic smile instead.

Obviously, Nicholai had used an attraction potion on *her.*

"Okay, class. Once you've finished filling your vial with attraction oil, we're going to make dragon's blood ink." Ms. Whalen held up a small jar filled with deep red liquid. "As you know herbs can have medicinal as well as magical responses on us and others around us, especially when used in the right combinations. Today, we will paint a protection talisman onto our skin using dragon's blood ink."

"A tattoo?" Sheila squealed.

"Temporary, I assure you," Professor Whalen replied dryly.

"A protection talisman? What do we need that for?" Mari asked, leaning close to Sheila so Ms. Whalen wouldn't hear.

"Got me. I'm just glad we're finally done with the attraction oils."

Mari smiled, but couldn't help wondering if the talisman had anything to do with Nicholai.

"Please come to the front of the room to collect your supplies and goggles then light the alcohol lamps at your stations."

Mari followed Sheila to the main table to collect the powders they needed. She logged into her notebook the genus of the herbs and then measured the correct amounts of each powder into a small bowl. Finally, she grabbed a jar of red ink and a brush and went back to her table.

"Heat your powders with the alcohol, then combine the mixture into the jar of ink. There's a box of templates making its way around the room. Pick up a template and infuse your partner's skin with the talisman, chanting the protection spell written on the board while you do. Please be sure to write the spell in your notebooks," Ms. Whalen instructed.

Ten minutes later, Sheila handed Mari a template of a dragonfly. "Here, paint this one on me."

Picking up Sheila's jar and the brush, Mari got to work. She liked the way the ink soaked into the skin. "This is really cool," she said, enjoying herself.

"Don't forget the incantations, ladies."

"Right." Mari muttered the words written in her notebook as she finished applying the last strokes of deep red ink to

Sheila's left arm. "There, perfect," she said, while admiring her work.

"What tattoo are you going to get?" Sheila asked.

Mari looked in the box and pulled out a template with a dagger piercing a heart.

"Little melodramatic, don't you think? You didn't know him long enough to get your heart broken."

Mari frowned. "What makes you think I have anyone in particular in mind?"

"Oh, come on. You can't stop thinking about Mr. Hottie-pants. You're not fooling me."

Mari grinned. "He sure was hot, wasn't he?"

Sheila bumped their shoulders. "Steamin'!"

Mari laughed. It felt good to joke around with someone who didn't know the truth about Nicholai.

Sheila opened her vial of attraction oil and added a drop to Mari's ink.

"What are you doing?" Mari asked under her breath.

"We're going to make sure you get another go-round with Hottie-pants."

"What makes you think I'll even see him again?"

"Considering you just saw him last night? I don't know."

Mari frowned. "How'd you know that?"

"I saw him with Ally outside the bookstore lurking in the shadows. She said he'd been there with you."

Mari's stomach soured. Ally knew she was with Nicholai? What if she told Sebastian? "I wasn't with him, I just ran into him there."

"Well, it looked to me like Ally was getting a little too close to him, if you know what I mean."

Suspicion, dark and cold, wormed its way through Mari's heart and quickly burrowed through her, leaving a deep chill in its wake. Goose buns rose on her skin.

Instantly, the alcohol lamp's flame snuffed out.

Mari rubbed her arms and stared at the lamp. *Did she do that?* Was Jacob was right? Were her powers getting stronger?

"Well, in case you're thinking of heading out there again tonight, I want you prepared for anything," Sheila said, completely unaware of Mari's unease.

"Great," Mari said dryly. "Except you didn't say the ritual. Now I'll have every man in New York hitting on me."

Sheila grinned. "Isn't life fun?"

Ms. Whalen circled the room, watching their progress with the talismans. "I want each of you to light your candles in your room tonight and when you leave today, take a stick of dragon's blood incense by the door. Recite your protection spells three times before you go to bed. We will make this house impenetrable to evil."

Mari frowned. "Impenetrable to evil?"

Sheila sobered. "Yeah, what's that about?"

"Is something going on?" a student at the next table asked.

Mari tensed as she waited to hear the answer.

Ms. Whalen sighed. "The weres have warned Sebastian that we all need to be extra careful. Something is afoot. I'm afraid that is all he knows at this time, but he will be sure to keep you updated as he discovers more."

"Weres?" Mari whispered to Sheila.

"Werewolves. You'll learn about them in your Shape-shifters and Demons class next semester."

"Oh, great. Can hardly wait for that one. Do they want to kill us, too?"

Sheila laughed. "The weres? No silly. They protect us."

Mari swallowed, and was almost afraid to ask. "From what?"

"Demons and vampires."

Vampires. Obviously that was what Sebastian was worried about. Two days ago she hadn't known vampires existed, now not only were there vampires, but werewolves and demons, too. How could she have been so oblivious to the world around her?

Because her mother wanted it that way. She had wanted her to have a normal life. And she had, for a little while. But not anymore. Apparently, it was up to her now. Her blood was the weapon they needed to hold back the vampire threat. Mari was responsible for the safety of all the people in this room, in this house.

Whether she wanted to be or not.

She couldn't let her libido overrule her good sense. Mari dug into the box, pulled out another template and slapped it on the table.

Sheila wrinkled her nose. "A skull and crossbones. What are you, a pirate?"

Mari nodded. "Just call me toxic."

After her last class, Mari climbed the stairs toward her room on the third floor. As she stepped onto the landing and turned down the hall, Ally grabbed her arm, her nails digging into Mari's skin.

"I need to talk to you."

Mari jerked her arm back. "What do you want?"

"I saw you last night." Her eyes glittered with the accusation. "With *him.*"

No need to deny it. Sheila had already warned her. "So?" Mari said, feigning nonchalance.

"So. Stay away from him."

"Or what? You'll run to Sebastian?"

"I should, but no."

"Then why?"

"Because he's planning something, and whatever it is, it involves you."

Mari took a step away. "Thanks, I'll keep that in mind."

"He's dangerous. Trust me. I know what these monsters are capable of."

"Then what were you doing alone with him in the dark?"

Ally's mouth opened on a breath of surprise. "Just be careful. Don't get too wrapped up in him. I know what it's like to want a vampire—their power, their strength. It's intoxicating. But they're dangerous. They feed on us. And they enjoy it."

Mari thought of the story Jacob had told her. Had Ally really watched her entire family die? "If you're so worried about me, why haven't you told my brother?"

Ally shrugged. "Sebastian goes a little over-the-top when it comes to the pointy-fanged beasts."

Mari stilled as wariness shifted through her. "How do you mean?"

"I have more reason to hate them than anyone else here, but plotting to destroy them all? That's beyond mad, and I worry they might…retaliate."

A chill fell over her at Ally's words. *But can she be trusted? Why had she really been alone with Nicholai last night? And why the sudden play at friendship?* "I heard about your family. I'm sorry for your loss."

A shadow darkened Ally's eyes. "Thanks."

Not sure what else to say, Mari turned toward her room. But Ally followed.

"I had to tell Sebastian about Nicholai that night," Ally said. "You were in over your head, and you weren't listening to me. You certainly wouldn't have believed me if I told you what he was."

"That's a fact."

"But you believe now?"

"Yes."

"And you're on board?"

Mari stared at her then lowered her voice to a whisper. "You mean with giving Sebastian my blood to develop a toxin that will wipe them all out?" She thought of Nicholai's skin last night and the pronounced veins under his eyes. He looked so…sick. And she'd done that to him. "Do I have a choice?"

"We always have choices. Vampires were once human. They know how we think and feel. Yet, something is broken inside them. They don't feel things the way we do, but they are very good at pretending they can."

"Is that what Marcos did? How he got to my mom?"

Ally's gaze shifted.

"Sebastian told me Marcos killed my mother."

"I'm so sorry about what happened to your mom. She was a nice lady."

"Thank you. Though, I must admit, I wish Sebastian hadn't told me. Ever since that night, I can't sleep. The questions and uncertainties keep chasing each other around in my mind."

"Just be careful, Mari."

"Of what?"

"Don't be so ready to trust everyone and…everything."

Something in her tone set Mari's alarm bells ringing. "What do you mean?"

"I've already said too much." She glanced around her, then dug into her purse and pulled out a small bottle of pills. "Here, take these. Get some sleep. Clear your head. You're going to need it."

Chapter 10

What did Ally mean by that? Mari wondered as she watched her walk away. And why was it every day she had more questions than she had answers? She walked into her room while reading the sleeping pills Ally had given her. She opened the top drawer of her nightstand ready to drop them inside when she saw her mother's recipe book that she'd taken from the basement.

Don't be so ready to trust everyone and everything. Ally's words replayed in her mind. Why had her mother's things been in that room in the basement? Had she really agreed to stay down there?

Mari dropped the pills into the drawer, grabbed the book and her mother's tin of herbs and dropped them both in her bag. It was time she discovered exactly what her mother had been up to, and why she'd been here in the first place.

An hour later, Mari settled herself at a corner table in her favorite Italian family restaurant. Her mother had been a witch, yet somehow she'd been able to hide it and keep Mari in the dark. But had she continued to practice her powers in their home in Vermont? Or had she put all of it, along with Vindecare, behind her?

Her mother had always been interested in herbs, but Mari thought it had only been for holistic medicinal purposes. Had she still practiced making her potions? Mari rested her hand over her mother's recipe book as if the mere process of touching the same worn leather her mother had touched so many times would bring her closer to her.

And give her the answers she needed.

She ordered a plate of spaghetti and a cup of hot tea. Discarding the store-bought tea bag, she stuck a diffuser filled with her mother's herbs into the metal pot of hot water. It had been a long time since she'd had a cup of her mom's tea. And now that she smelled the familiar scents of the herbs, she realized how much she missed it. How she missed everything about her mom, especially not having her around to talk things over with.

Tears pricked her eyes.

She blinked them away. All she had to do was pull out these herbs to be reminded of her. She just hoped someday she could drink her tea without the overwhelming sense of grief.

As the tea steeped, Mari went through the packets of herbs, listing their contents in her notebook, jotting down descriptions of the herbs that she knew and what their health benefits were:

Hogweed and parsnip were full of butyric acid to help increase normal hemoglobin.

Yellow dock root for iron deficiency.

Burdock root and raspberry leaf for the selenium.

Yellow and nettle leaf also for anemia.

Astragalus...

As she continued writing down the herbs, misgivings needled the back of her mind. So many of these herbs affected the blood. Had her mother been combining herbs for their flavors, to boost her immunity? Or had she been doing something else entirely?

She searched through her mother's book looking for a recipe that combined the items in the tin. After about ten minutes she found the list of ingredients. The heading on the page read: *Valetude Tea for use in masking a witch's powers.*

Mari's stomach dropped. Every day, for as long as she could remember, her mother made her this tea.

Every day!

Disbelief coursed through her. Had her mother wanted her to be normal so badly that she'd medicated her?

"Didn't your mother teach you not to play with your food?" The deep voice penetrated the shock numbing her mind. She looked up, shaken and slightly disoriented.

Nicholai.

Damn. How did he always find her?

He sat across the table from her, leaning back in the chair stretching out his long legs.

"I could say the same to you," she snapped.

He placed a hand on his heart. "Mariana, you wound me."

"What are you doing here, Nicholai?"

"I came to see you."

She grunted. "Stalking me, more like it."

He smiled, one corner of his mouth lifting in a sexy, confident lip-swagger. "You can't tell me you weren't hoping to see me tonight."

She thought of the tattoo on her arm with the drop of attraction oil in the ink and recalled Sheila's words. *Just in case...* She looked at him with narrowing eyes, afraid to give away the truth that yes, a small part of her had hoped. A very small part. For a very small moment.

He reached across the table and touched her hand. The contact was instant and went straight through her. It took every ounce of willpower she could gather not to snatch her hand back.

"It's good to see you," he said.

His dark eyes looked sincere, but she couldn't help noticing his skin still looked thin, almost translucent, with dark veins spidering out from under his eyes. The effects of the toxin still lingering? Were they permanent? What other damage had it caused?

She pulled her hand back and swept her mother's herbs into the tin, then replaced it, along with her books, into her bag.

"Potions? Hoping to make a love spell?" He waggled his eyebrows, his smile wide and confident.

"A protection spell," she said dryly.

He laughed. "Darling, silly little witches' spells won't protect you from me." To illustrate his point, he picked up the small metal teapot, poured her mother's steaming tea into a cup and took a large gulp.

A tremor of fear zipped through her. "Why not?"

His eyes locked on hers. "Because you don't want protecting."

She swallowed. "Don't I?"

Suddenly he was closer, his hand moving up her arm, tracing the skull and crossbones tattoo. Nerve endings fired along her skin, longing soared through her body.

He leaned in close. "What you really want is for me to kiss you."

Her heart fluttered in her chest. Could he hear it? Her gaze dropped to his sardonic mouth even as her breath caught in her throat. Yes, dammit. She did. The taste of his lips still lingered on hers and she couldn't stop remembering the way his tongue possessed her completely, leaving her unable to think or feel anything else.

"No. You're wrong." She pulled back, her gaze sweeping across his face. Was it the light, or did his skin look better? Not quite so pale. The veins not so exposed.

"No one is watching," he whispered. "No one will even care." He touched her thigh, exploring, caressing.

"Take your hand off me," she said on a shallow breath even as she longed for him to move it higher.

"Come on, darling. We're good together. I feel better now than I have for days. Your essence energizes me."

"Stop now or I'll scream," she said, her voice a harsh whisper.

He frowned. "Scream? Why would a willing woman scream? And if I remember right, you, my darling, were more than willing."

Heat filled her cheeks as images from that night assaulted her. Her blood thickened with desire.

"Are you sure you want me to stop?" he whispered, his hot breath close. "Your dilated eyes tell a different story."

"Yes," she said, more forcefully than she'd intended. She was furious at his audacity and at her own ramped-up desire. What was wrong with her? He was dangerous. He was all wrong for her. And yet here she was, hungering for him once more.

"I don't suppose I could get you to take me to Marcos," he said softly.

"Not on your life."

"I was afraid you'd say that." He stared at her. No, not stared—devoured.

Heat flooded her core.

"We were so good together. I can't stop thinking about how good."

"Well, you should. I have."

"Have you?" His smile told her he knew she was lying. Knew he was all she could think about. Knew he was the real reason she couldn't sleep at night.

He was dangerous, and yet here she was, moving closer and closer to the flame.

"A connection like ours doesn't come along every day. I've been around long enough to know."

"We have no connection, Nicholai. What we had was you manipulating me to get you into Vindecare."

"That might be how it started, but not how it ended. And to prove you can trust me, I came to warn you about that red-headed witch friend of yours."

"Ally? What about her?"

"She saw us at the bookstore together last night."

What was his game now? Why tell her this?

"She came up to me after you left. In fact, you could say she was 'all over' me."

Mari's eyes narrowed. "I have a hard time believing that. She knows what you are."

"True. But so do you. And yet, here you are."

"That's different."

"Is it?"

"Yes, I didn't seek you out. You found me. So, why would Ally go anywhere near you?"

"Because some witches like it hot."

Hot. Desire sparked though her body as he said the word. Yes. She liked it hot. She liked *him* hot.

"So, Mari. Tell me. What kind of witch are you?"

Nicholai watched Mari from the shadows, following her as she left the diner and walked back to Vindecare, cutting through the park that led behind the back of the estate. He could easily overtake her right now, drag her back to his penthouse and do whatever he wanted with her. Have his way with her luscious body and make her scream for more. And purge her from his mind once and for all before Helena worked her magic and made her a demon's vessel.

But as he let her slip away, he realized he didn't want to take her that way. He wanted her to come to him on her own. His victory over her would be that much sweeter. For now, all he could do was continue to plant seeds of doubt into her mind about her brother and the lies he'd been feeding her.

A whisper of arctic pressure moved over him. He stiffened.

"She's a beauty. Don't think I've seen her around before," the deep voice said behind him.

Christos.

Nicholai stiffened. There was something about the vampire he didn't trust. Though he wasn't sure if it was the air of meanness he carried like a second skin or the way he was always lurking around...*watching*.

"She's new," he said.

"Hmm...sweet. I'm going to have to keep my eye on that little witch."

"She's off-limits," Nicholai said, a little harsher than he'd intended. But just the thought of Christos laying a finger on her made his blood boil.

"Really? Because from where I stand, no witch is off-limits."

"She's taken."

Christos stared at him, his narrowed gaze perusing Nicholai's face. "So she likes to walk on the wild side, does she? Even better."

Nicholai didn't rise to the bait this time. "What are you doing here, Christos?"

"Better question is, what are you doing here? I would think one nasty go-round with the Vindecare witches would be enough for you. I thought you were hightailing it back to England."

Where you belong.

The unspoken words hung between them. "I'm not leaving without my clan."

"Noble, if not foolish."

Nicholai pulled back his shoulders and stepped forward, moving into Christos's space. "Again, why are *you* here?"

To his credit, the vampire held his own. "This is my town, and my favorite spot to watch what the little bitches are up to, and I'll watch or touch whoever I please."

Nicholai sucked in a deep breath and bared his teeth. This bastard was going to go after Mari just to prove he could. "All this watching, and yet you didn't notice them take a whole clan of vampires into their dungeons?"

"Ingenious, if you ask me. I didn't think this spineless crew had it in them."

"I'm fairly certain most of them don't know the vampires are there."

"Then aren't they going to be in for one hell of a surprise?"

"Something going on I should know about?"

"A rescue plan. And one I'm expecting will be quite…delicious."

"Were you planning to include me in your plan to rescue *my* men?"

"Perhaps. Though, frankly, Nicholai, I don't think you are up to it." Christos stared at him, his eyes glowing amber in the darkness.

Nicholai bit back an angry retort and evened his voice. "How do you plan to protect yourself from the poison?"

"I'm working on the antidote now. It will only be a matter of time."

Suspicion wound through Nicholai, tightening his already tense muscles. "And just how did you get a sample of the toxin?"

"Why from your blood, of course."

In the blink of an eye, Christos was gone. And the anger working its way through Nicholai's gut blossomed into full-blown rage.

"Darby!"

That night Mari took the pill Ally had given her, and still she was too ramped up to sleep. According to her mother's recipe book, the tea she'd been drinking her whole life masked her powers. Since she'd stopped drinking the tea, the anomalies in her blood were increasing, which was why her powers were suddenly becoming stronger. And why her blood had become more potent, more deadly.

To the vampires.

It hadn't been her that had made Nicholai look and feel better back at the restaurant, it had been the tea. Could it possibly be an antidote to the poison? There was no way to know for sure. Unless...

She could give it to Marcos and see what the effect on him would be. Her mother fed it to her every day to keep her powers muted. Would it also change the effect her blood had on a vampire?

She thought about Marcos as she turned off the light and slipped into bed. What did he think about as he lay in his box in the catacombs, unable to move, yet knowing what was happening to him and who was doing it? Was that why he'd killed her mother?

If Mari gave him the tea, would he get better? And stronger? Did she want him to get better? Or did she want him to suffer. To pay for what he'd done.

Most of the other witches in this house had no idea about the secret chambers beneath them and what her brother kept down there. If the tea rendered the poison useless and Marcos got out of that box, he could kill them all. She couldn't take that chance.

But what about Nicholai? He wouldn't give up until Marcos was free. He would be after her, day after day, trying to get her to relent and give in to him. But if somehow she could get Nicholai to take Marcos away without anyone discovering...

The thought crept unbidden into her mind. But how could she trust him? She hadn't forgotten the things he'd yelled at her that first night. He'd called for revenge.

If Marcos didn't kill them all, Nicholai just might.

She shuddered and closed her eyes, trying to still her mind, trying to stop thinking about *him.* She wondered what it would be like if he was just a normal guy and she was still in college? What if it were just the two of them and there was no such thing as Vampires and Weres and Witches.

Her eyes drifted closed and she tried to sleep. But she couldn't stop remembering how he felt, his mouth against hers, the touch of his lips, his fingers, the soft caress of his breath.

Stop it!

She turned over and beat her feather pillow. She couldn't think about him anymore. There was nothing she could do to help him. Sebastian and Ally were right. She had to put him out of her mind and forget about him.

Restless, she got out of bed, stood at the window and stared into the night. The room felt hot, stifling. Opening the window, she was tempted to stick her head out and suck in the cool night air. She caught a flash of movement, a shadow in the distance. Was that him? Was Nicholai watching her even now? Waiting for her?

She listened intently but heard nothing but the soft sounds of a boat on the river in the distance. After a moment of staring into the darkness, she saw nothing more and let out a deep breath.

There was no one there.

She climbed back into bed, listening to the wind rustle the tree's leaves and finally drifted off to sleep.

Chapter 11

The moon shone brightly, the clouds stirring restlessly across the sky. Nicholai stood in the bushes beneath Mari's window. It was a warm night and she had it open, the curtains fluttering in the slight breeze.

He laid his palms against the wall, feeling the porous stone digging into his hands as he climbed, scaling the wall until he reached her window. Her breathing was steady and even. She was asleep. Soundlessly, he climbed inside.

The room's subtle scent was sweet, like her. He watched the steady rise and fall of her chest and was tempted to climb into the bed next to her, to make her see what they could have together. And perhaps later he would, but right now, he needed to find Marcos.

He slipped out her bedroom door and down the darkened hallway. At two in the morning, everyone in the house slept soundly. He retraced his steps down to the basement. He needed to know where they were keeping Marcos and how many others were still down there.

And what about Christos's men? Darby had said the witches had them, too. He had no reason to doubt it, but he did. Christos didn't act desperate to find his men, in fact something about the way he'd stood in the darkness watching Vindecare told him the vampire had something entirely different on his mind. But what it was, he couldn't fathom.

One thing he was sure of, though, Vampire clan leaders did not befriend mortals unless they were after something. And Darby had played right into his hands.

Anger at the woman's lack of sense burned inside him as he descended the stairs to the basement. He hurried down the long hallway, wondering when Darby started losing faith in his abilities to lead and make decisions for their clan. As he slipped silently past the closed doors, he caught a distinctively garlic scent. Nicholai abruptly stopped. He wasn't alone down here in the dark.

He stood still for a moment, listening, and then heard the soft footsteps. He ducked into the nearest room, opened the door a crack and waited. Within a few minutes an armed guard passed, slowly patrolling the hallways.

Nicholai considered overpowering him, but he couldn't take the chance that the guard wasn't alone, or worse, that he might have the poison with him. One stick and he'd never make it out of the house.

And then they'd all be lost.

After the guard disappeared into the large room at the end of the hall, Nicholai realized he couldn't do this alone. He needed help. He needed Mari.

Silently, he made his way back to her room, plucking a long-stemmed red rose from a vase as he passed. She had seen Marcos. He was sure of that. But would she help him? Or would she pretend to help and trigger another alarm? He stood over her as she slept, staring down at her beautiful face, and hoped he was wrong about her. Hoped she was as innocent as she appeared.

If she was, and he could get her to help him, then maybe he wouldn't have to resort to the extreme measure of using Asmos. There were no guarantees with a demon that powerful that any of them would survive, but one thing he did know. She wouldn't.

He reached out and touched her cheek, running his fingers lightly down her jaw. She murmured quietly and leaned into him. Gently, he slipped into the bed next to her, running his hand up and down her body beneath the covers, loving the feel of her soft silk shift.

She moaned gently in her sleep, and he leaned close, nuzzling her neck, kissing her softly, loving her sweet scent and the delicious taste of her skin.

What was it about this woman that kept drawing him back to her? Was it because he couldn't figure her out? He couldn't tell if she was someone to trust, or a damn good manipulator who expertly hid her feelings while somehow wrenching his to the surface.

He drew the soft lobe of her ear into his mouth and sucked gently. It was then that he saw the bottle of sleeping pills on the bedside table.

He sighed. She wouldn't be waking up tonight.

Unless… He picked up the rose.

Mari stirred as desire pulsed through her, tightening her belly. She thought she smelled roses. She inhaled deeply, and smiled as she felt the velvety softness of a petal against her lips. Had she heard Nicholai's voice? Felt his loving caress? Was she dreaming of him again?

She opened her eyes and stared into the darkness. Her heart drummed in her chest, while a frustrating itch throbbed lower. No one was here. She was dreaming. Sensuous, erotic vampire dreams. *Again.*

She sighed and turned on her side, pulling her pillow closer. The sheer curtains billowed in the breeze from the opened window.

You going to scale three stories to see me? She recalled the words she'd asked Nicholai that night when he'd wanted to know which room was hers.

Her heart thudded, and dropped to the pit of her stomach. Could vampires scale walls? Could they turn into ravens or bats and fly?

She popped out of bed and rushed to the window. The night was dead silent. She shut the window, not caring how hot it was in the room. She stood there for a moment staring out into the darkness and tried to catch her panicked breath. Without the soft breeze the room became stifling. She pulled off her nightgown, dropped it to the floor, then turned around and gasped.

Nicholai stood before her. A red rose in his hand. "Shh. Don't scream."

She seized the nightgown from the floor and held it like a shield in front of her.

"You shouldn't hide your beauty. Not from me." He held out the rose to her.

She ignored it.

"How'd you get in here?"

"Does it matter?"

"You have to leave!"

"I know. I just wanted to see you. You are beautiful when you sleep, so peaceful."

Horror dawned inside her. "You've been watching me sleep?"

"Would you hate me if I told you yes?"

"How often?"

"Not too much."

Revulsion grabbed her by the throat. "If you don't get out of here right now, I will scream."

"And bring your brother and his poisoned arrows down on me?" He moved closer, one slow step at a time.

She stared at him. She couldn't move. Couldn't scream. Couldn't stop him. "I did the protection spell just as they told me. Why didn't it work on you?"

"Why would it? You've already invited me in."

Dread filled her, liquefying her insides.

"I would never hurt you," he said, and ran the rose across her cheek and down her neck.

Shivers followed in its wake, weakening her knees. She opened her mouth to speak, to demand he leave at once, but no words left her lips.

"We have something special, you and I. Something I don't want to lose."

"No. We don't," she said on a shallow breath.

"Don't we?" he purred, and dropped the rose even farther, dragging it down the valley between her breasts.

"Nicholai, please," she murmured, the velvety softness caressing her skin, soothing her nerves.

"You miss me as much as I miss you. I can feel it. Smell it." He stepped even closer, his lips brushing gently across hers, sending heat coursing through her body, fanning the flames low in her belly back to life.

She couldn't consider it. Not even for a second. "If anyone found out… If they knew…" she whispered.

"Who would tell them?"

His lips fell onto hers, crushing them. As if they had a mind of their own, her arms wound around his neck and she clung to him. She had to. Her knees were too weak, and if she didn't hold on to something, she would fall into a boneless heap on the floor.

He reached down and swung his arms under her legs, effortlessly picking her up. He carried her to the bed and laid her on it. Gently, he pulled the flimsy nightgown out of her grasp and tossed it away.

His breath caught as he stared at her. "You are so beautiful with the moonlight glistening on your skin."

He stood next to the bed, his gaze moving over her body in a slow, breathtaking perusal. She took a deep breath and licked her lips as he took the rose and brushed it across her feverish skin.

She arched her back as the soft fragrant petals moved over her more sensitive spots, and said his name on a soft sigh. "Nicholai."

She was crazy. Insane. And out of her mind with lust for this man.

But was he a man?

He sure looked like a man, felt like a man. And the way he was touching her... Man or not, she wasn't sure she had it in her to make him stop, even if she wanted to.

"We can't," she said on a moan, even though she wanted him, too. "I can't."

"What we have together is special," he replied and rolled the rose along the bottom of her foot, her toes and up her calves to the tender spot on the inside of her thighs. "You can't deny it."

She knew he was right. They were special together. She had never felt like this before and feared she would never feel it again. But it didn't matter. He couldn't be here. She couldn't let him touch her. No matter how badly she wanted him to. *Wanted him.*

She sat up, pushing the rose away. "This is crazy. What do you want from me, Nicholai?"

"Isn't it obvious?"

She took a deep breath. "Other than that."

"Marcos did not kill your mother. I can prove it to you."

She stilled. "How?"

"Help me help him."

"How will that prove anything?"

"I will find out the truth. I promise you."

"And I'm supposed to believe the promises of a vampire? You lied to me once already just to get into the house. How do I know you're not lying to me now? Forget it. Your game won't work this time. I'm not going to let you lie to me again, and I'm not going to help you find Marcos. I'm not going to have anything to do with you. Do you understand? Now go. Get out. Or I swear, I really will scream."

Maybe it was the desperation in her voice or the steely determination in her eyes—she didn't know, but in the blink of an eye, he was gone.

Nicholai stormed into the penthouse, furious and frustrated. Not only was he sexually frustrated, but the damned little witch refused to help him free Marcos. She was growing stronger, and seemed to be easily able to fight off his influence. She shouldn't have had the clarity of thought to stop him tonight, but she did.

One more time, he had roamed the halls of that blasted house and he still hadn't seen Marcos.

He went to the fridge and opened it, expecting to see a stash of blood Darby should have procured from a blood bank.

But the fridge was empty.

"Darby," he roared.

"What the hell, Nicholai? It's after three in the morning. What is it?" she asked, walking out of her bedroom in an oversize sleep shirt, her arms raised above her head as she yawned and stretched.

"Why isn't there any blood?"

"Because we're out, that's why. You've been drinking four times your normal amount."

"I need to flush the toxin out of my system. Is keeping enough blood on hand to be able to do that too much to ask?"

She raised her eyebrows as she glared at him. "We're in a fine mood this morning, aren't we?"

"Don't even start with me."

"Your little witch get you this bent?"

"Maybe it was your boyfriend," he sneered.

"What are you talking about?"

"I'm talking about the fact that you've obviously lost your mind, or else why would you be so stupid as to give that bastard my blood?"

"It wasn't like that. I was helping you. Christos was helping you. He needed a sample of the toxin to make an antidote."

"Christos has no intention of 'helping' me. Don't ever forget that."

"Listen, Nicholai. I have been a part of this clan for four years. I have proved myself to you time and time again. I stuck by your ass when you were high on demon essence and driving everyone else away! How could you doubt *me?* I love you. You know I would never betray you."

"Then how could you give him my blood? What were you thinking?"

"That you were going to die and he might be the only one who could save you. You didn't see what you looked like. You looked like you were dead."

"I am dead."

"You know what I mean." She scraped her hands through her long hair. "I have always been there for you. No matter how much of an ass you've been. And you know you can be a big one. I've stood by you through it all. And I'll stand by you through this, too."

Nicholai took in the dead certainty in her eyes. Yes, he'd

always believed he could trust her, but ever since she'd been hanging with Christos, her judgment had become questionable. Why was she so enamored with the cretin? Didn't she know he was dangerous? Couldn't she see what a bastard he was?

"Stay away from Christos," he said.

"Why?"

"I don't like him. I don't trust his motives. He's up to something, and until I know what it is, I don't want him around you. And I certainly don't want him in this house."

"Fine. And your little witch?"

"What about her?"

"Am I supposed to trust her motives?"

"You don't have to worry about her. Everything is moving according to my plan. I will take care of the witch."

Early the next morning, Mari woke alone in the bed. She swallowed the lump of trepidation in her throat. Had Nicholai really been there, or had it…had he, been just another dream? She saw the rose lying on her nightstand next to the bottle of sleeping pills and fought a shiver. Getting up, she threw the pills and the rose into the trash can in the corner. She had to take control of her life.

And to do that, she had to find out the truth about her mother's death and about what was really going on in this house. Before she lost her nerve, she quickly dressed then hurried to the third-floor lounge. She placed a diffuser with her mother's herbs inside a thermos and filled it with hot water.

For years, her mother had fed her this tea, masking her powers. And according to the blood tests Jacob had taken when she'd first arrived at the institute, the tea had worked. There weren't as many anomalies in her blood, and her powers weren't as strong as they were now that she'd stopped drinking it. If this tea could diminish the toxin in her blood, perhaps it could also diminish it from Marcos's? And if it worked, what would he be willing to do to get his hands on it?

Would he tell her the truth? Or just what she wanted to hear?

Clutching the thermos in her hand, Mari hurried down to the basement, toward the weapons room and the staircase that led to the catacombs. There was only one way to find out. Hopefully, she was early enough that no one would be up yet.

Careful not to put her weight on the step that would trigger the alarm, she crept down the stairs. She wasn't sure if she was doing the right thing, but she had to see his face for herself when she asked him the truth. Had he killed her mother? And if he had, why not let her brother kill him?

As she moved closer to his room, she heard voices. She wasn't alone. Silently she peered into the doorway. Ally leaned over the box. Mari could hear Marcos thrashing against his bindings, cursing under his breath. What was Ally doing to him?

Almost as if she sensed her, Ally looked up. Blood brightened her lips. Mari gasped then grabbed her stomach as it heaved and quickly stepped back into the darkness. She stood utterly silent, listening for Ally's approach, but she didn't come. She must not have seen her.

Feeling nauseated, Mari slipped past the room and hurried deeper into the catacombs, away from Ally and Marcos and whatever Ally was doing to him. As she turned a corner, she saw a light at the end of the hallway and hoped someone else wasn't down here, too. For a second, Mari contemplated whether or not she wanted to see any more of what was going on down here in the darkness. Some things she was better off not knowing.

But she couldn't bury her head in the sand any longer. She had to discover the truth. She edged deeper into the catacombs, moving toward the light. As she crept near the doorway, she listened intently for any sound or movement, but heard only the loud buzz of the fluorescent lights.

What else could they possibly be doing down here? She lingered near the doorway then, grasping the doorjamb, peered inside. She slapped a hand to her mouth to stifle her gasp. At least twenty steel boxes lay on tables. Jacob had a large syringe in his hand and was walking from box to box, injecting something into the IV lines.

Were there vampires in all those boxes?

How could they possibly have enough of the toxin to capture and keep incapacitated that many vampires? They would need a whole lot more blood than she could give them to keep all of them in a state of stasis. She thought of how often they'd been taking her blood. It was a lot, too much even, but certainly not enough for this?

What were they planning to do? Drain her dry?

Horrified, she turned away. More than anything she wanted to flee back to her room, back to the sunshine, outside into the fresh morning air. This was too horrible. She hurried down the hall, but before she could make her way back to the staircase, Ally walked out of Marcos's room, wiping the back of her hand across her mouth.

Mari ducked into another hallway and blended into the darkness. Ally stood still for a moment, staring in her direction. Mari held her breath and didn't move until Ally turned away and left. Mari blew out a relieved sigh then slipped into Marcos's room.

Chapter 12

Slowly, Mari approached the steel box and peered inside. Marcos looked up at her, his obsidian eyes filled with hatred and loathing. They shifted slightly when he saw it was her. He closed them and turned away. Had he thought she was Ally coming back again?

Mari sighed. She would not feel sorry for him. This monster killed her mother. All she wanted now was the truth. "I have something for you. I'd like you to give it a try and see if it makes you feel better."

"Why?" he asked, his tone defeated, his face still turned away.

"I told Nicholai I'd help you," she lied.

He turned to her then, his eyes now the beautiful shade of Caribbean-blue filled with suspicion. "I will never betray Nicholai. I won't help you get him for her."

"For her?"

"She will not have him, too." Anger and determination sharpened his words.

Ally? Why would she want Nicholai? Mari thought of the blood on Ally's lips and shivered.

"I promise. I'm not here about Nicholai. I'm here to help you. But you can't tell anyone. Especially not Ally. This has to be our secret."

He spat out a sarcastic laugh. "You witches keep a lot of secrets."

Didn't she know it?

"Whatever it is you have, I don't want it." He turned back away.

She ignored him, opened the thermos and filled the lid with her mother's hot tea.

"You'll want this."

She made sure his arms were still bound then reached inside the box bringing the cup near his mouth.

He faced her, his eyes widening with surprise as he caught the tea's scent. Gingerly, she reached inside the box and lifted his head.

His eyes locked onto hers as he drank the tea. Something akin to sympathy moved her, but she pushed it away, and instead forced herself to remember the way his beautiful eyes could turn black and dangerous. This man was a killer. She mustn't let his hopelessness get to her.

"Valetudo," he whispered, shaking Mari from her thoughts.

Stunned, she stared at him. Her heart raced as he repeated the name her mother had always called the tea. He knew about the tea, knew it could help him.

"Yes, how did you know that?"

"There was a woman who used to visit me. Lina."

As he said her mother's name, her stomach tightened. She pulled away from him.

"She'd bring me the Valetudo tea to take away my pain. But that was a long time ago. Where did she go, my Lina?"

His Lina? Mari didn't know what to say. "When did she bring you this tea? How long ago?"

"I'm not sure. There is no basis for time when you're held prisoner in the dark. Could have been months, or years." His gaze swept over her face. "She looked like you. You have the same kind eyes."

"She was my mother." Mari cringed as her voice cracked over the word.

"Was?"

Her chest muscles tensed and she could barely get the words out. "She died." To her horror, tears filled her eyes. She tried to fight them, to hold them back, but couldn't. They spilled over and ran in rivulets down her cheeks.

His eyes turned bleak and, for the briefest of moments, he looked pained. "I'm sorry. She…Lina was my friend. I asked her to help the others, but then I never saw her again. I hope…I hope it wasn't my fault."

Mari stiffened. "The others?"

"The others from my clan. They're here somewhere. I can hear them whispering in my mind." He looked crazed for a moment, and she wondered if maybe too much time alone in the dark was getting to him, but then she thought of the other boxes in the room down the hall, and felt slightly sick. Had her mother tried to help them, too? Had she gotten caught?

"I've missed her," he said.

Mari gave him another sip of tea, holding it up to his lips with trembling hands, trying to keep it steady as he drank. "Me, too."

After he finished, she replaced the lid on the thermos, confused and not sure what to think. Why would her mother help the vampires she was responsible for bringing here in the first place? If it weren't for her blood, her toxin, Sebastian never would have been able to capture them. So, why? Unless she never wanted to be a part of Sebastian's war to begin with. Had he forced her to give him her blood? Had they taken too much? Or had they caught her giving the vampires the tea?

Mari's head was spinning. "They told me you killed her," she said, hoping for an answer to the questions making her dizzy.

Marcos cried in outrage.

Startled, Mari jumped back.

"She was helping me!" he said. "She wasn't like the others. She cared about me. I would never have hurt her."

"Then who did?" she whispered.

"I don't know," he said through gritted teeth. "But when I find out…"

Why had Sebastian insisted Marcos had killed her? To keep Mari in line with his plans? Had he lied to her mom, too? Was that why she was helping Marcos?

Mari grasped the side of his box. "I'm so sorry," she whispered. So many secrets and lies. She thought she was going to be sick. Searching for air, she turned and ran, clutching the thermos to her middle.

She bolted out of the room down the long hallways and up the stairs into the weapons room, replaying everything that had happened, every conversation in her mind since she'd arrived. The only one who showed any true emotion over her mother's death, the only one Mari believed had even cared, was a prisoner locked in a steel box—a monster who was supposed to have killed her.

Only she no longer believed that was true.

She kept running, up to the main floor, ignoring the stares of those she passed, thinking of all the other vampires locked in the catacombs. Too many to help. Too many for her blood to keep incapacitated.

She raced up the stairs to her room, opened her closet door

and pulled down her knapsack. She filled it with her most precious items, including her mother's recipe book and her tin of herbs, then hurried down the three flights of stairs until she finally broke free of Vindecare and plunged into the sunshine.

She ran from this house of horrors and kept on going until the stitch in her side wouldn't let her continue any longer. She stopped, gasping, as she leaned against a building. Not able to stand any longer, she sank to the ground, buried her face in her hands and cried.

That evening Nicholai left the penthouse. He had one last chance to convince Mari to help him with Marcos. Tomorrow, Helena would be back to perform the ceremony. According to Darby, Mari had been out of the house all day going to the library, her favorite coffee shop, and was again at that small Italian place on Johnson Avenue. Playing hooky from witch school? Did she sense this could be her last day?

Not wanting her to pick up on the morose thought, he forced it from his mind and pushed open the door to the restaurant. He nodded to the hostess and made his way to the windows where Mari sat, slowly twirling pasta onto her fork.

"You're becoming fairly predictable," he said, as he sat across the table from her.

She didn't answer him. Didn't even look up, just lifted her wineglass and took a deep swallow of the burgundy liquid.

"What, no snappy comeback?" he goaded, leaning closer to her.

"Not from me. Not tonight," she said, barely lifting her gaze from her pasta.

"I'm disappointed. I've come to enjoy our sparring matches."

"Sorry, Nicholai. I don't have it in me right now."

"Why not?" He stared at her, his dark gaze perusing her

face. The skin around her eyes was red and puffy. Crying? "What's happened?" he asked, softly.

After a long pause, she took another swallow of wine. "I don't want to talk about it."

"Why not?"

"I can't." She pushed her plate away and picked up her bag.

Before she could stand, he gently placed his hand over hers. "Let me help you."

"There's nothing you can do." She got up and started walking toward the door.

He jumped to his feet, and in the blink of an eye, was standing in front of her. "Yes there is. I can cheer you up."

"Really," she said, dryly. "I don't think so."

He followed her out the door. "How about a ride?" He pointed at a Harley-Davidson motorcycle parked at the curb. "With the roar of the engine and the wind blowing your hair, all your worries will be lost. Trust me."

"I don't trust anyone anymore."

"Well, you need a ride home, don't you? Why not take a chance and let the bike work its magic?"

"I'm not going back to Vindecare. Not ever again."

He didn't have time to get another witch, another plan. He raised his eyebrows. "What about your stuff?"

She held her sack tight against her chest. "I have everything I need right here."

"What's happened? Is Marcos okay? Have you seen him?"

Unshed tears brightened her eyes. "I'm sorry. I know you care about him. Yes, I saw him this morning. For the most part, he's okay."

Nicholai sucked in a relieved breath. "For the most part?"

"They keep him in the dark. In a box. The poison constantly drips into his blood."

He thought of the debilitating, sick way he'd felt with the

toxin in his system and cringed. "Why are they keeping him alive? Why not just kill him?"

"They're trying different serums on him and the others, perfecting their formula."

"Others?"

She nodded, as her eyes once again filled with tears. "They're making a weapon to use against you. I'm so sorry. I won't have any more to do with it. That's why I have to leave."

She turned and started walking down the street, but after a few steps stopped and looked back at him. "Marcos said they're trying to get you, too. Be careful, Nicholai."

"That redheaded witch already tried the other night."

Mari stared at him a moment. "You didn't mention that."

"I didn't know if you were involved."

"I don't want to be," she whispered.

"Draw me a map. Help me."

"I can't." She turned and walked away.

He couldn't let her go that easily, couldn't lose this chance. In the blink of an eye, he was standing in front of her, blocking her path.

"Marcos didn't kill your mother. Don't let them do this to him. Help me."

Her eyes filled with tears once more. "I know," she whispered. "Marcos told me. My brother lied."

"What made you believe him?"

"He knew Mom's name. He said that she tried to help him. That he...*missed* her."

"Help us, Mari."

"I won't go back in that place."

"Then draw me a map. Tell me what I need to know."

She hesitated. "But what about the other witches? There are a lot of good people in that house, people who have no idea what is going on down in those catacombs."

"They won't be touched. We didn't come here to hurt humans. We only take what we need. Never more."

Her eyes searched his and he could see she wanted to believe him.

"Our witches' families have been slaughtered for years. They are only trying to protect themselves."

"Not by us. We have only been here since last summer. Before that, we were in England. We have done no harm. But you can't stand by and do nothing to help us. You know that. It's why you can't sleep at night."

He could see the fear in her eyes, could feel her getting ready to flee. "I know I'm pushing hard. Let's take a breather. Take a motorcycle ride, get a drink. Draw me a map of the house so I'm not wandering around aimlessly. Your brother has posted guards. I need to be able to get in, find Marcos and then get out quickly."

"I have a ticket on the 8:00 p.m. train back to Vermont."

His mind raced as he thought up a way to keep her with him. Whatever it took, she would not be making that train.

"That gives us an hour and a half. Come on, give the bike a chance, give me a chance. What else are you going to do, camp out at the train station?"

She looked at him, and then at the Harley. "What happened to your limo?"

"A man likes to have his toys. Come on, what do you say? Spend your last hour in New York with me. You won't be sorry."

"I don't know." She hesitated, but he could see she was thinking about it.

He took her hand in his, and gazed into her emerald-green eyes. "I care about you. You know the truth about what I am and yet you don't cower in fear. You match wits with me and take up a warrior's battle stance every time I see you. It's what draws me to you, and why I'd hoped we'd have more time together."

She opened her luscious mouth to speak, but he held up a hand.

"I realize we're in an impossible situation, but it's still one I want to explore. The truth is, I can't stop thinking about you. Wanting you. All the time."

She looked up at him, her eyes shimmering. "But don't you see? It doesn't matter what I want or what you want. We can never be together."

"Why not? We were together once and the world didn't fall apart."

"My world fell apart," she whispered. "That's why I have to be on that train. I have to go back to New England where my life was simple and fulfilled."

"But there's no one there for you now."

Pain glistened in her eyes.

"Stay with me. Just for tonight. Give me a chance, and if you still want to leave, I'll drive you to New England myself, tomorrow."

"I don't know."

He stepped closer, lifting her chin with a gentle touch of his finger. "Then how about this. Give me and that bike an hour, and then make up your mind."

She smiled, a small smile, full of sadness and heartbreak, then nodded.

An hour later, exhilarated and feeling immensely better, Mari had to admit, Nicholai had been right. The ride through the city was magical.

They stopped at a bar along the river and had another glass of wine. Warmth spread through her chest and she felt better than she had all day. Good enough that she was beginning to believe that maybe Nicholai was right. Maybe they could be friends.

Or even more than friends.

She found herself smiling and laughing at Nicholai's ridiculous attempts to cheer her up. If he only knew what had her so upset, he wouldn't be trying so hard. How could she ever confide in him that she and her mother were responsible for his friend's suffering? If she helped Nicholai and he discovered the truth about her, what would he do? Would he kill her, knowing the threat she posed?

It might have been Sebastian's sick and twisted plan, but without her blood, he never could have accomplished anything.

The best way she could help them all now, would be to leave. Without her blood, Sebastian would no longer be able to keep the vampires incapacitated. Then maybe he'd let them go.

She could hope, but she knew better. She remembered the rage simmering in his eyes. No, he'd never let them go. He'd kill them first. And if he knew she wanted to leave? Would he let her? She shuddered at the thought.

"Feeling better?" Nicholai asked as he moved closer and placed a hand on her waist.

She nodded and leaned into him, watching the moonlight shimmer across the surface of the water as the moon rose higher into the sky. No, she could never go back there. But that didn't mean she couldn't help stop the madness. Nicholai bent down and kissed her ear, nuzzling her neck, spreading warm melt-in-your-mouth goodness through her.

She should tell him to stop. But she didn't. Instead, she wound her arm around his shoulders, threading her fingers through his thick hair at his nape. Then she turned in his arms and found his lips with her own. Her mouth pressed against his, her tongue sweeping inside, exploring, battling, tasting. She kissed him as if this was the last kiss she might ever have.

As if she might never see him again.

Her heart broke at the thought and she pulled him closer to her.

"Please, stay," he murmured, as he rained kisses down her neck. "Just for a day. A night. A month."

She smiled.

"I will never hurt you."

But the way her heart was feeling right now, she knew that couldn't be true. It was too late for her. She had already been disillusioned and hurt.

"Give me a chance to show you how good we can be together. What we have is magical. Don't throw it away. Stay. Just for one night." He pulled back, looking into her eyes, his hope and anticipation rolling over her.

And in that moment, she knew if she left him, she would always wonder if he was right. Was she throwing away something worth fighting for?

She kissed him again, leaning into his hard, warm body. "Let's go to your place and draw ourselves a map."

Chapter 13

Mari walked into Nicholai's luxurious penthouse and looked around the spacious living room in awe. She didn't know what she'd expected from a vampire's lair, but it certainly wasn't warmth and sophistication. She stepped down alabaster marble steps onto thick cream carpeting and approached the floor-to-ceiling windows. She admired the view of the river with New York's cityscape in the distance. "It's beautiful," she murmured.

"Thanks. We like it."

She turned to him. "We?"

"There were more of us here, but now it's only my assistant, Darby, and me."

She nodded and, as she turned back to the windows, hoped she hadn't made a mistake in coming here. *In trusting him.*

He walked up behind her and slipped his arms around her waist. "Thank you for helping us." His deep timbre sent shivers cascading through her.

"Once I met Marcos, I couldn't have anything to do with my brother's schemes."

He turned her in his arms so she was facing him. "Come back to Vindecare with me. I need you."

She shivered at the thought of going back inside those tall stone walls. A part of her feared that if she went back, she would never be able to leave. That Sebastian would never let her leave. She looked up into Nicholai's chocolate-brown eyes. "I'm sorry, but I can't go back there. And neither should you. They want you, and they'll do anything they can to capture you, too."

He smiled and pulled her palms to his chest. "Everybody wants me."

"Be serious. Even Marcos is afraid for you."

"Don't worry. I will be careful. And I won't go alone. Will you at least draw me a map?"

She took a deep breath and nodded. That she could do. He led her to a large glossy black desk against a far wall. She picked up a piece of paper from the printer tray and started sketching the rooms in the catacombs below the basement floor.

"In this back room, there are at least twenty boxes like the one Marcos is in." She pointed to the map. "Maybe more. It was hard to judge. How many have gone missing?"

"Thirteen. But a clan in Manhattan has some missing, too."

"Do you think the members of this other clan are the ones killing the witches' families?"

His face turned grim. "Possibly. It sounds like we both got caught in the middle of something that started long before either of us got here."

"Maybe if we tell my brother that it might be the other vampires. If we try to explain…" She hesitated.

"Do you really think it would make a difference?"

She thought about the murals on her brother's walls and shook her head. "Probably not. To him, you are all the same. Evil killing machines."

"But you see us differently. Why?" he asked, his voice soft, as he stepped closer to her, his hands slipping to her hips.

"It's not something I can explain. It's just a feeling I have when I'm with you. I sense you are a man who cares deeply about those who are important to you. Someone who has that depth of feeling, who would risk his own life time and time again to rescue his friends, can't be evil."

Surprise glinted in his eyes. He bent down and kissed her softly. "You feel all that when you're with me?"

She took a deep breath, trying to explain how she felt. "I believe that those who will do anything to fulfill their own selfish agendas, regardless of who they hurt in the process, are the evil ones. You aren't like that. But my brother, Sebastian, is."

He held her close, the comfort of his arms almost lulling away the anger and disappointment teeming inside her. Sebastian was the only family she had left. She had wanted to live at his school, to learn everything she could and make him proud of her. Now all she felt was sick over how deeply he'd deceived her.

Nicholai brushed her hair back from her brow, his soft touch soothing to her jagged nerves. "How is it that you have that much faith in me when I'm not even sure I have it in myself?"

"Because I see all of you. I see what's in here." She tapped on his chest, and he kissed her again, his lips gentle and tentative, yet filled with sweet expectation.

His eyes met hers and all her doubts crumbled away. "When I'm with you, I almost imagine that there can be a life beyond this madness of running from one town to another, always searching, but never finding…" He broke off and stepped away from her toward the windows.

"Finding what?" she asked.

"Peace."

She walked up behind him and placed her hands on his back, massaging gently. "If peace is what you need, then come with me to Vermont. Our estate is hidden in the woods, away from everything and everyone."

"Completely isolated?"

"Only if you want to be."

He turned to her, taking her hands in his. "Sounds like heaven."

"Then you'll come?" she asked, surprised by the hope expanding her chest.

"After I find Marcos and the others, I will come," he said, but something about the sadness in his eyes revealed the truth. He didn't believe he would make it.

He held her once more. She stood there for a moment, her face pressed against his chest as the warmth he felt toward her washed over her.

He cared about her.

This she could believe.

She reached up and, standing on her toes, pressed her lips to his and kissed him and didn't stop even when he swept her into his arms and carried her up the stairs to his room.

Nicholai carried her up the stairs and laid her gently on his bed. He wasn't going to think about Helena or Asmos or what was going to happen tomorrow. Tonight he would only think about the fact that this beautiful woman was in his bed and willing to help him find Marcos.

And for that, he loved her.

She'd turned her back on the only family she had left and defied her brother's wishes. With her map he might be able to rescue Marcos without having to resort to using Asmos's power. And if it was true that Christos's men were being held prisoner, too, then Christos could be all the help he needed.

Perhaps by sunrise this whole nightmare would be over and he would be able to spend a few days in New England with a beautiful green-eyed witch.

He lay down on the bed next to her, brushing the hair off her face. She kissed him again, bold and brave, her lips moving over his, exploring, tasting, lingering, almost as if she were memorizing the feel of him.

"You are so beautiful," he said, liking the way the firelight glinted off her face. She looked at him differently than anyone ever had before—as a mere man, instead of a monster. It was exhilarating and a little unnerving at the same time.

She was a witch. She could read him. But she didn't know him well enough to know how many times he'd given in to his baser desires, ignoring what he knew was right in order to achieve what he wanted.

No, she couldn't know or she wouldn't be here with him now. She saw only his heart—a heart he thought had withered up and died.

He rolled over on top of her and took her hands in his, raising them above her head, lifting her breasts high.

He nuzzled her neck. "You smell delicious," he whispered. He longed to take a sweet drink, to really taste her, to know all of her. But he promised he would not hurt her. And he wouldn't. Not even a little sip.

Not tonight.

He released her hands. She reached for him, taking her time unbuttoning his shirt. "This time when we make love, I want it to be slow. I want it to last," she said, and leaned forward to kiss the skin exposed by each undone button.

He lay still, fighting to keep a strong grip on the control that was quickly slipping through his fingers as she swept his shirt off his shoulders. Her hands caressing his skin promised pleasures to come.

"I don't want the hurried frenzy of a noisy bar after we've had too much to drink, and not enough time to get to know one another," she continued, pressing her lips against his shoulders. He felt the soft, wet swirl of her tongue. His breath caught in his chest.

He pulled back and took her hands, bringing them up to his lips where he kissed the tips of her fingers. "I like the sound of that. But I must confess that you haven't given me enough time to really know you. Not the way you seem to know me."

He slipped her index finger into his mouth and sucked suggestively. She hitched a breath and, with her desire-laden eyes locked onto his, sat up and slipped out of her T-shirt. Swinging her legs over the side of the bed, she stood and unhooked her bra then let it drop to the floor. Her breasts, large and full, glistened in the light of the fire.

She unbuttoned her jeans and slid them over her hips then leaned forward and rolled them seductively down her legs, her breasts swaying back and forth.

She climbed back onto the bed beside him. "That's not true," she said. "You do know me. You know I grew up on an isolated estate with just my mother, and that we were very close."

Unable to keep his eyes off the rosy red buds dancing before him, he leaned over her breasts and took one pert nub into his mouth, rolling it around until it tightened with pleasure.

"True," he said.

"And you know that I trust people to a fault, until they show me otherwise."

Licking one nipple, then another, he sucked and nibbled until the tight little bead hardened against his tongue. He smiled as she arched her back off the bed, pressing herself closer to him, as she fought to catch her breath.

"True," he said again, though he was beginning to lose the thread of the conversation as desire, thick and languorous, moved through him.

She moaned, rasping his name across her lips, and after a stutteringly long moment, he released her.

"And I know how loyal you are and how it breaks your heart to betray your brother," he continued.

"True again," she said, her eyes glazing over as her sweet tongue swept across her bottom lip.

"And that you use your heart instead of your head to judge people's character," he added, feeling a slight twinge as the truth of his words mocked him.

She pulled him up to her mouth and kissed him, long and hard and thoroughly. As if she'd never been kissed before. And, for a second, he lost himself in it. He could think of nothing but her taste and her scent, and the fire she ignited inside him.

He broke the kiss and looked into her eyes. "I love that trait about you best, but it might not always be wise."

"Yes, but we all have our faults." With her hands braced on his shoulders, she flipped him over onto his back and, this time, held his arms stretched out above him. "Like you, always having to be in control of everything."

"That is not true," he protested, and couldn't help but grin.

She straddled him, her moist warmth teasing him and he groaned as his erection stretched to reach her. She leaned forward, her breasts hovering just out of reach of his gaping mouth.

"Isn't it?" she asked.

The she-devil was teasing him, moving back and forth, running her silky body across his; pleased to see the reaction she was having on *all* of him.

"You are a demon," he groaned.

"Ah, now who's calling who evil?" she chided, and relented, slipping her breast into his waiting mouth. He sucked on it feverishly, sending fire shooting straight to her core. Her nipple tightened almost painfully, and she moaned as desire burned through her, zapping her concentration.

He easily flipped her onto her back again, and showered her body with warm wet kisses, stopping just short of where she really wanted him to go.

"Nicholai," she pleaded.

"Your best quality is that you know when it is time to relinquish your power," he said on a husky breath.

"To you?" she asked, as her fingers skated down his abdomen, playing...teasing. She reached for his sex, circling his heat in her tight grasp, squeezing and releasing.

"And I know when to take things to the next level," she murmured, and slowly stroked the soft skin in her hand, smiling as it grew even hotter and overflowed her small palm.

"Yes, you always have great instincts," he said on a quickened breath. "Why you don't trust them, I will never know."

"Trust them? Of course I trust them." She gasped as he shifted, pulling out of her reach, moving until his teasing tongue found her sweet spot and for several long moments, she lost all conscious thought as he shook her world.

She reached down, grabbing his silky hair in her clenched hands and tried desperately to hold on. She wasn't ready to lose it just yet. Not until she had him where she wanted him—deep inside her.

Pressure, like molten heat, mounted within her...burning. Aching. She drew him toward her, pulling his sweet lips away from her, and tried desperately to catch her breath and just... *hold on*.

"If you trusted your instincts," he said, "you would have let me into your bed last night. Now I'm going to have to show you what you missed."

In one swift movement, he grabbed hold of her legs, parting them and thrust himself inside her. She gasped at the sudden intrusion, crying out as the burning sensation liquefied into a blazing, aching need as he began to move. She pulled him tighter, clutching his shoulders and lifted her legs, wrapping them around him, drawing him deeper inside.

She raised her hips and rocked in a rhythmic dance, skating on the edge of passion, searching for that elusive release that would soothe the fire scorching her belly. His long, deep strokes filled her and, as they moved, she knew she didn't want him to stop. Ever.

As her temperature rose and her belly tightened, she held on tight and wondered how it was possible that he could touch her like no other? Somehow, he reached right inside her, making her feel like she belonged. And now that she'd found him, no one, not Ally, not Sebastian, would ever separate them again.

And he felt it, too.

She sensed his emotions building inside him, felt it in his touch, saw it in the fathomless depths of his eyes as they locked on hers. He loved her. She was his hope.

His salvation.

As they moved as one, the depth of his feelings cradled her. She dropped her guard completely, letting him feel all of her—physically, mentally and spiritually.

They became one as they moved closer and closer to the edge of climax. No longer able to hold on, she let go, surrendering to their passion as it took her higher and higher until at last she screamed and fell into an abyss of pleasure so deep that when she hit bottom, she shattered into a million contented pieces that would never go together the same way again.

Chapter 14

As her breathing came back to normal, Mari tried to grasp hold of her senses. She turned her head and looked at Nicholai lying on his back, his eyes closed, his body flushed. God he was beautiful. Sexy. Happy.

And a vampire.

A chill shook her.

How was it possible that she had grown to care this much for a vampire? When had it happened? And how?

He turned his head and looked at her, a large grin filling his face and warming her heart. "What?" he asked.

"You are an incredibly sexy man."

"I know," he said, and waggled his eyebrows. She laughed and had an urge to throw the pillow at him, but she was too exhausted to move. Instead, she snuggled up beside him, resting her head against his chest, letting the warmth of their lovemaking fill her.

"When did you become a vampire?" she asked, realizing there was a lot about him, about vampires, that she didn't know.

"In 1761."

"Seriously? You must have seen and done so much. How did it happen?"

"A gypsy."

She smiled. "Brought down by a woman, huh?"

"A vampire with dark hair and emerald-green eyes, just like yours."

This surprised her. "Did you love her?"

He scoffed. "No. She was an animal. She tore our village apart, killing many and turning my brother and myself."

"You have a brother? Where is he?"

He turned solemn, then sat up, the sheet riding low on his hips. She trailed her finger along his skin at the sheet's edge, wondering if she had the energy to make love to him again.

"I'm not sure. We don't exactly…speak," he said softly.

"I'm sorry."

"Marcos is my family, now. This is why I must save him."

She raised her hand to his chest. "We'll get him back. I promise."

A shadow passed through him then, something so dark and so cold, it shook her to the core. And for the first time that night, she wondered if she'd made a mistake.

He leaned down and brushed his lips across her forehead. "I know we will," he said. "I will do whatever it takes to make sure we do."

Mari woke to the soft touch of Nicholai's lips as he brushed them against hers. "I'm sorry to wake you. I have to leave for a little while."

Mari sat up rubbing the sleep from her eyes. She couldn't believe she'd fallen asleep. "Where are you going?" she asked, yawning.

"To talk to Christos, the leader of the Manhattan Clan. I need his help."

She reached out and stopped him with a hand on his arm. "Promise me no one will get hurt."

"I can't do that. I won't lie to you by pretending I can."

"But, Nicholai, so many people at Vindecare don't even know what Sebastian and Ally have done. It's not right."

"We will go in while they're all sleeping. If everything goes according to plan, we'll get Marcos and as many of the others as we can out before any one knows any different. We don't want to take any more chances than we have to. This isn't my war, Mari. I only want my own back."

Mari nodded, heartbroken and terrified for what was about to happen. Sebastian was the one who had set this game in motion; there was nothing she could do. But then she thought of Sheila and Mr. Hoskins. She could at least warn them. She swung her legs over the side of the bed and searched for her jeans. "All right, I'm going with you."

"No way. I can't let you."

"Why not?" she asked, while searching the crumpled covers for her shirt. Unable to find it, she picked Nicholai's up off the floor, pushed her arms into the sleeves and started buttoning the buttons.

Suddenly in front of her, Nicholai placed his fingers over hers, stopping her. "I can't let you get hurt."

"I'll be fine. You'll be there, won't you? You can protect me."

"From twenty rabid vampires hell-bent on getting out of there and ready to plow down anyone who gets in their way? Do you really want to take that chance?"

She shuddered at the thought. "But I have to warn Sheila to stay in her room. If anything happened…"

"I won't let the vampires go up the stairs. That I can promise."

"Do you think you will be able to stop them?"

"Not if I'm distracted by worrying about you. Trust me on this one."

She nodded, not seeing how she really had much choice. "All right. I'll stay here."

"Good plan." He leaned down and kissed her. The press of his lips against hers started a little flutter in her heart. Before she could wrap her arms around his neck and pull him closer, he was gone.

She blinked and ran to the doorway but saw no sign of him. She would never get used to that.

After he left, Mari climbed into the bed and tried to go back to sleep. It was almost midnight. By the time he found this other clan leader and made it to Vindecare with the map and security codes it would be closer to 2:00 a.m. No one should be up. She hoped.

She trusted Nicholai, but things didn't always go the way they should. And she certainly didn't trust the other one— Christos. He could easily be the one Jacob had been talking about, the one who was killing the witches.

She shivered and burrowed deeper under the covers. She didn't know anything about Christos, had never met him, had no reason to believe he'd hurt anyone. But he would. She knew it, because Nicholai knew it. She'd sensed it from him. Nicholai didn't like him and certainly didn't trust him. But what else could they do?

She tossed and turned, rolling different scenarios around her mind, all of them bad. She got out of the bed and paced the room, then finished buttoning Nicholai's shirt all the way to the bottom and went down the stairs to the kitchen. She had to think. She needed coffee.

She wanted a caramel latte. Java Blue would still be open. One of the perks of living in a city that never sleeps. She considered pulling on her jeans and going, but she wanted to be here when Nicholai came back. A water bottle would have to do. Her bare feet curled against the cold tiles as she stepped into the kitchen. She hurried over to the massive stainless-steel fridge, opened it and gasped.

Several bags of blood filled the top shelf.

"A little disconcerting, isn't it?"

Surprised by the voice, Mari turned to find a tall, slim woman sitting on the sofa in the adjoining living room. She'd been so deep in thought when she'd come down the stairs, she'd totally missed seeing her sitting in the dim light.

"Um…yes," Mari said, and shut the door, wishing she'd taken the time to put on her jeans.

"So, who are you?" the woman asked, her eyes skimming down Mari's bare legs.

"Mari. Sorry. I'm a…friend of Nicholai's." She took a step toward her, ready to offer her hand. But stopped. From the growing cloud of antagonism rising off the woman, Mari guessed she knew exactly who she was, and she didn't like her.

The woman's eyebrows rose. A slight smirk lifted her red-stained lips, as her gaze swept over Mari again. "I can see that."

"And you are?" Mari prompted, praying she wasn't a vampire, too.

"Darby."

The assistant.

And obviously more, from the evil eye she was getting.

As a familiar wave of jealous hostility rolled over her, Mari realized it was the same feeling she'd had in the bar the night she'd first met Nicholai. At the time, she'd thought the anger had come from Ally. Apparently, she'd been wrong. Now, more than ever, she wished Nicholai had taken her with him.

"You know, I think I'm going to get dressed and go out

for a cup of coffee," Mari said with a nervous laugh as she backed out of the kitchen and toward the stairs.

"I can make coffee." Darby sprang from the couch then flicked a switch on the wall, filling the kitchen with bright light.

"That's all right. I don't want to put you to any trouble."

Darby smiled, transforming her face into a picture of beauty. "No trouble at all. I'd be happy to do it. Go, rest. Do you want something to eat?"

Mari thought of the blood in the fridge, and whatever appetite she'd had, vanished. "No, I'm good. Thanks."

She should leave. She wanted to leave.

Would this woman let her leave?

"I'm sure Nicholai would be very unhappy if he came back and you were gone," Darby said, as if reading her thoughts. She opened a cabinet door next to the fridge and pulled down a large bag of coffee.

On edge, Mari watched her, trying to decide what she should do.

"This machine is awesome," Darby said, as she loaded the complicated-looking contraption sitting on the counter. "It can even make those caramel lattes you like."

A chill snaked down Mari's spine. She took another step backward. "How do you know what kind of coffee I drink?"

One corner of Darby's mouth lifted as she turned toward her. "I've been watching you."

Mari's mouth went dry. "Why?"

"Because Nicholai asked me to."

Mari turned then and ran back up the stairs to Nicholai's room. She threw on her jeans and searched for her bag as tears pooled in her eyes. That was how he always knew where she was and what she was doing. What had she expected? He wasn't a psychic with a big crystal ball.

Her nerves stretched taut as she raked her fingers through

her hair. She spotted her knapsack on the chair by the fireplace. She snatched it up and held it clutched against her chest as she stepped into her sneakers. What was she going to do? She'd missed her train and she wasn't about to go back to Vindecare.

She dropped onto the edge of the chair. Was she really going to let this jealous girl chase her off? Or was she going to wait for Nicholai to return and ask him why he was having her watched? The answer could be something simple, even something innocent. Like maybe he was interested in her, but didn't know if he could trust her. Or more likely, that maybe he just needed her help.

Instead of bolting, she leaned back into the soft leather and took a deep breath to calm her nerves. For a moment, she stared into the flickering flames of the fire and thought back over all the impressions she'd ever gotten from Nicholai. Not in any of them had he ever meant her harm. Her heartbeat slowed and her breathing evened. This girl, *his assistant,* was the only one who didn't want her there. Not Nicholai.

She flicked on the light next to the chair, and as she did, her gaze fell upon a large crystal sitting in the center of the mantel. She stood and reached for it, watching the prisms of reflected light dance off its sharp edges. Holding it in both hands, she sat back on the chair and stared into its smoky depths.

"Do not be afraid, Mariana. You are the daughter's daughter of a powerful witch. You were meant for great things. Together, you and I can overcome anything and anyone. Even a vampire. Call me. Let my name pass your lips. Invite me in. I'm waiting for you." The soft whisper, like an elusive tendril of smoke, curled through her mind.

Mari stood quickly, a pervasive chill spreading through her body. She dropped the crystal to the ground where it rolled across the carpet. "What the hell was that?" she muttered, and rubbed her arms.

"One of Nicholai's prized possessions," Darby said, as she walked through the door, a tall coffee mug in her hand.

"It spoke to me." Mari's hand fluttered to her chest as she tried to shake the apprehension seeping through her bones.

"Here." Darby handed her the warm mug then bent over and picked up the crystal, turning it over in her hands. "You're tired. I'm sorry I spooked you earlier. Didn't mean to. I watched where you went a few times. It was no big deal."

Mari's eyes stayed riveted on the crystal in Darby's hands. It couldn't have really talked to her. Crazy. She was tired and imagining things.

"Go ahead and try it," Darby said, gesturing toward the coffee.

Mari glanced down at the mug in her hand complete with frothy foam and caramel sauce dribbled across the top. It looked good, but more than that, it felt warm. "Thanks," Mari said, fighting back another shiver.

Darby walked toward the fireplace and placed the crystal back on the mantel.

Mari sipped the coffee, feeling its heat spread through her. "Mmm. It is good."

"Caramel is my favorite, too," Darby said with a slight smile.

Mari took another long drink. "Where did that thing come from?" she asked.

"Who knows?" Darby said, glancing over her shoulder at the rock on the mantel. "It's a prison of sorts."

"A prison?" The coffee was working, Mari thought, as soothing warmth moved through her. She took another long swallow, licking the sweet foam off her upper lip.

Darby walked toward her. "For a demon."

A demon?

Ridiculous. Demons didn't live in rocks. Mari shook her head. She wouldn't believe it. Vampires were one thing, but this? It was too much. "Demons?" she murmured, and shook her head again.

"Yes. This one is fairly primitive. But if you said he talked to you, he must like you. His name is Asmos."

"Asmos," Mari whispered, as she struggled to make sense of her thoughts that had suddenly turned muddled and fuzzy.

"Yes, Mari. I'm here. I'm waiting for you. Waiting for you to call me...."

She let out a soft cry.

Darby was suddenly standing next to her, placing a steadying hand on her arm. "Are you all right?"

"Did you hear that?" she asked. But as she stared down at Darby's hand, images flooded into her mind: glowing red eyes, rivulets of blood and the howling of wolves, a cacophony echoing on the wind and ringing in her ears.

The room started to spin. Slowly at first and then faster. Suddenly Mari felt as if she were going to be sick. But she couldn't; she had to pull herself together. She had to get out of there, because now she knew the truth. How had she forgotten that first night when she had tasted the darkness that lay in Nicholai's heart? Now she knew what he'd been hiding.

Nicholai was going to use her to free a demon. To free Asmos.

Mari jerked away from Darby, her eyes widening as a new impression filled her. "You're terrified."

"Yes," Darby said, matter-of-factly, but she wasn't scared for herself, only for Nicholai.

Mari shook her head, trying to break loose from the thickening fog. She didn't know what was happening, or why Darby was so afraid, but one thing she saw with clarity— she was going to die.

And Nicholai would be the one to kill her.

Mari turned toward the door as pain seared her chest and her heart broke into a million pieces.

He didn't love her.

He had tricked her again. All he wanted her for was something…horrible. *Something evil.* How could she have been so wrong? She had been so sure of him. Of her abilities to know!

She took one step, then two, wobbling on shaky legs. "What have you…?"

Her stomach lurched, her strength left her and, in what felt like slow motion, she watched the coffee mug with the remains of her caramel latte drop to the floor.

She felt drugged.

Had Darby drugged her?

Fear stole her breath. She gasped as she fell. Landing on the carpet, she watched wide-eyed as the dark liquid trickled from the mug and seeped into the cream fibers.

"Now look what you've done," Darby said, and reached down next to her to pick up the cup. "Nicholai might think he loves you, but soon you'll be gone and it won't matter. He'll be all mine again and there will be nothing you or anyone else will be able to do about it."

Chapter 15

Nicholai looked in the park behind Vindecare, fielding his vampire senses along the river. He traveled down into Manhattan, searching one block after another, but there was no sign of Christos anywhere. Not even his clan members knew where he was.

After several long hours, he left word for Christos to contact him, and then finally gave up and headed back to the penthouse. Helena would arrive at sunrise to make the transfer. He needed to be there to inform her that he wanted to wait one more day. With the help of the ten men still left in Christos's clan, they should be able to get into Vindecare and rescue the others without having to resort to using Asmos's power.

Without having to kill Mari.

Surprised by how much the thought devastated him, he pondered how totally she had gotten under his skin, and into his heart. He pressed down on the throttle, pushing the motorcycle to its limits as he pictured her lying naked in his bed, waiting for him to climb in next to her and make tender love to her. He recalled the sound of her sweet voice as she cried out his name, begging him for more. He couldn't seem to get enough of the witch and couldn't wait to get back to her.

With a roar of the bike's engine, he pulled into the parking garage beneath his building and took the lift up to the penthouse. As he entered his home, he hurried up the stairs, taking them three at a time until he was in his bedroom, the door closed softly behind him.

He stood next to the bed for a moment, watching the light from the fire's flames dance across her face. Gently, he eased next to her then pressed his lips against hers. She stirred slightly. He pulled back. Something was wrong. She didn't feel right. She didn't smell right.

"Nicholai?" she asked, her voice sounding raw. She could barely open her eyes.

"What's the matter? What's happened to you?"

Mari cringed and brought a trembling hand to her head. "It hurts."

Nicholai swore under his breath.

"There's something…horrible," she whispered. "Can't… quite…grasp it."

Nicholai took both her hands in his and felt her pulse. "Your energy is too low. I'm going to get you some food. Rest. Don't think. Just sleep. I'll be right back."

He bounded out of the room. He hadn't been gone more than a few hours. What in the hell could have happened to her? Realization suddenly hit him.

"Darby," he roared, as he leaped down the stairs.

Tucked into a chair by the fireplace, Darby looked up at him. "I'm here," she muttered so softly he almost didn't hear her.

"What in the hell happened?" he demanded, instantly standing before her.

"I drugged her coffee," she admitted. "I had to."

He clenched his fists, keeping them glued to his side as he towered over her. "Why?" The one word was all he trusted himself to say. He had never been more furious at her than he was at this moment.

"She was going to leave. I had to do something to stop her," Darby insisted. "It's what you would have wanted."

What he would have wanted?

"And why was she leaving?" he asked through clamped teeth.

She stared at him for a moment, her small mouth opening and closing as her big brown eyes bored into his. "Asmos said something to her. He really freaked her out."

Nicholai pulled in a deep breath, calling up every ounce of patience he could muster, but he was just about tapped out.

"Asmos can't talk to her."

She was lying to him. He could sense it. Something else was going on, something she wasn't telling him. Out of patience and no longer caring, his teeth descended, sharpening into fine points. He would get the truth, even if he had to drink every last drop of her life source to do it.

She shrank farther into the chair, her dark manipulative eyes growing wide. "Apparently he can, because he did." Her voice was high-pitched and squeaky. "The witch picked up the crystal from the mantel and her face turned as white as yours. She was terrified. I had to stop her."

Nicholai turned toward the fire and anchored his fists against the heavy wooden mantel. Was it possible? Could Mari have heard Asmos? "What did he say to her?"

"How would I know? I didn't hear him. But I saw her right after she dropped the crystal, and she was getting ready to bolt. I did what I had to. What I thought you would want me to do."

Nicholai fought for control, fought to extinguish the fire fueling the fury that raced through his blood. He couldn't give in to his anger. He needed to keep a cool head, to do what he could to discern the truth from her, when all he really wanted to do was rip her throat out.

"We need her," she said with a shaky voice. "*You* need her. I couldn't let her go. I…I thought you'd be pleased."

"Does she know about Helena? About our plans," he insisted, without turning to face her. If he had to look at her right now, he'd snap her neck. She had always hated Mari. He knew that, had felt her raging jealousy more than once. She hadn't hurt Mari for him; she had done it for herself.

Because she enjoyed it.

That much he was certain of.

"I don't know," she said. "I didn't tell her."

"Helena will be here soon. When she arrives, I'm sending her away."

Darby gasped. "What? No! Why?"

"Go out and get Mari something to eat," he said, ignoring her outburst. What he did, and when he did it was no longer any of her business. As soon as Marcos was back, she was out of here, and if she gave him any trouble about it, he'd serve her up in a silver goblet and give her to Christos.

"Something with a lot of protein and do it fast," he continued, staring into the fire, but not really seeing the flames. He heard her tentatively rise out of the chair and turned to her. "And Darby…"

Wariness played across her face as she looked up at him.

"No more tricks. No more chances. Don't screw this up. Do you understand?"

Surprise filled her eyes as she bobbed her head then hurried out the door.

Nicholai clenched and unclenched his fists. He had to find out what Asmos said to Mari and how much she knew about Helena and their plans. And he had to do it before Helena arrived within the next hour.

But how?

He hurried back up the stairs to his room. She was so drugged she wouldn't be awake enough to give him a straight answer for hours.

But there was one way he could find out. Not only what Asmos had said to her, but if Darby had been lying about it. And if he was very careful and very gentle, perhaps Mari might never know.

Nicholai stood next to the bed and pulled back the comforter. Mari was still wearing his shirt, a pair of panties, and nothing else. She looked beautiful and enticing. And once more, he felt his fury rise over Darby's stupidity and for her ruining his chance to wake Mari up properly, with his mouth and his touch.

Now, he'd have to wait. And he didn't like waiting.

He brushed Mari's silky hair off her brow and pulled it through his fingers. It was soft, shiny and baby fine, just like her. She stirred and murmured his name, then drifted back to sleep. He hated that she was in pain and hated even worse that she'd been frightened. He wondered once more what Asmos had said to her.

It was time he did what he'd been meaning to do since the first night he saw her in The Chamber. He slipped into bed next to her and burrowed down beneath the blankets. The sheets were warm from her body heat and still carried the scent of their lovemaking.

He settled down between her legs and pressed his lips to the inside of her thigh. She gave a soft moan, but didn't move. He kissed the soft skin more deeply, rolling his tongue around in a circle, feeling for the artery that thumped slowly beneath his lips—one…two…three.

He sank his teeth into her leg. Warm blood filled his mouth, sluicing down his throat. With it came the images he'd been waiting for: he saw her reaching for the crystal on the mantel. She thought it was beautiful.

"Do not be afraid, Mariana. You are the daughter's daughter of a powerful witch. You were meant for great things. Together, you and I can overcome anything and anyone. Even a vampire. Call me. Let my name pass your lips. Invite me in. I'm waiting for you." Asmos's whisper slithered through his mind.

The demon wanted inside her. He knew what Nicholai was planning. He wanted it to happen. He would be free of his crystal prison and he knew Nicholai wouldn't be able to control him. Asmos would be in control, walking the earth once more, not demon, not human, but a vampire.

An immortal who would never die.

Was Asmos powerful enough to overtake him? How much did he really know about Asmos, other than that he was primal, and powerful? Not at all in the same league as the other demons whose essence he'd stolen.

Images flashed behind his eyes. A room full of stainless-steel boxes lined up row after row. Marcos staring up at him, his eyes black, his expression wild as a man sliced him open with a knife. Nicholai's stomach twisted as outrage roared through his mind.

Mari sitting in a chair, a man in a lab coat smiling at her, his hand on her arm as he stuck a needle into her vein and drew blood, filling one tube after another with the crimson liquid. His fingertips lingering…

Why was he taking so much of her blood?

"We are trying to develop a poison that will protect us from the vampires." The man's words echoed in his mind.

"One bite, and those little spiral cells of yours would travel straight to their brains, attaching to their synapses, blocking them and rendering them useless."

Uneasiness turned to horror as Nicholai realized what he was seeing, what he was hearing.

Mari had been involved from the start.

"I won't have any more to do with it. That's why I have to leave." Her words, finally clicking home, filled him with dread.

His Mari. Not as innocent as she seemed.

As he'd wanted her to be.

As the realization dawned, pain speared through Nicholai's head. He grabbed his temples and sat up. What the hell was happening to him? The room spun, his stomach turned. He pulled himself up next to Mari, but was suddenly unable to move. The burning pain was unbearable.

She'd poisoned him.

The thought arced in a burst of fire across his nerve endings, searing the truth into his mind. He tried to pull away from her, to get off the bed, but he couldn't move.

How had she done it? She didn't have one of those pens, she hadn't even woken up. Then the truth hit him like a sledgehammer to his brain. *The toxin was in her blood.*

And suddenly it all made sense. Why she was so willing to come with him. Why she was never afraid. She'd fooled him. Taken him down with his own seductive game. Made him fall for her, knowing either way, one day he would bite her and when he did, he'd be hers.

She was the witch's secret weapon. Her blood was the poison that would destroy them all.

Mari woke to a dull throb in her head. She cracked open her dry eyes and gasped. Nicholai was lying on the bed next to her, blood smeared across his lips, his eyes opened wide and his mouth slashed in a grimace of agony.

Quickly she sat up and shook him. "Nicholai."

Pain sliced through her head and she fell back against the headboard. "God, what happened to me?" Then she remembered the coffee.

That woman had drugged her.

Mari pushed her fingertips gently against the throbbing in her temples until it subsided enough that she could glance once more at Nicholai.

He still hadn't moved.

Had that bitch drugged him, too? She had to get up. She had to get help. Her bag was still lying in the chair by the fireplace. Keeping her upper body as still as possible, she pulled back the sheets and froze. Dried blood was pooled around her upper thighs and a huge circle of crimson stained the sheet.

Her blood?

She brushed her fingertips along her upper thighs, stopping when she reached a tender area. Gingerly, she probed her skin, then stopped as she realized what she was feeling—two small puncture wounds.

Wide-eyed, she turned to Nicholai. "You drank from me?" she accused, her voice hoarse with raw emotion.

Stunned, her gaze fell to the blood staining his lips.

Her blood.

An ice-cold wave of anguish broke over her. "You drank from me!" she cried, once more in disbelief.

Moving one leg at a time, she carefully got out of the bed. As she stood, her legs wobbled and almost gave out from under her. She clutched the side of the bed. Closing her eyes, she focused on calming the nausea rolling in her stomach.

She had to get out of here before that woman came back. Before the effects of the toxin on Nicholai wore off. Wincing at the throbbing in her head, she forced herself to get out of bed and move toward her bag on the chair by the fireplace. After what seemed like an excruciatingly long time, she finally had her bag in her hand. As she sank into the chair her gaze fell on the crystal on the mantel. Then she remembered what Darby had said, and what Mari had seen in her mind—Nicholai was going to use her to free the demon. Horror rocked through her. She dug in her purse for her cell phone and called the only person she could tell, the only one who would understand. She called Ally.

"You have to come for me. Please," she pleaded, after she quickly explained what had happened.

"What about Nicholai?" Ally asked.

"What about him?"

"Are you just going to leave him there?"

Mari forced herself to look at him again. He still hadn't moved. How long would the poison keep him like that? However long it was, she knew it wouldn't be long enough. "Yes. I don't ever want to see him again. I can't."

"Think about it, Mari. If you don't do something about him, you'll be a prisoner in your own home. He'll come after you again. You'll never be able to leave the house."

Mari thought of the tall walls and the statues in the garden. Did she really want to be just like them? Trapped forever at Vindecare?

Ally was right. Nicholai would never let her go. And then she recalled his recent late-night visit to her room and she knew she would never be safe from him. He'd be able to come after her anywhere at any time.

Her gaze moved to the crystal once more. A violent shiver shook her as she recalled the slithering voice within, and how it had spoken to her.

As if it knew her.

Nicholai was planning to put that thing into her. Her stomach turned once more, and she dropped her head between her knees. She couldn't let him do that. Wouldn't. "What can I do?" she asked Ally, her voice no louder than a squeak.

"I'll bring a retrieval team with me. We'll lock him in the basement with the others."

"At Vindecare?" Terror filled her at the thought of Nicholai trapped in his own steel box in the catacombs beneath her room.

"Do you have any better ideas?" Ally asked.

No. She was right. Mari had no choice. "All right. But don't tell Sebastian. He can't know I had any part of…this."

Ally laughed softly. "Don't blame you there. Just make sure you're gone before we arrive."

"I'll leave the door open. But hurry. I don't know where his assistant is."

Her stomach heaved once more and she broke out in a cold sweat.

"Don't worry. We can handle her."

Before Mari could disconnect the line she bolted for the bathroom and threw up into the toilet. After a few minutes, she splashed cold water onto her face, then pulled a large plush towel off the rack and pressed it against her eyes.

For a moment she stood there, her face smothered in luxurious Egyptian cotton. This couldn't be happening to her.

She swiped the tears from her eyes and walked back into the bedroom to look at Nicholai one last time. She thought she'd loved him.

She did love him.

And for that, she'd almost died.

Or worse.

She spotted her jeans on the side of the bed and carefully stepped into them, trying not to move her head too much. She then approached the fireplace and pulled the crystal down from the mantel and wrapped it within the towel.

No matter what happened, even if he was able to escape

his box and get to her in her room, he would never be able to infect her with this demon. Ever. She stuck the crystal into her knapsack and zipped it up tight. She would find a place to bury it where he would never find it again.

She crossed the room to the door, cracked it open and listened for a moment, then without looking back, crept down the staircase, careful not to make a sound in case Darby was sitting on one of the sofas again, waiting for her. But she didn't see Darby or anyone.

As quickly as she could, she hurried to the front door. She propped it open with a large sculpture that had been sitting on a nearby table then pushed the button for the elevator that would take her to the street. Her heart thumped in her chest as she watched the numbered floors light up as the elevator drew closer.

Twenty-eight.

What if someone was inside? There was nowhere she could hide in the small alcove outside his apartment, nothing she could use to protect herself with.

Twenty-nine.

She contemplated running back into the kitchen for a knife, but knew she didn't have time. The elevator was almost there.

Thirty.

She took a deep painful breath. The shiny doors slid open. No one was inside.

Relieved, she closed her eyes and stepped inside.

Chapter 16

Nicholai writhed in pain. Every nerve ending was on fire. The pressure in his head was excruciating. He tried to lift his arms, but couldn't. Something held him down. He opened his mouth and roared, the sound of his torment echoing through the dark chamber. Grit filled his eyes, making them sticky, and his tongue felt like sandpaper. What in the hell had happened to him?

Then he remembered.

Mari.

She'd done this to him. She'd tricked him and played him for a fool. Brought down by a witch for the second time in his life. The first time he'd lost his family, his humanity. What would it be this time? Torture for all eternity?

"Nicholai."

The quiet voice filled his mind and it took him a second to realize he was actually hearing it. "Marcos?"

"They got you, too," his friend muttered.

Four little words and yet they conveyed so much—sadness, anguish and, most of all, dashed hopes. No, Nicholai thought. He wouldn't be able to rescue him. There was no help now. Not for any of them.

"I'm sorry," he pushed through a clenched jaw. Pain and fury comingled in his heart and pulsed through his veins. Being sorry wouldn't help. It wouldn't accomplish anything and there was no one left to count on, no one to save them. How could he have been so foolish as to fall for the witch? He knew better, and still he had let down his defenses, let her sucker him in.

He roared once more as he struggled against his bonds. But all he managed to do was scrape his wrists as the hard plastic of the tie wraps dug into his skin. Suddenly, the room filled with light. Pinpricks of pain were like darts in his eyes.

"Calm down there, big boy," the redheaded witch said as she stood above his coffin and looked down at him. "I'm so glad you could join us. Your friend, Marcos, over there was getting lonely."

Nicholai clenched his jaw. He would not say a word. Would not give her the satisfaction.

"Look what you've done to yourself." She brushed a finger down his arm. Every fiber within him repulsed at her touch.

He turned away and squeezed his eyes closed. The only part of his body he had any control over.

"Come on, now. I want you to meet Jacob," she said, her voice coated with sugar. "He is going to be your new best friend."

Nicholai opened his eyes and saw a man in a lab coat step into his line of sight. Nicholai recognized him from Mari's vision. He had a large syringe filled with blood in his hand. He shot the crimson liquid into the IV Nicholai noticed had been inserted into his arm.

He tried to jerk away, but his arm didn't do more than

flinch. "Don't do this," he blurted, but to his horror, his voice sounded more like a plea than the demand he'd intended.

"Don't worry," the man said. "This will take away the pain and keep you calm."

For a second, Nicholai thought he read pity in the young man's eyes and, for the first time since he woke, fear grasped hold of him and squeezed. But true to his word, the fire in Nicholai's veins started to recede and along with it, all the feeling in his body.

"There, now, isn't that better?" the witch said. "Don't you worry that beautiful head of yours. Ally is here, and I'm going to take real good care of you."

Mari woke to Nicholai roaring in her head. Her eyes sprang open, her heart hammering inside her chest, sweat pooling beneath her T-shirt. She bolted upright and switched on the bedside light, half expecting Nicholai to be standing above her, his face a sneer of ragged, blood-dripping teeth. But he wasn't. Her room was empty.

She pushed out a relieved breath, got out of bed and pulled on a robe. She must have been dreaming. Whatever it was, she was glad she couldn't remember it. The throbbing in her head had finally subsided to a dull ache. She rubbed her temples and took two more aspirin out of the bottle on her nightstand then chased them down with a gulp of water from her bathroom sink.

Three o'clock in the morning and she was wide-awake. She paced her room, trying not to think about what would happen in a few hours. Should she get up and go to her classes and pretend she hadn't decided to run away only to return with her tail tucked between her legs and a new vampire in the basement?

Thank God, Sebastian didn't know. It was the only thing about this situation that made it bearable. She couldn't face him and the diabolical fury in his eyes right now. Though she guessed it would only be a matter of time before he discovered the truth. Secrets like what happened between her and Nicholai didn't stay buried for long.

She tried not to think about Nicholai. She thought what she had with him was real, that it was special. She was ready to give up everything to be with him. And he knew that.

Bitterness soured her stomach. He showed his true colors when he bit her. She was unconscious, unable to protect herself and he took advantage of her. What kind of man did that?

Not a man at all. *A vampire.*

Why did she keep forgetting that?

As she stared out the front window into the darkness below, she wondered what Ally and the containment team had done with him. Was he here now, lying below her? What was he thinking? Feeling? Was he scared? Angry? Did he blame her? Hate her?

He should. And if he did, she didn't care. He was planning to…her gaze moved to her knapsack in the bottom of her closet, and she shuddered. She wouldn't think about what he was going to do.

She wouldn't think about him at all.

She removed her robe, switched off the light and climbed back into bed. Then tossed and turned. Like a fish out of water, she searched for comfort, for relief and peace. But it was nowhere to be found. Somewhere in the bowels of this house, Nicholai was waiting for her.

After thirty more minutes of flopping back and forth, she sat up. She couldn't continue like this. She couldn't stop thinking about him. Wondering. Worrying. She had to see for herself.

She had to tell him why she hated him. And why she would never forgive him for what he'd done.

And for what he'd planned to do.

She got out of bed, slipped into her robe then hurried out of her room. As she walked barefoot through the dark house, her feet sinking soundlessly into the plush carpet, she berated herself over and over again. But she couldn't stop. She had to see him. She had to know if everything had been a lie.

As she crept down the stairs into the darkness of the catacombs, she couldn't help thinking of how many vampires her brother was holding down there, and how they all must hate them. *Hate her.*

Because now Nicholai must know the truth—the poison came from her.

She walked into Marcos's room, not at all surprised when the lights flickered to life to show a second box placed next to his. Slowly, she approached them. Nicholai lay in the first one, staring blankly at the ceiling, blood pooling in his eyes, and dripping in tiny rivulets down the side of his face.

Her heart lurched. "What did they do to him?" she muttered, and had to stop from reaching inside and wiping the blood away.

"Tea," a hoarse voice said from the box next to him.

She hurried over to Marcos.

"He needs the tea."

She couldn't. If she did, if he came out of this stupor, then he would be able to see her. To accuse her. To tell the others the truth. That it was her.

All her.

"I can't," she muttered.

"Yes. He needs it. The pain…it's unbearable."

"You don't know what he was planning to do, what he has already done. The lies. The deception…it was horrible."

"This is horrible. Death would be better. Please, help us."

His brilliant blue gaze held her captive, and though she wanted to, she couldn't pull away. "He bit me," she squeaked.

"He's a vampire. Why are you surprised?"

"Because I thought he…loved me."

"Maybe he does."

She listened to his calm rational words and continued staring into his fathomless eyes, as if she could find the answers to all her questions buried within.

"I trusted him. Why would he do it?"

"Vampires bite for more reasons than food. For sexual intimacy, perhaps?"

"I was unconscious," she muttered.

"To connect with a person," he added.

"How?" she asked, thinking of all the times Nicholai had said that they'd had a connection.

"When you drink the blood of another, you can see their thoughts. Nothing is hidden. Maybe he was looking for answers?"

"Maybe he was."

"Give him the tea and ask him yourself."

That would be one way of finding out, but would he give her the truth or would he deceive her again?

"You are like your mother. You are a good person. It is in your heart to help us. Follow your instincts. What do they tell you about him?"

She almost laughed out loud. Her instincts had been completely drowned out by her hormones. She didn't know what to think. But one thing was certain, she was like her mother and, like her, she had wanted to help them all. But now?

"I will make it for him just this once. Just so I can look him in the eye and ask him why he did what he did."

"Whatever his reason, sweet one, it did not warrant this. Death would be a welcome respite to the constant pain in this cold, dark prison."

His words echoed in her ears as she turned and hurried from the room. She ran up the stairs longing for the sanctuary of her room. But Marcos was right. She would rather be dead than tied in a box, withering in pain alone in the dark. It was too horrible to contemplate.

And she was responsible for it.

How would Marcos feel about her once he found that out? Would he still think she was as "good" as her mother? And if he found out the truth about "his Lina"? He would feel betrayed and furious.

Was that how Nicholai thought about her?

But it wasn't her fault. He did this. He bit her!

Back in her bedroom, she went over to her nightstand and took out the loose tea from her mother's tin and the thermos, then hurried to the lounge to fill it with hot water. The tea steeped inside as she continued down the stairs back toward the catacombs.

She paused as she heard something, her hand resting against the wall as she listened intently, but continued forward when she didn't hear it again. She was every kind of fool, she knew that, but she also knew there was no way she was going to be able to sleep until she talked to Nicholai. Until he admitted what he had planned to do to her.

And maybe he would tell her it was all a mistake. *A horrible misunderstanding.*

And then what?

She walked back into the room, stepping between the two boxes. She leaned over Marcos's first. He turned to her. "Give it to Nicholai. He needs it more."

She pulled in a fortifying breath and turned to him. Nicholai's crimson eyes still gazed upward toward the ceiling. Did he even know she was there? Could he hear her? Or was he lost in the pain?

"Please," Marcos pleaded.

Mari inched closer to the box. She would have to reach inside. *She would have to touch him.* Her heart thudded erratically in her chest. She leaned down and reached beneath him, then gingerly lifted his head. His silky hair filled her palm and tickled her hand.

Just a few hours ago, she had been running her fingers through his hair, loving every part of him, with her hands, her mouth, her heart. She loved him. She knew it was crazy. She'd tried to fight it, but she hadn't been able to. She'd wanted him. Worse, she'd craved him.

And he had betrayed her.

As she turned his head toward her, tears pricked the back of her eyes. She held the cup of tea to his lips. But he couldn't drink from it. He couldn't even open his mouth. Anguish tore at her heart.

She set the tea down, lifted her fingers to his lips and gently parted them. She remembered how he'd drawn her finger into his mouth and sucked on it. How those lips had kissed her...*everywhere.*

Unable to stop them, hot tears filled her eyes. She gulped a loud breath as they spilled over and ran down her cheeks. Her heart ached. A pain so sharp and so strong, it tore a cry from her lips. She focused on trying to keep her hand steady as she slowly poured the tea into his mouth.

Her knees weakened as the amber liquid ran down his chin and pooled beneath his shoulders. She tried once again, and this time got more of it into his mouth and down his throat. She had just finished with the second cup, when she heard a sound coming from upstairs.

"It's the guard," Marcos said.

"Guard?" Since when did they have a guard? Since she invited a vampire into their home. She quickly surveyed the room looking for somewhere to hide, but couldn't find anything that would keep her from sight.

She twisted the lid back onto the thermos. "I'm sorry, Marcos. But I can't let my brother find me here. I have to go."

"You will return?" Marcos asked.

"If I can."

As fast as she dared, she rushed from the room, flipping the switch to keep the lights from automatically turning on in the hallway. As she crept toward the stairs, she listened intently for the guard, but heard nothing.

She climbed upward toward the weapons room, carefully avoiding the step with the built-in alarm when she heard it again. The jangle of keys on a belt.

And close.

She scanned the room and saw a large desk against the far wall. Hurrying to it, she crouched down into the desk's well, and pulled a chair in front of her. Before she could catch her breath, a guard walked into the room. He shone his flashlight into the corners, sweeping it along the walls, before descending the staircase.

She took a deep breath and after a few moments, when she was sure she could no longer hear him, she scurried out from under the desk and hurried down the hall. She hadn't made it far when she heard the jangle of keys again.

Another one? Or had the first one come back? She slipped into the nearest room and shut the door behind her. As she stood leaning against the door in the dark, she realized she was in the same room she and Nicholai had hidden in before.

Her mother's room.

When she had been here with Nicholai, standing close to one another in the dark, all she had thought about was his touch, and how he made her feel all tingly inside. Nothing else seemed to matter, but the press of his lips against hers.

Boy, had things changed.

She pushed him out of her mind. She was in her mother's room. If she was going to leave, she was taking the painting of her parents with her. After giving the guard enough time to get past her, she flipped on the light.

The room was completely empty.

Her heart plummeted and she fell back against the wall. What had Sebastian done with it all? The furniture? Her perfume? The painting of her mother and father? She hadn't realized the comfort she'd taken from the knowledge that a small piece of her mother was still with her in this house.

But now, like her mother, it was all gone.

Now, she was truly alone.

Clutching her middle she slid down the wall, staring at the empty carpet. There was nothing of her left. It was as if she'd never been here. As if she'd never mattered to anyone.

As if she'd never been loved.

Chapter 17

Mari was back home in Vermont. She stood barefoot on the shore of the lake behind her house, her toes sinking into the wet sand. In the distance, on the far side of the lake, hawks circled above the trees, at least thirty of them. What were they hunting? A rabbit? A mouse? She shivered at the way they circled, round and round, gliding through the air. There were so many.

She heard footsteps behind her and turned, a smile warming her heart. "Mom, look at all—"

Only it wasn't her mother.

Nicholai stood behind her. It was him, and yet it wasn't. His brown eyes had turned into inky pools of black anger that leeched into his skin, fanning out in dark veins down impossibly white skin. His lips were a purplish-blue slit.

She gasped and stepped backward, sinking into the icy-cold water. The sand turned to muck and pulled at her ankles. A rabbit screamed from the other side of the lake.

"You did this to me," he rasped.

"No, I—" She backed up farther, the freezing water rising up to her knees.

"I wanted us to be together. To be happy. Here!" He gestured wide, and was suddenly in front of her, his angry breath fanning her cheek. "You betrayed me."

"No. It was you. It was you!"

He grasped her arms. Wickedly long, sharp nails dug into her skin as he yanked her against him. All she could see was teeth. So many, so sharp, each one dripping blood as his head dipped closer. "I loved you."

Thunder clapped in the sky. Booming overhead. The gods were angry. Pain seared her neck, hot and burning.

He loved her?

"Mari!"

She stirred, rolling over in her bed. Someone was pounding on her door.

"Mari. Are you in there?"

"Yes," she called out, her voice cracking. She opened her eyes and looked around the room as confusion swam through her brain. She was at Vindecare.

She touched her neck expecting to find torn and bloody skin, but it was smooth and untouched. And yet, it had felt so real. It was a dream. A horrible dream.

I loved you.

"Mari?"

"Coming." She swung her legs off the bed and stood, then leaned back onto the mattress for support as the room spun. She smacked her tongue against the roof of her dry mouth. She needed something to drink. She needed coffee. She walked over to the door and opened it.

Sheila burst in. "What is going on with you?"

"What do you mean?"

"Mari, it's ten o'clock. I've been pounding on your door

forever. You missed your classes yesterday and your Persuasion and Techniques class this morning. Now you're late for Potions. Professor Whalen let me come check on you." Her narrowed eyes scanned Mari's face. "Have you been taking those sleeping pills again?"

"No. I—" Shocked, Mari turned to the clock on her bedside. "I don't know. I guess I slept in."

"Are you sick?"

"No. Just tired."

Sheila eye's narrowed again as she studied her. "You really don't look good. You look pale. Maybe you should go to the infirmary."

A rolling wave of intense heat followed by dizziness broke over Mari. She reached back against the bed for support. "Wow. Maybe you're right. I don't feel good. Can you tell Professor Whalen that I won't make it to class again today?"

"Sure thing." Sheila touched her shoulder. "Take care of yourself, okay?"

"I will. Thanks." Mari sank back onto the bed as Sheila shut the door behind her.

That was one helluva dream.

Still feeling out of sorts after her shower, Mari went down to the cafeteria for a light breakfast then to the infirmary to talk to Jacob.

She carried her knapsack with the crystal, her mother's herbs and recipe book inside. They were the only items she wanted to take with her from this place when she left. And she would leave. Soon.

She made another thermos full of tea and stuck it in her bag. She wasn't sure if she could face Nicholai again, or if she even wanted to. Especially after the nightmare she'd had that morning, but a part of her wanted to see for herself. To see what they'd done with him, and to see if she was safe.

"Heard you missed your classes this morning," Jacob said as she walked into the infirmary.

"Now, there's a big surprise," she said. "Does anything get by you in this place?"

"And yet, she's still feeling her cheeky self."

Mari smirked. "I'm not sick. Just tired and a little dizzy."

He held her wrist and felt her pulse. "All right. Take the rest of the day off and get some rest. I'll inform your afternoon teachers."

She nodded. "Thanks, Jacob." She walked toward the door, then stopped and turned back. "Jacob? Do you know where Sebastian put my mom's stuff?"

Surprise hiked his eyebrows. "No idea. Why?"

"It's not in the room where she'd been staying."

"I don't know. But I'm sure if you ask him, he'll be happy to tell you."

Mari wasn't so sure. Instead of leaving, she walked back toward him. "How was my mother's health while she was here?"

A shadow passed in front of his eyes. "Good," he said. "She was a little tired, too. That's why we want to make sure we take real good care of you."

"Because you didn't with her?"

"That's not what I said or meant." He turned away from her, picked up a clipboard and started flipping through the pages.

She wouldn't be so easily dismissed. "What aren't you telling me?"

He took his time reading the last page, then set the board down on the counter and slowly turned back to her. "There's nothing to tell."

"Isn't there?" She probed his face, reaching with her senses, trying desperately to read him. Something was there. Something she couldn't quite grasp.

"You're hiding something from me, Jacob. Now spill," she demanded.

He leaned back against the counter. "Your mother was ill. Maybe we took too much blood, maybe it was all those herbs she always insisted on drinking—we don't know for sure. All I do know is that she became very ill and very weak, very quickly."

If her mother had drunk the tea to lessen the potency of the toxin in her blood, it wouldn't have made her sick. Mari had drunk it for years. But taking too much of her blood would have.

"And that's how the accident happened?" she guessed, pushing to see what he'd say.

Jacob's expression grew pained. "Yes. I don't know why she had been down in the catacombs, but that's where we found her, lying at the bottom of the stairs. I'm really very sorry."

Mari's body stilled. She thought she'd be angry once she'd discovered the truth, but all she felt was sad. Her mother didn't want to be here, didn't want to be a part of Sebastian's war with the vampires, so she'd tried to help them, sneaking down to the catacombs at night to give them her tea. Probably drinking it herself so they had to take more and more of her blood to get the same effects. Until one night she was too weak and perhaps even dizzy and, in the dark, tripped and fell down the stairs.

She could almost see clearly the way it could have happened.

"Thank you, Jacob, for finally telling me the truth."

"I'm sorry, Mari. I was only following orders."

"I know. So why tell me now?"

He stepped closer to her, reached out and softly touched her cheek. "Because I think you need to know. For your own peace of mind. So you can stop wondering and worrying, and start to feel at home here. So you can move on."

Mari kept her eyes focused on his to keep herself from flinching away in disgust, from screaming her fury. How dare he presume to tell her when she should *move on?*

"Promise me you'll take care of yourself."

Not trusting herself to speak, she kept a stranglehold on her voice and nodded. Then without another word, she walked out the door, scrubbing her hand across her face to remove the imprint of his touch.

The bastard. She would never move on. Nor would she ever feel at home here. Especially with him, and certainly not with Nicholai, Marcos and a whole lot of others tied up below her.

She didn't go back up the stairs to her room to rest as he wanted; instead she went back to the basement, to the catacombs, to Nicholai. There was no sign of the guards today and she figured they probably worked only at night.

As she crept down the stairs, she wondered how it was possible that her mother could have fallen down them. The stairwell itself was very narrow. It would have been easy for her to brace herself against the wall had she tripped. Unless she really had been too weak. Or if she'd been pushed.

The thought crept into her mind, like a soundless serpent slithering through the grass. She tried to reject it, but the more she pushed it away, the stronger it became.

She dug the thermos out of her bag as she walked into Marcos's room and approached the boxes. She was somewhat disconcerted to see Nicholai still staring up at the ceiling. Had the tea she'd given him earlier been no help at all?

"You've come back," Marcos said.

She turned to him. "How are you feeling?"

"Better, now that you're here. It's okay, Nicholai. This is the one I told you about. She's here to help."

Nicholai turned toward her, his black eyes gleaming with hatred. The raw emotion, so dark and so cold, reminded her of the Nicholai she'd seen in her dream. Her hand moved instinctively to her neck. His eyes, like the hawks from her dream, followed her slight movement and shook her to the core.

"Did you bring the tea?" Marcos asked.

She nodded, and tried to answer, but her voice wouldn't come.

"Give it to him first."

"No," Nicholai spat through a clenched jaw. The one word hung in the room like the sharp icicles that dripped from her roof during the brutal New England winters.

At once thankful for the ties that kept Nicholai bound, she turned away from him and poured out the tea. She brought the cup to Marcos's lips, and as she held his head she thought of all the wrongs that had been done to her. To her mother. To Marcos and Nicholai and the others. It made her want to cry, but she couldn't. Not anymore.

She didn't feel anything but numb.

"You wouldn't drink anything she gave you if you knew the truth about her," Nicholai said from behind her, his voice raw with unleashed fury.

She stiffened. She saw the confusion enter Marcos's eyes. He drained the cup and she refilled it, her fingers shaking, her heart racing. When he didn't respond, she lifted his head and helped him drink from it once more.

She waited with her breath trapped in her throat for Nicholai to continue. To say the words she knew he would, to spill the toxic truth that would make her risks, and her mother's sacrifice, worth nothing.

She didn't have to wait long.

"She is the poison, Marcos. The weapon those bloody

witches have been using against us. It comes from her blood. It's how I got here."

Marcos spat out the tea.

Mari gasped, stepping away from him, and in her haste bumped into Nicholai's box. He roared, and she knew in that instant he'd kill her if he could. If somehow he could reach her, he'd do what he'd almost done to her in her dream. He'd rip her throat out. She ran from the room and didn't look back.

Bolting up the stairs, she barely hesitated before breaching the weapons room. Luckily for her, no one was there. She hurried down the hall then up and out of the basement. As she reached the main floor, she hesitated, leaning against the wall and trying to catch her breath.

The loathing and anger she'd felt pouring off both Nicholai and Marcos had been so strong she'd felt it deep down in her pores. She still couldn't shake the acrid scent of it. Was it possible that she could now smell other's emotions as well as feel them?

If so, she didn't like it.

She couldn't go back down there again. They hated her, and would kill her if they could. There was nothing more she could do for them. And no reason to stay here any longer.

Once her heart slowed to its normal rhythm, she continued walking down the hall, but hesitated as she heard her brother's voice booming in anger down the hallway from the infirmary.

"Why has this happened again?" he said. "Is it her blood? I thought you said it was getting stronger."

"It is," Jacob answered, though she had to move closer to hear him. "They must be building up immunity. Or perhaps the older ones are stronger than the rest. I don't know."

"What the hell do you know?" her brother demanded.

"That I'm not making any significant progress with the serum. And we've already taken more of Mari's blood than is prudent. She's weak and tired. I want to wait at least three weeks before taking any more. Give her a chance to regain her strength. We don't have enough serum in storage to keep them incapacitated long enough until we can make a new batch."

"Damn!"

"I'm sorry. But I'm not taking any more chances. We can't risk losing her, too."

Losing her, too? Mari's stomach rolled. Was that all she was to them? All her mother had been? A blood supply? Was there really no one left in the entire world who gave a damn about her?

Not anymore. Thanks to Sebastian.

Anguish consumed her. This man and his obsession with monsters had destroyed her life. She would not help him any longer. She had to get out of there, and she had to get out now.

"Fine," her brother said, before she could turn and go. "Keep one to continue your tests then bury the rest."

"Bury?" Jacob's voice cracked.

"Or stake. Burn. I don't care. Just get rid of them."

Nausea rose in Mari's throat. Marcos and Nicholai weren't responding as they'd hoped, not because they were older or stronger, but because she'd been giving them the tea to counteract the poison. Because of that, because she tried to help them, they were going to die.

Suddenly she couldn't breathe. The walls were closing in on her. She had to get out, to disappear and never come back. There was nothing else she could do. No one left here she could help, no more secrets to unbury. The past three months had been a living nightmare, and it was time she woke up.

Clutching her knapsack, she ran out the front door and into the drizzling rain. She kept running until she was out of the gate and on the tree-lined street. Once on the sidewalk and out of view of the estate, she bent over, hands on her knees, and tried to catch her breath and still the anxiety in her stomach.

Where could she go now? What could she do? She thought of the train station, but then knew she couldn't wait for the next train, and she didn't want to leave any trace for her brother to find. She'd rent a car and drive, not stopping until she was far, far away from Vindecare, from New York State, from Nicholai.

Mari started walking, but hadn't gone more than ten feet, when Darby stepped out of a limo and onto the sidewalk in front of her.

"Stay away from me," Mari said, and continued forward.

"Where is he?" Darby demanded.

Mari ignored her and kept going, moving past her.

"He was furious at me for what I did to you," Darby called after her. "I didn't know he'd changed his mind about…everything. Or I wouldn't have drugged you. I swear."

Mari stopped and turned, keeping under the thick canopy of branches. "What are you talking about?"

"He'd fallen for you. Don't ask me why," she said, as her gaze swept over Mari. "But he wasn't going through with his plans."

"And what plans would those be? Sucking my blood or feeding me to a demon?"

Before she could continue, a window opened in the back of Darby's limousine. Mari leaped away from the curb, and away from a dark-haired man in the backseat wearing large mirrored sunglasses.

"Ah, now I can see why he wanted you all to himself," he said, his voice deep and smooth.

Mari let out an exasperated sigh and took another step away from the limo. God, not another one. Were they everywhere? "I don't want to have anything to do with any of you.

Do you understand? Just stay away from me." She turned and continued walking quickly up the street.

"It was my fault," Darby continued, following after her.

"Leave me alone!" Mari yelled over her shoulder.

"Please. You can't leave him in there. It was my fault. Not his."

Mari turned on her. "You weren't the one who bit me. He was."

"He had to."

Mari hesitated, more because of the definitive statement than anything else she'd said. "Why?"

Darby stepped closer to her, turning her back on the limousine that had been keeping pace with their progress up the street. "He needed to know what you'd heard," she said softly.

"What I heard?" Mari questioned.

"From the crystal," Darby mouthed.

Mari looked over her shoulder at the man sitting in the darkness of the limousine. Why was she with him if she didn't trust him? If she didn't want him to know about what Nicholai had planned to do? And then she realized who he must be. The only one they could turn to for help, even though they didn't trust him.

"You must be Christos," she said stiffly.

"Yes." His face broke into a perfect smile, oozing charm and confidence. He made her skin crawl.

"And you want to rescue Nicholai, too?" she asked, her doubt weighing heavily in her tone.

"Oh, you are good. And you're right. I couldn't care less about rescuing Nicholai. But I have men in there, too. And if I have to bring him out to get to mine, so be it."

"Charming," she muttered.

"As long as he promises to leave. One clan in New York City is one too many."

"Why didn't you help him last night?"

"I wasn't there when he came round or I would have."

"Well, whatever you were doing, I hope it was important because it's too late now. Sorry, but I can't help you."

"Can't or won't?"

"Is there a difference? Even if I could, Nicholai doesn't want my help."

"Fine. Stay out of it. All I need from you is an invitation into the house. Once you do that, you can go on your merry way and never look back."

For a moment she stared at him, remembering how uneasy Nicholai had felt about him. She could feel how nervous Darby was around him now. And he wanted her to invite him in?

"Not on your life," Mari said.

"Why not? Are you just going to walk away and leave him?"

"Absolutely."

"Sexy and cold. I think I'm in love."

She turned away and started walking again. She refused to have anything to do with him. With any of them.

Darby ran after her and grabbed her arm. "Please. Don't leave him to die in there because of something that I did. I saw how he felt about you and I was jealous. I thought with you out of the way, I could have him back to myself. I didn't know he'd changed his mind. I didn't know he wasn't going to go through with it."

"With what?" Mari asked, suddenly too tired for this.

Darby lowered her voice again. "With Asmos. He wasn't going to go through with it. He didn't want to lose you. He loves you, Mari. He's angry and confused, but he's a good man."

"He's a vampire," Mari gritted, realizing the truth of her words as they finally sank in.

"True. But he was a man first. And that man is still in there.

Help him, please," she begged. The sincerity of her words, mingled with her fear and desperation, filled Mari and suffocated her.

"Even if I wanted to, I can't let that one in there," she said, gesturing toward the limo. "You know what he'd do to all those people in there. He'd kill them. I can't let him do that. Not for anyone."

"I won't," Christos said from behind her.

She gasped a breath and turned quickly. He stood behind her under the thick shade of the trees; heavy drops falling from a gray sky peppered their faces.

"And why should I believe you?"

"Because all I care about is getting my men out of that house as quickly as I can. I won't have time to stick around and play."

"Not good enough."

"Sharp, as well as cold and sexy. But you're wrong. Just like Nicholai was wrong about you. You aren't courageous and you aren't special. You are just a scared little human who is willing to walk away and let the man who loves you be tortured and killed."

"Or I'm a woman who's strong enough to stand up to you rather than let a house full of innocent people die."

He nodded his head, his long fingers pulling on his lower lip. "One thing is for certain, someone is going to die today. Any guesses as to whom?"

Chapter 18

Mari stared at Darby and Christos, torn and not sure what to do, but knowing she could never invite that monster into Vindecare. No matter what her brother had done, none of them deserved that. She opened her mouth to say so, when pain as sharp as an ice pick stabbed her temples. She cringed, and with both hands, pushed against her head. Then she heard it. The scream. The roar of hatred-filled anger so strong and so loud, she looked up, certain it had to be reverberating through the air. But it wasn't. It came from inside her.

Nicholai.

"I...I have to think about it," she muttered. "I'll call you." She turned back and ran for Vindecare. Whatever Jacob was doing to Nicholai, she had to stop it. He might hate her, but she couldn't stand by and let him suffer and die.

She ran into the house and hurried down the stairs to the basement, dashing along the corridors until she finally made it down to the catacombs.

Nicholai was screaming, his voice roaring through the rooms. She rushed toward the sound, turned the corner into his room, then skidded to a stop.

"Ally? What in the hell are you doing?" she asked, as shock slammed into her.

Ally straightened and pulled away from Nicholai, wiping his blood off her chin and licking the last remnants off her lips. "Oh, hey, Mari. I can see next time I'm going to have to gag him. What are you doing down here?"

"What am I doing? Seriously? What the hell are you doing?" Mari walked farther into the room, and peered down at Nicholai. Outrage tightened her grip on the side of his box as she noticed his pants were open and a long gash sliced his lower belly.

"You shouldn't be down here, Mari," Ally said, her voice turning hard.

Mari tore her gaze away from Nicholai and glared at Ally. "Honestly, Ally, I really don't care what you do and who you do it with, but you will not do this—" she gestured wildly, unable to verbalize her overwhelming disgust "—with him."

A slow grin crept across Ally's face. "Saving him for yourself, are you? Even after he drank from you? Even after what he'd planned to do? Don't be so high and mighty. Why should you care if I take a little sip? You're the one who called me for help, remember? Now stop acting like his personal doormat and back off. Forget he ever existed. Trust me—he'd do the same to you. Oh, wait. He already did."

Tears sprang to Mari's eyes at the brutal truth of her words.

"I wasn't going to do it," Nicholai said from inside the box, his voice grating like sandpaper.

"Yeah, right." Ally laughed. "Let me guess. Because you love her."

"I did love her." The words were so soft Mari almost didn't hear them.

"That's what they all say."

"Leave us alone," Nicholai insisted.

"Not a chance."

"What's wrong with you?" Mari asked, unable to comprehend what was happening to the other woman. She had a feverish gleam in her eyes and was almost acting high or drunk. "You're the one who convinced me to bring him here. Was this why you wanted him? Is there no decency left in you at all? From where I stand, you've become worse than the vampires you supposedly hate."

"Me? What's wrong with you? Here you had this hot babe in your bed, and you threw him out? You should have been the one drinking from him. Give it a try, girl. Go ahead. Trust me. There is nothing like it." Ally handed her the bloody knife. "See you around, boys."

Mari shuddered as Ally sauntered out of the room.

"I'm so sorry," she said. She reached down and closed Nicholai's pants. She was afraid to look into his face, to meet his eyes. She felt horrible. Ally was right. She had called her; she brought him here, but she never believed that Ally, that anybody, was capable…that she would hurt him in this way.

"Why didn't you tell me?" he rasped.

"Tell you that I'm the reason all your friends are gone? When I met you, I didn't know. It wasn't until after you were here that my brother told me the truth about my blood. About my mother's. It's why she took me away from here when I was little, and why she kept me from Sebastian all these years. If you knew the truth, you would have—" Her throat tightened and she couldn't say the words they both knew were true.

She dropped the knife onto the counter then walked over to Marcos's box. "My mother didn't want to help my brother. She didn't have a choice. If she hadn't helped him, he would have come after me. She'd spent her whole life protecting me from the truth of what I am. She died protecting me. But I came anyway. I didn't know," she whispered.

"That's why she wanted to help you, to make up for everything Sebastian was making her do. Please don't hate her."

Marcos's eyes softened. "I do not hate her. And I do not hate you."

At the softness of his words, her tears rose and spilled onto her cheeks. "Thank you."

She turned back to Nicholai. "Christos and Darby are outside. They want me to let them in. They want to help you."

"Are you going to do it?" he asked, his voice hesitant.

"I don't know. I don't trust either of them."

"We won't let him hurt the others. I swear," Nicholai said, his eyes widening with emphasis.

She wanted to believe him, but how could she? She couldn't stop remembering the way he'd looked at her earlier, and the pure, raw hatred in his eyes. At this point, he'd say and do anything he could to get out of that box.

And she couldn't blame him.

"Bring more of the antidote," Marcos said. "They have stopped the treatments, and I can move. With a little more of the tea, I'll be able to help you with the others and I'll be able to protect you from Christos."

"Are you sure?"

He flexed his fingers and toes and lifted his head, all on his own. "Yes, I'm sure."

"All right. I'll be back as soon as I can," she said, and hurried from the room. They stopped his treatments because they were going to kill him. Her insides turned over and tightened in on themselves.

What was she going to do? How could she live with herself if she left them there to Ally's twisted sex games or Jacob's orders? But could she live with the consequences if she let them out? Maybe, if Marcos was strong enough, he could help her get Nicholai out of the house. Then she wouldn't have to involve Christos.

Then she'd only have Marcos and Nicholai to worry about. Could she trust them? Did she have a choice? Calling Ally and allowing her to bring Nicholai here had been her decision and a huge mistake. She could not leave this place without doing something, and yet she couldn't stay here any longer. She would free them, and then she'd disappear for good.

She reached the main floor then went toward the cafeteria, intent on making another thermos of tea, but as she rounded the corner, she ran smack into Sebastian.

"Mari, you've been a hard one to find lately," Sebastian said, loosely grabbing hold of her arm.

"Oh? I can't imagine why," she said, smiling, making her tone as light and innocent as she could, then she cleared her mind of all thoughts. She still wasn't sure what Sebastian's special gift was, but if it was anything like hers, she didn't want him to know how she was feeling about him right now.

"You seem winded. Are you going somewhere?" he asked, dropping his hands and perusing her face.

"Actually, I'm on my way to Java Blue. I have become addicted to their caramel lattes." Details, she thought. Add in lots of details.

"Unfortunately I have a call coming in, or I'd join you. But I wanted to take a moment and check in with you to see how you're doing."

"Everything's great. I love my classes, and Sheila and I have become really good friends."

"And this…" He glanced around them, then leaned in closer to her. "This vampire you were involved with?"

"Nicholai? I haven't talked to him since that night," she lied. She wished she could confide in him and share her fears about Christos and Ally but, as was always the case with him, she could feel his anger simmering below the surface.

And she knew to try and talk to him, to try and make him see reason, would be like throwing jet fuel on a fire.

"I'm glad to hear that. I've taken the liberty of speaking with some of your teachers. Mr. Hoskins seems especially taken with you."

Mari forced a laugh. "He is sweet. But I don't think his Persuasions class is my thing."

"On the contrary, he seemed quite impressed with your abilities. Considering you've only been here for three months, all your teachers are amazed by your progress."

"Really?" she asked, genuinely surprised.

"Mr. Hoskins said if you keep up your studies, you will be even more powerful than your mother was."

Mari stared at him for a moment, trying to determine exactly what was happening. She was feeling something coming off him, but couldn't quite determine what it was.

"I...well, I've been trying pretty hard, but I didn't think I was making much progress. Although it was pretty cool finding out that Mr. Hoskins had also taught my mother," she added, trying to figure out what he was hiding.

He stiffened, and shoved his hands into the pockets of his blazer. "When my father and I first came here, your mother was the life of the house. He couldn't keep his eyes off her. She was all he could think about."

She smiled. "Sounds romantic."

He cleared his throat, his expression guarded. "She was a student. It was highly inappropriate."

And then it became so clear. He'd hated her. He'd been jealous of her. She'd taken his father's attention away from him. Was that why he hadn't come with them when they left?

"How old were you at the time?" she asked.

"Eleven."

"And then came me."

His jaw tightened. "Yes, you were a squalling, messy little thing."

She forced another laugh, squashing a shudder at his sudden hostility. Had he always hated her? "Well, I hope you never had to change my diaper."

"Good God, no."

She stepped forward and, taking a chance, touched his arm. His hatred and jealousy came flooding over her. It was overwhelming and toxic.

Unable to bear it, she snatched her hand back. His brow furrowed, and he looked at his arm then his hard gaze locked on hers.

"Sebastian, I would like to see my mother's things," she said quickly, before he had a chance to say anything more.

"Her things?"

"Yes." She waited.

"There wasn't much. Just a small suitcase. I'll have it taken to your room."

"What about when we were here before? Was there anything left?"

"No. I'm sorry. That was many years ago."

She nodded, knowing he was lying and wondered if there was anything the man said that was truthful.

"Thank you, Sebastian. And don't worry, I will work hard at my classes to become as strong in my abilities as I can. I don't ever want to be fooled again. *By anyone.*"

He relaxed, and took a step backward. "I'm glad to hear that, Mari. Just take care of yourself. And do everything Jacob tells you to do. We want you strong and healthy."

Of course he does. Can't damage the blood supply, she thought with bitterness, then quickly wiped the thought away. But for the first time, it occurred to her how much he resented being dependent on her for his plans. He was the one who had never wanted her here. Who had never wanted her born.

"As always," she said, and gave him a big smile then started to walk past him.

"One more thing," he said, stopping her. "I know you've been going down into the catacombs to visit your lover. From this moment on, the catacombs are off-limits. Do you understand? I'm sealing off the room and posting a guard." He looked at his watch. "In fact, right about now. Now, if you'll excuse me, I must get upstairs in time for that call."

She turned cold as the blood drained from her face. She hadn't been fooling him. He knew she'd been lying to him, knew about her visits to Marcos and Nicholai.

What in the hell was she going to do? Marcos wouldn't be able to help her. She couldn't save them on her own. Her mother had tried and look what had happened to her. She had no choice but to depend on Darby and Christos, and hope to God Marcos and Nicholai would honor their word and keep Christos from hurting anyone.

Slowly, she walked back out of the house and into the gloomy day, out the gates and around the corner. To her surprise, the limousine was still parked at the curb. As she approached, the window rolled down and Christos peered out at her. "We were hoping we'd see you again."

"I will let the two of you in. Only you two," she emphasized. "Under no circumstances will you go up the stairs to the sleeping quarters. We will go straight down to the catacombs and rescue those we can. Bring lots of blood. They have been…dehydrated," she said for lack of a better word.

"Those who can walk out on their own, you will keep in line. No one will be hurt. Including the guards my brother has posted in the basement. Do we have a deal?"

"Absolutely," he said, and grinned. He took off his sunglasses and she peered into his amber-colored eyes.

"How do I know you will keep up your end of the bargain?" she asked.

"I suppose you're going to have to trust me."

"Oh, joy," Mari muttered, and not for the first time that day she wondered if she was doing the right thing.

And if she had any choice.

"Come at midnight," she said, then turned and walked away.

Chapter 19

At midnight, Mari crept silently down the stairs, her stomach tangled in knots. Was she doing the right thing? Would Christos keep his word? It didn't matter how many times she rolled it round and round her mind, she always came up with the same answer—she couldn't leave Nicholai down there to the mercy of her brother.

She loved him.

She couldn't stand what was happening to him. Even if she never saw him again, at least she'd know she wasn't responsible for whatever horrible fate Sebastian had planned.

Now if she could just get them out of Vindecare without anyone getting hurt. She wanted to warn Sheila, to send her to a club, to send her anywhere, but how could she without giving herself away? She only hoped Sheila would never have cause to find out what was about to happen, and how Mari was the one who set it all in motion.

She slipped out the door and hovered against the wall,

staying out of range of the outside lights until she reached the gates. Darby and Christos were standing in the shadows, Darby a bundle of nervous anxiety, while Christos practically hummed with excitement. She was giving him exactly what he wanted. She knew that. She only hoped the pencil sharpened to a point in her pocket would be enough if worse came to worst and she had to use it on him.

She knew it could barely function as a stake, but where did one go to buy small wooden vampire-killing weapons? It would have to do. Without a word, she opened the gates and let them in, then hurried as fast as she could to the main house before she lost her nerve.

But she hesitated at the front door, her hand lingering on the doorknob.

"It's okay," Darby said. "You can trust us. We just want our friends back. You're doing the right thing."

Was she? She still wasn't sure, but it was too late for second guesses now. She opened the door and invited them in. A strange flutter lit her stomach as Christos walked past her through the door.

"Not everyone is asleep," she whispered. "But I didn't want to wait any longer. We'll have to be extra careful." Her gaze met Christos's. "Especially you."

"Don't worry. Tonight is a night for rescue and triumph. Not revenge."

Tonight? It occurred to her that now that she'd invited him in, he'd be able to come back at any time. Whenever he wanted. A shudder of dread moved through her.

"Let's go," she said.

As quietly as they could, they moved through the main floor down to the basement. And to his credit, if she hadn't known, she wouldn't have guessed Christos was even there. The silence in which he could move frightened her more than she wanted to admit. As they crept down the hallways, Mari listened for the jangle of the guard's keys, but heard nothing.

Had her brother lied? Or had he already gotten rid of Nicholai and the others alleviating the need for guards? Her heart skipped painfully at the thought and she quickened her pace.

She should have checked. She twisted and pulled at her fingers until they entered the weapons room. "There's an alarm embedded into the second step," she whispered.

They followed her down the stairs. As she reached the bottom, she hurried down the hall and into Nicholai's room. Again, there were no guards. Where was Ally? Sebastian? Why was it so quiet down here? Anxiety pulled at her. Something wasn't right.

Slowly, she approached the boxes, terrified she'd find them empty. She glanced inside. Nicholai looked up at her. She pushed out a breath full of relief.

"What took so long?" he asked.

"Oh, my God," Darby said as she stepped up behind her and looked down into the box, her eyes wide with shock, her mouth opened in disbelief.

"I'm sorry. I—" Unable to explain, Mari turned to Darby. "Did you bring the blood?"

Darby nodded, slipped off the backpack and dug inside. She pulled out what looked like a bag of blood from a hospital, opened it then started pouring it into Nicholai's mouth.

He gulped at it like a starving baby.

"Where are the others?" Christos asked, as he watched Darby.

"In the back. We'll get them next," Mari said.

"I'll get them now." He leaned down and picked up Darby's bag.

"Wait," Mari said, loudly. Too loudly. She cringed as her

voice echoed around the chamber. "I don't want you going alone. Darby, go with him."

"I can't. Nicholai's not done."

Mari grabbed the knife still sitting on the counter, still coated with Nicholai's blood, now dry and flaking, and cut the plastic tie holding down his wrists. Nicholai blew out a relieved groan and flexed his hands, then held the packet of blood for himself.

Darby turned to Christos and grabbed the pack out of his hands. She dug inside and pulled out another bag of blood. "For Marcos."

"Thanks," Mari muttered, taking the blood. Then told them how to find the last room where the others were being kept. Anxiety tightened her insides as she watched them walk away, but she couldn't go with them. Not yet.

Quickly, she cut the ties on Marcos's hands so he could drink from the packet of blood. They both looked tired and worn and she wondered how long it had been since they'd been fed. He sucked it greedily as she cut the bindings around his ankles, and then did the same for Nicholai.

"Can you stand?" she asked Nicholai as he finished the bag.

He nodded, but he had to grab the side of the box when he tried to sit up. She pulled the thermos out of her pack and handed it to him. "Here, drink some of this."

He took it, and she turned back to Marcos. "You promised you'd watch Christos. Make sure he doesn't hurt anyone."

"I will," he said, and climbed out of the box. He'd been drinking her tea longer and seemed in much better shape than Nicholai. He walked over to Nicholai's box and helped him out of it and down off the table.

"We should get you out of here," Marcos said to Nicholai. "Then I'll come back and help Darby and Christos with the others."

"No. I won't leave them."

"What help are you going to be? You can barely walk. You'll only slow me down."

"I'll be fine. Just give me back that thermos."

Mari handed it to him, and he drank until it was empty. She had to admit, he was starting to look better.

"This way," she said, anxious to join the others in the back room. She didn't like leaving Christos alone.

As Marcos ran ahead of them down the hall, Nicholai grabbed her hand. "Mari?"

Surprised, she stopped and turned back to him.

"I know how hard it was for you to bring him in here, to rescue us."

"I couldn't leave you here to die. My brother is an evil monster."

He smiled. "What kind of monster is he?"

"The human kind."

He pulled her against him. She stood stiffly, mentally guarding herself. She was afraid to let her defenses down, to give her heart to him again, but after a moment all her resistance broke down and she succumbed to the feel of his arms, the tenderness of his embrace.

"I meant what I said before. I wasn't going to go through with the transfer. I couldn't hurt you."

"I believe you." And she realized as she said the words out loud that she did. It wasn't just a false sense of hope that she'd grabbed on to; she felt his love. And it was real. She hadn't been lying to herself.

He leaned down and pressed his lips to hers and kissed her gently.

She shuddered.

He pulled back, looking confused.

"Sorry," she said. "But you're freezing."

He smiled. "I need more blood."

"Then let's go find Darby and the others and get you some so we can try that again."

Mari led the way through the darkness of the catacombs to the last room at the end of the hall. As they reached the end, she was surprised to find the door shut. She stepped forward, opened it and gasped.

Sebastian stood in the center of the room, holding Darby's arms extended behind her. His two guards held Christos up against the wall, their guns pushed up under his chin on each side of his head.

"Hello, sister. I've been waiting some time for you to come. I see you've brought guests." His eyes glittered dangerously.

Stunned, Mari stared at him. How had he known what she'd planned?

"You look surprised. I don't know why you should. I'm not the fool you believe me to be. I know how you feel about that one," he sneered as his eyes fell on Nicholai. "Like mother like daughter."

"What are you talking about?" She turned back to Nicholai, who was leaning against the wall and put her shoulder under his arm to give him support. Not that he needed it. She just wanted to touch him. To hold him. Because she knew it would most likely be for the last time.

"Your mother had been sneaking down here, too. I followed her one night. Watched her with that demon scum. Listened to her declarations of love. She made me sick," Sebastian continued.

Mari glanced at Marcos, but his face was a blank mask. Had he loved her mother?

Sebastian walked closer to her, pulling Darby with him. "Your mother left my father because she didn't love us enough to stay, but she loved that demon."

"Left you?" Mari asked, confused. "I thought our father had died."

"Is that what she told you? The woman told nothing but lies. No. My father was very much alive when she left. She broke his heart, told him she couldn't live with his obsession with the vampires any longer. She wanted a peaceful, happy house to raise her daughter in. Her daughter!"

Mari shuddered as his anger washed over her, so thick and greasy, she could smell its acrid scent.

"All because of her love for the vampires. My making her come back here and forcing her to poison them, well, I call that poetic justice."

"How did you do it? How did you get her back?" Mari asked, her voice shaking. Though she already knew. Had already guessed.

"To keep me from coming after you. You were always the only one who mattered to her. Her precious baby girl with the extra special gift." He snarled as he said the words, and Mari knew that even though she might be related to him this man wasn't her family and never could be.

"I thought that maybe she'd changed while she was here," he continued. "Maybe she understood what my father and I were trying to accomplish in ridding the world of these vermin," he said, gesturing around the room. "But then I saw her with him. *Kissing him.*"

His eyes fell on Marcos and, for the first time, Mari was scared. Because now she knew the truth. She could feel it so clearly.

"You killed my mother," she accused Sebastian.

He smiled as he turned back to her. "When I walked down here and saw her with him, heard what she'd said and discovered how she'd planned to help him escape, I lost it. How could she betray me for that…thing?" He spat, pointing at

Marcos, whose eyes had once more turned blacker than the night.

Mari shivered. "What are you going to do now?" she asked, her voice barely a whisper.

"You've given me no choice. You're coming with me. I have a box of your very own waiting for you."

Horror liquefied her legs. "What?"

"Don't worry. Jacob insisted on putting you in a coma state so you won't even know what's happening to you. Jacob!" he called.

From behind her, Jacob walked into the room, a syringe, like another appendage, hung from his hand.

Coma? He was going to put her in a coma, feeding her with a tube, keeping her barely alive, just so he could steal her blood and continue his experiments?

Disbelief spread through her. She thought Jacob cared for her. And here she'd been so worried about him. About what Christos might do. How many others in this house were in on her brother's sick and twisted plans? Sheila? Mr. Hoskins? Ms. Whalen? A cry escaped her clenched throat.

Jacob walked toward her and grabbed her arm. Nicholai protested but, too weak, fell back against the wall. Mari yanked her arm out of Jacob's grasp.

"How could you do this?"

"How could you do him?" he asked, his mouth turned down into a disgusted sneer as he glanced at Nicholai. "He's an animal. He isn't even human."

"He's more human than you!"

He grabbed her arm once more. Nicholai lunged for him.

"Guards," Sebastian yelled, throwing Darby to the ground and running toward her.

The guards who were surrounding Christos turned and pointed their weapons at Nicholai. Christos reached forward and smashed their heads together so hard their skulls crumbled inward and blood splattered on the concrete blocks behind them.

Sebastian grabbed her. Mari screamed, pushing him away. She turned back to Nicholai and saw him with his teeth imbedded into Jacob's neck. His eyes a feverish glow of black obsidian as he drank until Jacob slipped to the floor and gazed blankly at the ceiling.

A cry filled Mari's throat, but before it could escape, Sebastian slipped out the door, slamming it behind him.

"No!" She ran toward the door and pushed on it, but it was locked.

She turned back around and saw Nicholai and Marcos drinking from the unconscious and barely living guards. Darby was digging into her pack pulling out blood packets.

"Christos, break their binds," Darby said, as she ran to place the blood packs into each of their boxes.

"They haven't had blood for a while now. They're shriveled up. We have to get them hydrated again if we're going to be able to get them out of here," Darby said.

Mari stared at her in horror.

"Don't," she said, her voice barely audible. "Don't wake them up."

"Why not?" Darby asked, as she turned back to her.

"Because we're locked in."

Chapter 20

Locked in a room full of starving, angry vampires and they were the only two humans left alive. Darby's face went ashen. Mari turned and pounded on the door.

"Let us out!" she cried.

Christos looked at her and smiled. "At least he's left us with a blood supply."

Mari wrapped her hand around the pencil in her pocket. The smart thing to do would be to try and kill as many of the vampires still locked in their boxes as she could. But she knew Christos, and probably even Marcos and Nicholai, would never stand by and let her do it.

Desperation bordering on panic filled her. Her gaze swept the room as she searched for a way out. But she saw nothing except Darby casually placing the bags of blood back into her backpack. Hopefully they could keep the others from waking up.

"You can hand those over to me, now," Christos said, walking toward her with his hand extended.

Darby's eyes widened with fear as she handed him the bag.

"That's a good girl." He reached out to touch her, but she flinched back.

"Afraid of me now, are you? Are you worried that your precious Nicholai isn't strong enough to protect you?" His mocking words echoed through the room.

"Leave her alone, Christos," Nicholai said. He was sitting on the floor, leaning against the wall.

Mari's chest clenched. Her hand fluttered to her throat. There was so much blood. Everywhere. She turned away.

How had everything gone so wrong?

"Don't worry, Nicholai. With the help of both of these beautiful and delectable young ladies, all my plans have finally come to fruition. I've been trying for years to get into this house and, thanks to you, Mari, I'm finally here," Christos said.

"Yes. Trapped here," she muttered. "You're locked in. Buried deep beneath the ground. We're not going anywhere."

"Do you think I'd come in here without a backup plan? In the morning, a FedEx driver is going to drive in to the estate a van big enough to carry all my vampires. He is going to need a signature for his delivery. With luck, it will be that tall, pretty blonde who will answer the door. He'll ask her if he can use the restroom, and considering how much she likes Latino men, well, she's going to invite him in. And thanks to the map you left at the house for Darby to discover, he and a few of my friends will easily be able to find their way down here. And luckily for us, there is plenty of fresh meat right here in the house to help get my men get back on their feet."

Mari's stomach dropped. "But you said…"

He laughed. "Yes, I know. The gullible little witch who believes everything she hears. Even when she hears it from a vampire. I thought you would have learned your lesson the first time around from that one." He gestured toward Nicholai, and Mari couldn't hold back the shudder.

She was such a fool. A stupid, naive, love-struck fool.

Nicholai eased off the ground, using the wall to push himself up. He walked toward the boxes, looking in at his men, one after another.

"Are they in pain?" Darby asked.

He lifted one of the dried arms. "Not anymore. They can stay like this indefinitely, never feeling, or thinking, just lying in limbo waiting to be resurrected."

He started ripping the tie wraps off their wrists and ankles, one by one.

"Stop," Mari said, stepping forward.

"Why?" He turned back to her and all she could see was the pain in his eyes.

"We can't let them hurt—"

"Who? The witches in this house that did this to them?" His mouth turned down.

Christos laughed and walked toward her. "So much for your knight in shining armor."

After everything they'd been through, Nicholai wouldn't turn against her. Mari wouldn't believe it. She might be naive when it came to men, and yes, she was probably gullible, but she also had good instincts, and they told her to believe in Nicholai. Even as he walked from box to box, breaking open the ties, pouring bags of blood down the throats of his friends until every last bag was drained.

She held fast to her belief even as she watched in horror as the vampires rose in their boxes, their eyes filled with bloodthirst and rage. He wouldn't feed Darby to them, or kill Mari. She wouldn't believe that.

Not for a second.

He walked toward her and, stopping in front of her, brushed the hair back from her face.

"I love you," he said. "I have since that first night in the bar, when I lost myself in your emerald-green eyes. I promised myself that night that someday they would be mine."

He leaned forward to kiss her. But the guard's blood staining his lips was all she could see. She turned her head away.

"This is what I am," he said. "See me for what I am. Open your eyes, your heart and really look at me. Do you love me?"

Tears burned the back of her eyes as she looked up at him and saw him. Blood and all. Not a man, but a vampire. Did she love him? Could she?

Yes.

She nodded her head as her tears ran down her cheeks. She did.

Nicholai turned around to Christos who was hovering dangerously close to Darby.

"Stay away from her, Christos. She's mine and I don't share."

"That's hardly fair. You can't have both of them and you've used up all the blood."

Mari didn't like the determination in Christos's eyes, or how long it was taking Nicholai to consider his words. But what could he do?

What would he do?

"All right, then. Here." He thrust Mari toward him. The imprint of his hand hard on her back, his betrayal even harder on her heart. "She's all yours."

"No," Mari cried, and tried to push away from Christos.

"I thought this one was off-limits? I thought you *loved* her?" Christos asked.

"I did. But that was before."

"Before what?" he probed.

"Before she showed her true nature."

Panic stole her breath as Mari watched Christos turn into a beast—his fangs long and wickedly sharp, his face as white as stone. She turned back to Nicholai, her heart shattering as his gaze locked onto hers. What if he was wrong? What if he killed her before the poison could take effect? With razor-sharp pain, Christos's teeth pierced her skin.

"Trust me." She heard Nicholai's voice clearly in her mind. Warm and soothing. *"Think only of me."*

Images flashed through her mind—his touch, soft and gentle, and the way he held her as he made love to her, holding her tight, his forehead resting on hers, their warm breath mingling as they lost themselves in each other.

"Hey! Make sure you save some for me," Marcos demanded. "I'm the starving one over here."

Christos pulled back, her blood running down his chin. "Boy, has she got it bad for you, Nicholai. It's almost…heartbreaking." He laughed as he pushed her at Marcos. "She's all yours."

Weakened, Mari fell into a heap at Marcos's feet. Marcos pulled her up into his arms, and buried his face beneath her long hair.

"Don't worry," he whispered, "it shouldn't take long now."

And it didn't.

Christos grabbed his head and screamed as the pain hit him. Within minutes he was lying on the floor, paralyzed, a look of disbelief etched into his frozen face.

Then Nicholai was next to her, pulling her up into his arms, cradling her against his chest. "Are you okay?"

She nodded. "How'd you know he would stop?"

"It was an estimated guess."

"A guess?" she said in outrage and punched his chest.

He laughed, and held her closer. "If he hadn't then I would have had to pull him off you. I couldn't let him eat my favorite witch."

"Oh, gee, thanks."

At that moment, they heard a tentative knock on the door. They all quieted and listened.

"Mari?"

"Ally!" Mari made it to the door and banged on it. "Ally, we're trapped in here. Let us out."

"I can't," she said, her voice torn with indecision.

"You have to." Mari turned back to glance at the vampires, who looked more and more hungry by the minute. "You can't leave me in here with them," she pleaded.

"Make them promise not to hurt me. Even after everything I did."

"They won't. I promise. I won't let them," she said, though when she turned to Nicholai and Marcos, she wasn't so sure they would live up to her word. She looked at them pointedly; Nicholai nodded first, then Marcos. She let out a relieved breath then turned back to the door.

"Ally, you have to let us out. There's a van with Christos's people coming in the morning. They're planning on killing everyone. Now hurry, before my brother finds you."

"It's almost daybreak now."

"Then open the door, Ally!"

After a moment of silence, the lock clicked and Ally pulled open the door. Mari ran into her arms almost knocking her over in her haste to get out of the room. "Thank you, Ally."

But Ally didn't respond. She was staring wide-eyed at Jacob and the guards, and then her gaze fell onto Christos and she started to shake. Small mewling sounds filled the air.

Surprised, Mari tried to pull her back out of the doorway, but Ally wouldn't move. "They won't hurt you," Mari said.

"It's him," Ally cried, her voice a high-pitched wail. "He's the one who killed my family." She turned back to Mari. "He took everything from me—my sisters, my parents, my power. By drinking the vampire's blood, I could get my power back. I could make sure *he* never took anything away from me again."

Mari led her out of the room, away from Christos, away from Nicholai and Marcos. "I see," she whispered. And she did see. She just hoped Marcos and Nicholai would see. "He can't hurt you anymore. I promise."

"You swear?"

"I swear." Mari led her out of the catacombs, and as she did, she could hear Nicholai and Marcos, helping their men out of their boxes and carrying them out of their nightmare. Slowly, one by one, they took them out of the house and to the limo waiting on the street.

"Sebastian and Jacob ran out of the poison," Ally muttered. "Then they stopped giving them blood, too, hoping they'd shrivel up into raisins so they could lock them up down there forever, unable to move, unable to do anything. But I couldn't let Sebastian lock you in there with them. I just couldn't."

"Come, on," Mari said, and led her up the stairs. "We have to protect the others. We have to make sure no one comes up the stairs. If they do, can you fight them?"

Some of the brightness seemed to come back into her eyes and she pulled a stake out of her pocket. A real one, thick and pointy, making Mari's pencil look really pathetic.

Mari smiled. "Good."

But they didn't need the pencil or the stake after all because, true to their word, no vampires came up the stairs. Later, after the sun shone high in the sky and all the vampires were gone and the FedEx truck had come and had been sent away, Mari and Ally returned hand in hand to the catacombs. Not a trace of the guards, Jacob, the vampires or even Christos was found. They were all gone, except for Sebastian, who lay in a crumpled heap at the bottom of the stairs, his neck twisted at an awkward angle.

"Looks like he fell down the stairs," Mari said.

"We really should install a railing," Ally said, and linked her arm through Mari's as they climbed back up the stairs.

Epilogue

Mari stood barefoot on the shore of the lake behind her house, her toes sinking into the wet sand. She gazed off into the distance at the forest of trees as far as the eye could see on the far side of the lake, almost expecting to see hawks circling. But the orange-and-pink-tinged sky was clear. Not a bird in sight.

This wasn't a dream.

She heard footsteps and turned, a smile warming her heart. "Good evening."

Nicholai stood behind her, wrapping his arms around her waist. He nuzzled her neck, kissing her gently. They'd made love all night long, and slept the day away.

"I love your home," he said, planting a kiss on her shoulder.

She turned in his arms. "I hope you'll stay."

"I hoped you'd ask."

She smiled. "Consider yourself invited."

He lifted her hair and kissed her nape. "I was hoping you would say that."

"What about Marcos and Darby and the others?"

"You want to invite them, too?"

She laughed. "No. I think one vampire is enough."

"Good, because they will do just fine without me and it is better that they don't know the truth about you."

"But Christos…"

"Yes, there's a possibility when he comes out of his coma, he'll tell them. That's why you can never go back to the city, and you can never let them find you."

She shivered. "No worries there. I'm happy here. Especially if you stay."

"And Vindecare?" he asked.

"Ally is in charge now. The school is still functioning, and most of the students and teachers have no idea what happened, though I think some suspect. She's installed a first-rate alarm system and hired more security. I think she'll be okay. Though she's terrified Christos will wake up and come after them. I left her a little more of my blood, just in case. I'm hoping she'll never have to use it." She hesitated, wishing she didn't have to ask, but needing to know. "And Marcos? Will he retaliate?"

"Marcos wants the whole ordeal behind him. He said he'll leave her alone if he never has to see her again."

"Then she's safe?" she asked, slightly disbelieving.

"From Marcos. As long as she stays away from him."

"Trust me, she wouldn't be that foolish." Mari hoped. Though Ally did have a strange obsession with Marcos that worried her. Surely, she was smart enough after everything that had happened to keep her distance.

Nicholai reached down and picked up her knapsack he'd brought out of the house. "We have one last thing we need to talk about."

He pulled out the bundled towel she'd taken from his bathroom and unwrapped the large crystal from within its depths.

"The demon," she whispered.

"Asmos, the Demon of Wrath. What do you want to do with him?"

"It's your crystal," she said. "You should decide. But I'd rather not have it in our house."

"Our house," he repeated. "I like the sound of that." His smile sent flutters of desire moving through her.

"Me, too."

He reached back as far and he could and chucked the crystal out into the middle of the lake, where it landed with a loud splash and sank to the bottom of the dark depths. "I don't think you'll be able to hear him from there."

He kissed her then, his mouth moving against hers, his tongue sweeping inside and claiming hers. "I'm staying," he said. "I'll never let anything happen to you. You're stuck with me."

She liked the sound of that. "I love you," she said, and without a second of hesitation or doubt.

He held her face in his hands and kissed her again. "I love you more."

* * * * *

*If you loved this heart-wrenching, sensual story
about lovers uniting against impossible
odds, be sure to turn the page and read
HIS MAGIC TOUCH,
which was first published in electronic form
in Harlequin Nocturne Bites.
We hope you enjoy it.*

Chapter 1

Trent Drouillard's stomach turned as he approached the door. Evil he could face. Restless spirits and angry demons he could handle. Sera Barnhardt with her big brown eyes and bouncy, soft curls? No way. He had to, though. He had to face her well-deserved fury. Worse, he had to convince her to trust him when there was no reason she should.

If she didn't, their daughter would die.

He stood in front of the door of the small cottage in a small town in a Louisiana bayou and swallowed the frustration building within him. He'd sacrificed his life, his family, and yet, no matter how far he'd run, the demon still found them. Trent looked over his shoulder, reaching with his senses, searching for the demon's presence. He was close.

Trent took a deep, calming breath, then reached forward and rang the bell. He listened impatiently to the sound of footsteps moving within the house. Over the years, he'd watched from a distance this place grow from cold and empty to teeming with life. Exotic tropical plants lined the walk to the front door. Off to the side, a hot pink bicycle with its metallic streamers flowing out of the handlebars lay on its side in the grass, waiting for Aimee to come home and take it for a ride. A sign of innocence soon lost if he couldn't save her.

With a pang of regret, he remembered the big smile brightening her face, the tinkling sound of her laughter ringing through the air the first time she'd ridden it. He'd watched her, unseen from his car, wanting to scoop her up and spin her around. But he didn't dare. A few stolen moments at a time was all he'd ever been able to chance.

The door opened. Sera stepped into the doorway, her beautiful brown eyes widening in shock, her luscious mouth falling open. He caught his breath, hoping to still the anxiety hammering inside him.

After all this time, the sight of her still weakened him. Her sweet scent filled his nose and spread like warm molasses through his being, drawing him to her. He took a step back, trying to distance himself before he lost control. His heart quickened in his chest, he clenched his fists at his sides to keep from moving a muscle, from pulling her soft body up against him.

"Trent?" The voice that had haunted his nights all these long years pierced him.

He forced a wide, cocky grin. "Hello, beautiful."

"What are you doing here?" she demanded, her tone sharp, her gaze icy.

"I wanted to see you...and Aimee."

Her face paled. The sharp scent of fear rolled off her in waves. The sound of her heart ramping up to a wild staccato pounded in his ears.

He held up both hands. "Don't worry. I just..." *Miss you.* "I need..."

Her mouth closed abruptly, thinning into a straight line.

He stepped forward again, opening his arms at his sides in a welcoming gesture. "I know this must seem out of the blue." What could he say to put her at ease when he was nowhere near at ease himself?

Her eyes narrowed.

"It's been a long time and…" The words he couldn't say choked him. *You're in danger. Aimee is in danger.*

Anger sent color rushing back into her cheeks. "What is it you want, Trent?"

"I need to talk to you about Aimee."

"What about her?" Her knuckles whitened as she clutched the edge of the door. "You have about thirty seconds before I completely lose it. Talk. And talk fast."

"She's in trouble."

"How would you know anything about Aimee? You haven't seen her in eight years."

"Trust me, I know."

Sera blew out an exasperated breath. "Twenty."

"Aimee needs me. *You* need me."

"Like hell."

"She's in danger. You haven't given her the amulet."

Surprise, then skepticism wrinkled Sera's brow. "How would you know that? Have you been watching us?"

He stiffened under her direct gaze. "Does it matter? Aimee needs my protection."

"Taking care of my daughter is my responsibility. You gave up that job when you walked away from being her dad."

Trent stiffened. Low blow, and from her perspective one he deserved, but she was wrong. "Are we going to stand out here all day and become a spectacle for the neighbors, or are you going to invite me in and listen to what you're up against?"

A moment later, two women pushing baby strollers turned the corner and walked past the house, their eyes riveted on them. Sera gave them a halfhearted wave, then turned back to him with suspicion darkening her eyes.

"Come on, Sera. Give me a break."

"You don't deserve a break and time's up." She stepped back and slammed the door so hard the front windows shook.

Damn, but she was even more hot-tempered than he remembered. "I will protect my daughter."

Nothing.

"Give Aimee the amulet. The demon can't touch her if she's wearing it."

Trent dropped his head against the front door, knowing she was standing on the other side. He could hear her shifting from foot to foot, could hear the pounding of her heart, her blood rushing through her veins. His gift. His curse.

For a moment, he wished he could touch her and hold her like he used to, then maybe she'd listen to what he had to say. Maybe she'd believe the unbelievable. But she was afraid. Not of the demon he knew was close by. She was terrified of him—the father of her child. The man she'd once promised to love forever.

But her fear didn't matter. He would protect his daughter whether Sera helped him or not. They could do this the easy way or the hard way, but either way, he was taking Aimee.

Sera waited until she saw Trent drive away, then rushed out to her car and drove quickly to Voodoo Mystique. If anyone on the planet knew what that man was up to, it would be Mary. She pulled around back of the store and ran in through the delivery entrance.

"Mary," she called, as she entered the empty shop.

Mary sat at a table by the window, worry lines creasing her brow as she flipped over a tarot card and set it on top of a row of others. "They've been saying the same thing all day. The threat I've warned you about draws near."

Fear needled Sera as she stared down at the cards spread neatly across the small table.

"*He's* here now," Mary whispered.

"I know. He just left my house."

Mary looked up at her, surprise widening her eyes.

"Trent," Sera whispered through the tightening of her throat. She still couldn't believe it, after all these years, he'd just shown up and damned if he didn't look better than she remembered.

"No, not Trent," Mary muttered, shaking her head. "He's not the threat."

Sera slapped both palms down on the table. "Of course he's a threat. The man has been missing in action for eight years and suddenly he decides to show his smug face? I'd say that's a threat."

Mary pursed her lips and placed a hand over Sera's. "He can help you fight the demon who seeks Aimee. Listen to what he has to say. Let him in."

Sera yanked back her hand. "Demon? What would a demon want with Aimee?" Ridiculous. "Besides, there are no such things as demons." She'd heard Mary talk like this before, but had never paid much attention to her ramblings. But now? Now she was talking about Aimee. Uneasiness twisted Sera's insides.

Mary leaned forward, her fear-filled gaze capturing Sera's. "I've told you for years she's different. She's special."

"Of course she's special. She's my baby."

"Magic is in her blood. It makes her desirable and easy to find. You won't be able to protect her on your own." The look in Mary's eyes, the tone of her voice…she was dead serious.

A shiver shook Sera. "You're scaring me, Mary." She turned away from her aunt, her gaze moving over reptile heads that stared at her through cold, glassy eyes. Voodoo dolls hung suspended from the ceiling by the hundreds, and apothecary jars of powders and herbs lined the shelves of the shop.

Why was she surprised her aunt had finally lost it? Look where she spent all her time.

Sera inhaled a sharp breath. "Mary, Aimee's smart, beautiful and talented, but she can't do magic. No one can."

"You can't deny her blood heritage. That's why you must listen to Trent. He is here to help you. There's a lot about him you don't know."

"And why exactly is that? Perhaps because he never let me know anything about him. He's never kept in contact, has never been worried about his daughter before, and now suddenly *he* has to protect her? I know all I need to know about Trent Drouillard. He can't be trusted. He has never been there for me or for Aimee."

Mary leaned back in her chair, her gaze narrowing. "Hasn't he?"

Sera bristled. "Yes, he's provided for us financially." Handsomely, in fact. Their cottage was paid off. Life for them was good. Lonely, but good. "But that doesn't mean I owe him. *He* was the one who abandoned us. I wanted him to stay." Her voice broke over the words, and tears burned behind her eyes.

Tears of frustration and outrage. Tears she wouldn't let fall. She'd shed enough tears over that man.

Sera flung her arms wide. "Why am I having to defend myself to you? You are the one person I thought would be on my side."

Mary sighed, her dark eyes softening. "I am on your side. But turning your back on the one person who can save Aimee is not the answer. You have to see him. You have to listen to what he has to say. You have no choice here. Do it for Aimee's sake."

"Of course I have a choice. It's my job to protect my

daughter. I'm not going to let him waltz in here and worm his way into her heart only to leave her in shambles when he waltzes out again."

Mary's lips pursed. "Is it her heart you're worried about? Or yours?"

Sera stiffened and looked away. Her aunt had always been able to read her too easily.

"Sera, what matters here is that Aimee's in danger and Trent is the only one who can protect her."

Why did everyone keep saying that? What proof was there other than a picture on a tarot card?

Bells tinkled throughout the shop as the front door opened. Trent strolled in, acting as if he owned the place, as if he'd never been gone. Sera's eyes widened and dread turned her stomach.

For the first time she noticed his faded blue jeans and worn black leather jacket, probably the same clothes he'd left with. His shaggy blond hair was overdue for a trim and he hadn't shaved in a few days, but that only made him look more appealing. And more dangerous.

Mary stood and reached out her hand to him, a large traitorous smile on her face. "As I live and breathe."

"Hello, sweetheart," Trent said, his blue eyes sparkling as he kissed her cheek.

Sera's insides twisted and burned. She clenched her hands, certain that if she stared at him much longer she would self-combust.

"What are you doing here?" she said through gritted teeth.

"I thought neutral territory might make it easier for you to listen to what I have to say."

Neutral? Hah! "Sorry. I'm not interested." Sera stood.

"Are you going to let your anger at me endanger our daughter?"

Her eyes widened in disbelief. "Our daughter is not in

danger. This is some ploy you've made up. Some game you're up to, and I'm not playing."

"For chrissakes, Sera. Wake up!"

She stood stiff as a board, sputtering. Her wake up? Her? She was the only sane one in the shop. She couldn't speak. Refused to speak, and instead gnawed on her tongue until she tasted blood. And then adrenaline surged through her system. "Get out!" she demanded, flinging her arm toward the door. "You are not seeing Aimee."

In two steps, he was on her. Before she could think, he had her in his grasp. He pulled her up against his hard chest.

"No," she blurted, placing her hands between them, trying to brace herself as his spicy scent overcame her. She couldn't breathe. Anger, heartache and betrayal rose in her throat and choked her. With a twist of pain, she remembered his smell, his touch and how safe she'd felt in his arms. Once she'd thought nothing or no one could destroy what they'd had together.

And then he'd left her.

She pushed against him, a roar of outrage building within her. Then his mouth crushed hers. In a blinding rush of shock and humiliation, she cried out against his lips. But he held on tighter, pulled her closer.

And then the images came.

Nightmarish images of blood and pain: black waters sloshing against the knees of bald cypress trees as a man pushed a young girl into the water again and again. The head flying off a beautiful burnt-orange rooster, its blood seeping into the dirt at her feet and splattering across her white shoes. A man with emotionless, coal-black eyes smiled as a trickle of blood seeped out the corner of his lips. And Aimee, crying as he came toward her, a wicked knife raised high above his head.

Sera jerked free from Trent's grasp. She rubbed her lips

and swiped at the tears streaming down her face. "What did you do to me?"

"I'm sorry, *chère*. But I had to show you the truth. You need to know what we're up against. It's not pretty, I know. But I had to get you to listen."

Disgust filled her. "Who are you? What are you? How did you do that?"

Pain slashed through his eyes. "I'm a demon hunter. I was born one. I can see them, sense them, just as they can sense me. I had hoped you'd never have to know. But after Aimee was born, I knew we were in trouble. Demons can smell the blood of those like us. As a baby, she was too young to be detectable, but they could have found me. I couldn't chance bringing them to her door."

Sera stared at him. The only man she'd ever loved was certifiable. "That's insane."

"Maybe, but it's my life. And it will be Aimee's—if I can keep her alive. Aimee will grow up to hunt demons, she will have no choice. She will hunt or die."

"You're crazy."

"Am I? Has Aimee been having night terrors lately?"

Sera stared at him, a worm of doubt and fear wiggling through her. "All kids have nightmares."

"Night terrors so bad she has to sleep with you or she won't sleep at all?"

"How did you know about that?" Sera turned accusing eyes on Mary. "Did you tell him?" She turned back to Trent. "Is that why you're here? Why you're spouting all these insane notions?"

"They're not dreams, Sera. They're visions. The monster she sees in her sleep is the demon who has found her. She's getting old enough to put out her own scent and they've been able to pick it up. I had hoped the amulet would have given her more time to be a kid, to be normal before I had to come for her. I'm sorry."

"What do you mean, come for her?" Sera's heart lurched in panic.

"She needs to be trained. She needs to know how to protect herself. She needs to come with me."

"You are not taking my daughter anywhere." Tears sprung to Sera's eyes. God, no. This couldn't be happening. She looked to her aunt for assistance.

Mary stepped forward and placed her hand on Trent's arm. "You can't just take Aimee and run. You must stay and fight. You must protect the ones you love."

The cloying scent of sandalwood incense filling the shop grew stronger, making Sera's head spin. She looked at Mary, at Trent, and felt the walls closing in. Sera didn't believe in voodoo or demons, but was she wrong? Was there really a demon after her baby? Would Trent really steal Aimee away from her? Nausea made her knees weak.

"I need to get back to my daughter," Sera said and clutched her stomach. She had to get away from him. She had to get to Aimee. "She'll be home from school soon."

"I'm going with you," Trent said.

"No!" Sera stepped back from him. "Don't come anywhere near us."

Sera felt Mary's gentle touch on her arm and turned to her aunt. "Don't take this threat lightly. Trust Trent. This demon wants her blood."

A chill moved through Sera, shaking her to the core. She ran from the shop, rushing home, driving faster than she should have down the small tree-lined street. She checked her rearview mirror constantly, hoping Trent wasn't following her. She couldn't deal with him. Not now. Not ever.

She looked at her clock. Two thirty-nine. The bus should

have arrived at two thirty-five. Four minutes, nothing could have happened in four minutes, right?

This demon wants her blood.

Crazy. The whole thing was insane. And yet, Sera couldn't help bolting from the car and running toward the house. She needed to see her daughter, to hold her and assure herself that Aimee was okay. That they were okay and all was right with the world.

But as soon as she opened the door and stepped inside, she knew something was wrong. The house was too quiet. Too still. "Aimee?" she called, though she knew Aimee wasn't there.

Panic welled up inside her. Unjustified, but overwhelming. Sera looked once more at her watch. Six minutes late. Six. You could set your watch by those damn school buses. Had it already come by? Had Aimee gotten off and gone next door to Hanna's? Had she come home at all?

Her heart was thudding painfully, stealing the breath from her chest. *Had the demon been waiting for her?*

Stop it! There's no such thing as demons.

Sera rushed to the phone to call Hanna's mom and the school, but before she could dial, the door bell rang. She bolted toward the door and pulled it open, hoping to see her daughter's smiling face.

But instead Trent stood at the door with a squirming puppy in his arms.

"What are you doing here?"

His smile was halfhearted. "You know why I'm here. And this little girl is going to help me." He set the puppy down and held tight to the leash.

"Now's not a good time." Sera's eyes scanned the street over his shoulder, searching. Aimee's bike was still lying in the grass under the tree. There was no book bag on the porch, no sign that she'd come home and then left again.

Trent's gaze narrowed. "Where's Aimee?"

"I don't know." Sera's voice broke. She looked at him and almost lost it. "She isn't here," she whispered through a tight throat. Then she heard the roar of the bus's diesel engine coming up the street. Relief bubbled up inside her and she swayed against the door.

"The bus. Oh, God. It's just late," she said, more to herself than to him. She'd panicked, which she never would have done on a normal day, on any other day that Trent wasn't standing on her doorstep babbling about demons. Annoyance surged through her as the bus pulled to a stop outside the house and Aimee climbed down the steps and ran toward them.

"Oh, my gosh, look at the puppy," Aimee squealed, and dropped to the ground at Trent's feet. "What's his name?"

Trent grinned down at her. "Her name is Shirley."

The small black puppy covered Aimee's face with sloppy puppy kisses.

Sera stood there fuming and at a complete loss as to what to say. How was she supposed to introduce Aimee to her father when he'd never even bothered to write, or call, or visit? And now he shows up with a puppy? The bastard. She could rip his eyes out.

"She likes you," Trent said.

"Is she for me?" Aimee looked up at her mother with hope shining in her eyes.

Sera stiffened, then sucked in a deep breath. She stood frozen as she waited for Trent to say the dog was his, but he just stared at her little girl, at *their little girl,* with his face looking awestruck.

"Aimee, why don't you take the puppy inside while I talk with Mr. Drouillard, okay?"

Aimee beamed, scooped up the puppy and hurried inside.

Sera pulled shut the door behind her, then turned back to Trent. She couldn't deal with him right now. After the trick he'd pulled on her at Mary's shop—the things he'd shown her, what Mary had said and then her scare with the bus, she needed to sit down, regroup, think. Make a plan. A plan that didn't include him.

A plan that didn't include him trying to take her daughter away from her.

"I can't believe how big she is. How beautiful," Trent said, his voice rough.

"Yeah, well that's what happens when you aren't around for a while." A long while, she thought bitterly.

His eyes darkened. "It was better that way for both of you. I explained why."

His audacity sent a line of fury coursing straight down her spine. "No, it was better for you, Trent. We were a complication you didn't need or want, but you're not taking my child away from me. Not now. Not ever."

He rocked back on his heels. "You're right. I'm sorry. I didn't mean for it to sound that way. It's just…" He paused, as if searching for the right words. "I know what's coming after her. Next time she might not be on that bus. I can't let you face what's coming alone. She needs to be trained to protect herself and you need to learn that there really are monsters hiding under the bed."

Sera's stomach dropped and something distasteful caught in her throat.

"I don't believe you," she whispered. But for reasons she didn't understand, she did believe him. She just didn't want to.

His blue eyes locked onto hers and her stomach tightened. "Now, are you going to invite me inside and introduce me to my daughter?"

Chapter 2

Trent placed a hand on Sera's arm as he stepped up beside her onto the doorstep. He looked down into her gorgeous eyes and thought—*it will be all right. Trust me.* The words pulsed through his mind. He inhaled sharply and pushed them toward her, hoping to influence her thoughts.

For a second, she relaxed, then she pulled away from him, breaking eye contact. She was still hurt. He didn't blame her. He just hadn't expected there to still be so much fire between them—pain from his betrayal, sadness for what might have been, anger for making her feel it all again, and beneath it all the burning embers of a passion that had consumed them both.

He had to help her without being sucked back into her world. He couldn't stay now any more than he could have stayed then. The danger was still here, if anything, greater than before.

He followed her into the house. "I can help you. If you believed that, it would make this easier."

Her eyes flashed. "Nothing could make *this* easier. You can't come and go from Aimee's life whenever you please. You can't make her love you and then abandon her again."

He stiffened at her words. That wasn't why he was here. That wasn't what this was about. "Do you still have the amulet?"

She nodded without looking at him and left the room. He had to get her to calm down. Aimee would never trust him if she sensed her mother's animosity.

He walked toward the large back window and watched Aimee playing with the puppy in the backyard, a huge grin on her face as the puppy chased its tail.

For reasons he couldn't understand, a demon was close by in a Podunk town of less than a thousand. A demon who never should have found Aimee. Trent closed his eyes and reached with his mind, searching for the demon. He was close. Trent could feel him. Worse, Trent could smell him on Aimee. *He's already made contact.*

A few more days and Trent would have been too late.

A rush of anxiety filled him. He felt drawn to Aimee in a way he hadn't expected. As he watched her play, he allowed himself the luxury of wondering…what if?

Sera returned, the amulet dangling from her outstretched hand.

He took it from her. "The demon won't be able to touch Aimee if she's wearing this."

"Fine, I'll put it on her and then you can go."

Resistance and distrust rolled off of her. He took a deep breath, trying to calm the frustration growing within him and decided to try a different tactic. Knowing he was plunging into dangerous waters, he asked, "Isn't Aimee the least bit curious about me?"

Sera's eyes darkened, her mouth hardened. "We don't talk about you. As far as she's concerned, you're dead." Anger seeped out of her pores, so thick he could almost feel it.

He scraped his hand along his jaw. "Ouch."

"What did you expect, Trent?"

What had he expected? Certainly not to feel so…attached to Sera and their daughter. Part of him wanted what he'd always wanted: to stay and put the hunting behind him, to be a part of their lives, to take care of them. But Sera was right; he'd given up that option a long time ago. For good reasons.

"I want you to be safe," he said, softer than he intended.

"We're fine."

"You are now." He slung his pack off his shoulder and unzipped it. "But give it a day or two, even a week, and you might not be so sure."

"What are you doing?" she asked, eyeing his pack nervously.

He pulled out a stack of candles and some powerful juju.

"No way," she said, taking a step back. "You are not spreading voodoo around my house."

A musky scent filled the air. She crinkled her nose.

"Come on, *chère*. Be reasonable. This one's been blessed for protection."

Sera glanced out the window at Aimee throwing a ball to the puppy, then back down at the pack. "This isn't negotiable. She's already plagued with nightmares, what do you think will happen once she sees that stuff?"

"Voodoo is a part of your heritage. *Her* heritage. You may go to Mary's shop and pretend it's not a part of your life, but it is and it always has been. It's nothing to be afraid of. And we need it. We have to use everything in our arsenal to fight this beast."

"We'll have to find another way. A different way."

Trent swallowed his mounting frustration. "Okay, if you're

against bringing voodoo into the house, then we should leave. We'll go to my place in Tennessee."

Sera's eyes widened. "And how long do you expect us to hang out at your place?"

"As long as it takes for this demon to lose her scent. The amulet and distance should do the trick."

She crossed her arms against her chest. "There must be another way."

"Stubbornness doesn't suit you."

"If it's okay for us to go to 'your' place in Tennessee now, why wasn't it then?"

"My house isn't a long-term solution, it's an extreme measure. You have a demon after you."

Sera shook her head. "Aimee has friends here, a life here. She's on the soccer team and she's in the school play. I'm not uprooting her just because you and my aunt have seen a few signs that say a demon is coming—a demon I'm not even sure I believe in."

He placed a gentle touch on her arm, willing her to listen to him, to believe. "Whether you believe in this demon or not, he is real and he is coming after Aimee."

Sera flinched and pulled away from him. "Fine." She looked out the window once more. "I'll allow the voodoo, but we're not leaving."

How could she be so resistant to his mental suggestions? If she wouldn't pull away from him every time he touched her, perhaps he'd make more progress. He picked up his pack and walked down the hall toward Aimee's sweet scent, toward her room.

Sera stayed right on his heels. This would not work if he couldn't get her to trust him. She'd grown hardheaded over the years, or maybe it was just him she was resisting. She'd built a powerful wall around herself, blocking him.

He stepped into his daughter's pink and frilly room and stood in the doorway. "Cute."

She didn't say anything, just watched him warily.

"You're a good mom, Sera."

She stiffened.

He gave her his melt-them-in-their-pants smile. "Thank you."

"For what?" she snapped, totally unfazed by his charms.

"For doing what I couldn't. For raising our daughter. I know it couldn't have been easy raising her alone."

Her brown eyes narrowed. "Stop trying to butter me up, Trent. Let's get this over with. I want you out of my daughter's room, out my house and out of our lives—once and for all."

Stung, he turned from her. This was going much harder than he thought it would. He walked over to the large window that looked out onto the backyard. He strung slips of gossamer silk with bells tied to the ends across the top of the window. Beneath them, he lit a candle, poured some oil into the burning wax, then set an especially large juju bag sewn in the shape of a brightly colored dog next to it.

"And what is all that supposed to do, other than cause a serious fire hazard?"

"Consider it an early-warning detection system."

Sera stared at the candle and shivered.

"What's going on? And what's that smell?" Aimee asked, crinkling her nose as she walked into the room.

"Aimee. This is…an old friend of mine. Mr., uh, Trent."

He turned to Aimee, his mouth suddenly dry.

"Hi," Aimee said, and approached him. "I like your dog."

"Thanks." Trent sat on the bed and patted the spot next to him.

Aimee took a step toward him, but remained standing. He tried not to let her rebuff bother him. It was exactly what she should do for an old…friend of her mother's. She didn't know him.

He cleared his throat. "Aimee, I came here for a reason today."

Her gaze swung to the bells and the juju sitting in her window. She turned big, wary eyes on him.

"You see, your, um…daddy wanted me to give this to you." He held out the amulet dangling from a chain, a ring of brightly colored gemstones circling a polished silver center.

Aimee looked at it, but didn't touch it. Instead, she walked past him toward the dog-shaped juju.

He glanced up at Sera, whose surprised gaze followed Aimee. "Aimee, don't you have something to say to Mr. Trent?"

"I don't remember my daddy." Aimee's voice sounded small and vulnerable, twisting something deep in Trent's chest.

"He loves you very much," he said, his voice tight. "He carries your picture around with him everywhere. Pulls it out for anyone who'll listen and tells them all about his beautiful baby girl."

"Really?" Aimee asked, suddenly interested enough to turn back and face them.

"Cross my heart and hope to die." He brushed his hand across his chest.

"Then how come I never see him?"

Good question. "Well, you need…"

Sera stepped forward. "Aimee, we talked about this. About how your daddy's work took him far away for a very long time. We're not sure what's happened to him. We think maybe he got lost."

Aimee turned back to him. "Is he? Is my daddy lost?"

Trent stared into her beautiful blue eyes so much like his own and wanted to deny it. To shout from the rooftops that no, he was right there, and he was never going to leave her again. But could he guarantee that? Could he stay? Would it be fair for her to grow attached to him, only to have him leave her once more? He looked up at Sera and saw the stark fear in her eyes.

No, he wouldn't hurt his child. Not again. Sera was right. He wasn't here for the long haul. No reason to take Aimee's heart with him when he left.

"Your daddy has a very dangerous job and he stays away to keep you safe. This necklace was your *grand-mère*'s. I know she would be real happy if you wore it."

"My *grand-mère* is dead."

"Yes, sweetheart, I know."

Sera walked forward and took the necklace from Trent's hand. "How about we see how it looks, okay?"

Aimee nodded and Sera clasped it around her neck.

"It looks beautiful," Sera said softly. "Go see for yourself."

Aimee ran out of the room and down the hall to the bath-room.

"Thank you," Trent whispered, surprised by how hard that was. "I thought all girls loved jewelry."

"It depends on who's giving it to them. They don't have to be grown up to know not to accept gifts from strangers."

"I'm hardly a stranger."

"To her you are. To both of us."

His eyes caught hers, and for a moment, it was just the two of them. No demons or excuses or secrets. "So I got lost, eh?"

"It was the best I could come up with."

"I'm sorry," he said again, and he genuinely was. Fighting demons was in-your-face and dangerous, but at least you could see them coming; you could predict what they wanted and how they would act. But raising kids? Now, that was like walking an emotional minefield. One wrong step and *boom*.

Sera stared at him, one eyebrow raised.

"I should have realized how hard this must have been for you."

"What, you mean being run out on? Don't know why that should be a toughie."

He stood. "You got someplace I can rest up for a while?"

Sera stiffened.

"I won't make things any more difficult than they need to be. But I have to stay here to protect Aimee."

Sera nodded and led him into the guest bedroom. "A couple of days, that's it."

"That's all I'll need." He shut the door as she walked away and hoped for both their sakes he wouldn't need more than that.

For a second, Sera had felt sorry for him. As she'd watched Trent with Aimee, a part of her had wanted to tell her daughter the truth. That standing right before her was the daddy she'd always asked about. How many times had Sera wished he'd contacted them, or just come back?

But she knew better. She knew he wouldn't be staying for long. It would be better if Aimee didn't grow to care about him. Better for them both.

Sera let out a deep breath. How was she going to function with Trent in her house? Every time she looked into his eyes, she couldn't help remembering…feeling everything all over again.

And when he'd kissed her in Mary's shop? The touch of his lips against hers sent her heart lurching with an old familiar ache she thought had long since healed. And then the images came, nightmarish and frightening. How had he done that? Were the images real? Were demons real?

She'd grown up in the swamp. Her aunt owned the local voodoo shop. Folklore had been a part of her everyday life. Then there were the whispers in town that Mary was a witch, a priestess who did more than just sell sour-smelling candles and ugly dolls. But Sera hadn't believed it.

Hadn't wanted to.

But was it all really true? Could there possibly be a demon after her baby? She shivered as the image of the coal-black dead eyes surfaced in her mind. An image planted there by Trent's very warm lips. She shook the thought away. Why Aimee?

Demon hunter's blood.

Aimee was a tough little girl, always had been, but a destined demon hunter? No way. Sera gave an uneasy laugh, wondering what her God-fearing mother would have thought about that?

Her parents had died in a car crash when she'd been a teen. She'd always thought that was why she'd fallen so hard for Trent. He'd made her feel taken care of, loved. But it had all been a charade. He hadn't been the man she thought he was. He hadn't been there when she needed him, and he hadn't loved them enough to stay.

Spine stiff, she walked into the kitchen and set the kettle on the stove. She thought about Trent sleeping in her guest room and shook her head. How did this happen? And how was she going to get through the next few days with him here?

Once the water boiled, she filled the porcelain teapot and took it into the living room to watch Aimee and her friend, Hanna, from next door play with the puppy. She settled on the love seat, and poured herself a cup of hot tea from her mother's tea set. It was a self-indulgence she loved, and a comfort she fell back on in times of stress.

But nothing could soothe her nerves right then. Usually when she sipped orange spice tea from the dainty cup while watching her child play, she could almost convince herself that their lives were normal. Happy. Fulfilled.

That they weren't alone.

Almost.

"Hey," Trent said as he walked into the room and slipped into one of the chairs next to her.

No, definitely not alone, though right then she wished she were.

He leaned forward, propping his elbows on the worn knees of his jeans. He looked relaxed, but she could tell by the tightness in his jaw that he was primed and ready for action. And it scared her.

"I know this is all very difficult. And again, I'm sorry."

For breaking my heart into a million pieces and running away? Or for coming back and turning my world upside down? "You keep saying that."

He smiled, and the sight of it tweaked her heart. "I know."

She held his gaze with her own, one eyebrow raised…waiting.

"The last time I was here—"

Sera closed her eyes and took a deep breath. She didn't want to think about the last time he was here, the things he'd said, or the way he'd left her.

"When you told me about the baby, I knew she'd be special, that she'd need extra protection. I wanted to be able to do that."

There he went again, talking about Aimee being different. "But you didn't. You left. You weren't here. Okay. There's no going back and changing that. I don't want to talk about this."

"We need to talk about it. About us."

She set down her tea and stood. "There isn't any *us.*"

He stood, too, effectively blocking her escape. "Isn't there?"

"Not anymore."

He placed his hands on her arms and held her. His warmth seeped into her skin, bathing her in a wash of calm. In fact, that seemed to happen each time he touched her. She tried to pull back, to break free, but his grip tightened.

"I should have come back sooner. I know that."

He was so close she could smell his warm breath fanning her face. Her knees weakened. He raised one hand and grazed the pad of his thumb gently across her cheek. Even though his touch was warm and gentle, a shiver moved through her. Of fear? Desire? Trepidation? She wished she knew, but her emotions were a tangled mess.

"It's been eight years," he whispered, the low timbre of his voice caressing her nerves. Her anger dissipated, replaced by a warm feeling of trust.

He was doing this to her. Somehow he was twisting her emotions, turning her inside out.

"Eight years and I haven't been able to stop thinking about you out here in this bayou all by yourself." He moved closer.

Her breath caught in her throat as heat flooded through her. "I'm not by myself," she protested, suddenly panicked. "I have Aimee. We don't need you. We don't *want* you."

She pulled free, then looked up at him, wide-eyed, as the false sense of security fell away and her anxiety returned full force. "What have you been doing to me?"

He took a step back and cocked his head to the side, his forehead wrinkling with confusion.

"Can you affect my feelings?" It was crazy. She knew it sounded crazy, but every time he touched her... "How were you able to put those images in my head? Back at Mary's shop."

He shrugged his shoulders. "You needed to see the truth."

"I asked how."

"I told you before that I'm...different. Aimee's different. It's in our blood."

He'd told her, but she hadn't believed him. Now she wasn't

so sure. Her head was spinning. What exactly did he mean by *different*? How different?

He sighed. "I never meant for any of this to happen. The first time I saw you working behind the counter of Mary's shop, I was drawn to you. You were so innocent, so unaware of the effect you had on me. I should have stayed away, but every moment I was with you, you pulled me in deeper. Before I'd realized it, I'd fallen in love with you. Do you remember?"

She stepped away from him. She wouldn't go there, wouldn't let him pull her back to that dark place. The emptiness she'd felt after he'd left had created a hole in her that had never healed, had only been buried. No, she wouldn't remember.

"I knew it couldn't work, but I couldn't make myself stay away from you." He stepped forward, closing the distance between them.

Why was he saying all this? What did he want from her? Fear rolled off of her. It seemed that with just a touch, he could influence her emotions. Was that possible? Was that what he'd done to her back then? Was that why she'd fallen so hard for him? Why she'd needed him so much?

Why she'd let him back in now?

"I wanted to make it work," he continued, sounding honest and sincere. Everything she knew he wasn't. "But then the unthinkable happened."

She followed his gaze out the window. *Aimee.*

"I was a fool to think I could be normal. Worse than a fool to believe I had a right to put you and Aimee in danger by staying."

"What's different now?" her voice broke.

"Now it's Aimee who is drawing the demons. Aimee is the prey."

Sera shivered.

He took her hand in his. Warm. Comforting. She should pull away and run. But she didn't.

"I was born into this life. I didn't choose it. You think I wanted to leave you? To leave our daughter? Our life here? I had no choice." He pulled her up against him. They were touching, her thighs against his, her stomach against...

Her body hummed. Were her feelings real, or was he creating them? She didn't know anymore. She closed her eyes to hold back tears that threatened to overwhelm her. "Stop it, Trent. I want my feelings to be my own."

"They are your own," he whispered. "I still care about you and you still care about me. That's why we're so potent together." He released her and moved back a step.

And she wanted to pull him back. He was right, they'd always been something *more* together than they each were on their own. Her eyes met his, and it took all her strength to hold on to her resolve. "You made your choice a long time ago, whether you believe you did or not."

She couldn't take much more. She felt cut open and exposed. Raw. But she had to focus on what was important. Aimee. She collapsed back down onto the love seat and took several deep breaths to steady her nerves.

He sat down next to her, thankfully keeping a respectable distance between them. It didn't help that she could still smell his musky scent, sense his warmth, see his passion for her burning in his eyes.

He wanted her. *Still.*

She turned from him and watched her...their daughter playing outside the window, looking no different from any other eight-year-old girl. Sera had to know. "You said Aimee was different.... How?"

"It starts with the dreams. If a demon has caught her scent, she will dream of him, nightmarish images she won't understand. When she's older, her range will grow farther. She will be able to sense the demons before they are anywhere near her. But they will also be able to sense her."

A chill shook Sera to the core. She rubbed her arms, trying hopelessly to warm herself. "And affecting people's emotions? Putting images in their heads? What about that?"

"That talent is mine. We won't know what special gifts, if any, Aimee will develop until she's older.

"Are there others? Demon hunters, I mean."

"More than you would think."

Sera's stomach churned. "I don't want this life for her."

"I know. Listen, this is a lot to take in. Sit back and relax. Enjoy your tea. I'll watch Aimee."

Doubt rushed through her. "That's all right. I'm fine."

"No, you're not. Here…" He stood and pushed a throw pillow toward her. "Rest. I'll go out back with Aimee and Shirley and their friend."

At that moment, Sera yawned. She was exhausted, she thought as her eyelids drooped. "Shirley?"

"Her new puppy."

"Hers? No. We don't want a puppy."

He leaned down and laid a hand on her arm. "The puppy is special. She can protect her."

Sera wanted to laugh, but she didn't have it in her. She was out of her element and unfortunately would have to trust this man who'd taken so much from her. But only as long as it took to discover if what he said was true, and what it would take for her to learn how to keep Aimee safe.

On her own.

Chapter 3

As Sera rested on the sofa in the living room, a breeze whispered across her cheek from an opened window. Under heavy lids, she watched Trent dump supplies from his pack onto the table. In a matter of minutes, he had put what looked like herbs, bones, powders and God-knew-what-else into small leather pouches and tied them tight with leather straps. He then went around the house, placing a bag in each room.

Anxiety pulled at her insides. She sat up and rubbed the fatigue from her eyes. "Is that really necessary?"

"That and a white candle under each window."

"I don't understand how some dirt and wax can stop a demon."

"Oh, it won't stop him," Trent said, coming closer to her. "This will just make the house a little more inhospitable for him." He placed one of the bags on the windowsill behind her, leaning so close the musky spice of his cologne seeped into her senses, evoking images she'd rather not think of.

"I'll stop him," he said with a confident grin.

And when he looked at her like that—so self-assured and full of confidence—she remembered why she'd found him so attractive all those years ago. And why he still appealed to her now. She shook the thoughts away and twisted her lips with skepticism. "And how exactly are you supposed to stop a demon?"

He stopped in front of her now, and damn if he didn't have an impressive chest and strong, wide shoulders. If a human was after her daughter, she didn't doubt for a second that those rock-hard biceps could handle anything that came along.

But the threat wasn't human.

Trent eased onto the sofa next to her, his weight tilting her in his direction until they almost touched. His body heat reached out to her, making her yearn to lean closer.

He brushed her hair away from her face. She froze, knowing she should jump up and go, but instead she found herself unable to move.

"You know," he said softly. "I've missed you."

His gaze caught hers and she read his intent in his eyes. He wanted more than to make sure she and Aimee were safe. He wanted her.

Her heart raced. Her palms felt damp. *Damn.*

Hunger emanated from him, she could see it in his gaze, feel it in his touch. Her temperature rose, making her skin flush. He placed his hand on her shoulder and slid it slowly down her arm. "We were always good together, *chère.*"

She tried not to think about *how* good, and yet her body remembered and responded. "Trent," she whispered, but knew it was no use. His lips pressed gently against hers, barely touching her, yet leaving her breathless. Leaving her wanting more.

"We should work on our protection circles," he murmured against her lips.

Yes, protection circles. But instead of taking the out he offered, instead of pulling away like any rational sane person would do, she wrapped her arms around his neck and deepened the kiss.

"Later," she murmured. Right now, she didn't want to think about juju spells, protection circles or demons. Right now, she wanted to think about his hands on her breasts. He'd always had a magic touch, his hands warm and gentle, knowing exactly where and how to caress her.

Time hadn't changed that. His hand moved up the inside of her arm, down her side, across her breasts. Her nipples tightened, extending, longing for his sweet touch, for the gentle pull of his lips.

She was surprised by how strong her desire for him was. She'd been so lonely. Would it hurt to have just a moment of bliss? Even if she knew it couldn't last? Even if she knew it was wrong?

A soft sigh escaped her lips as the insistent tingle started between her legs. It had been too long since she'd allowed herself to feel like a woman, to want and need.

And she wanted Trent now.

Even if it was only for this one time.

She let her mind wander back, remembering how she had felt nestled in his arms, lying beneath him, moving in a slow, steady rhythm as the pressure inside her mounted, growing, pushing her toward the edge of complete fulfillment.

There had only been two other men over the years since Trent had left her. But they hadn't been able to make her feel the way he had—safe, secure, loved.

And completely satisfied.

No one had come close to touching her the way he did, with the pads of his fingers, the breadth of his palm, the gentle tips of his nails. But it was so much more than a physical touch;

he touched her inside, too. She sighed and shifted, trying to find relief as the pressure built within her.

Yes, she remembered. Even now, she could feel his feathery caress moving up her thigh. She smiled, her lips spreading in a grin as a desire-laden purr filled her throat.

His light touch turned to long, firm strokes.

"Trent," she murmured, and his lips were on hers, hard and demanding. She opened her mouth as his tongue pressed inside, possessing, conquering. As she lost herself in his taste, she knew she shouldn't be doing this. She was letting her loneliness, her desire, overrule her good sense. She wanted to resist, but she couldn't.

For all she knew, he was manipulating her thoughts. She shouldn't give him that much power over her mind, her body. She shouldn't let him in. But then his hands were under the waistband of her pants, moving downward. His finger found her moistness, and slipped inside, and all logical, rational thought disappeared. She groaned and shifted, allowing him in deeper. It had been so long, and it felt so good as he pulled out and pushed in, again and again.

"Trent," she whispered, his name rolling off her tongue.

Tension tightened the nub between her legs. If he didn't touch her there, if she didn't find some relief soon, she would scream.

"Trent," she called again, and shifted, then reached down to move his hand where she wanted it, but his hand wasn't there. He wasn't there.

"Trent?"

He'd left her again. Left her wanting…left her needing. Her eyes flew open and she was lying on the sofa.

Alone.

Embarrassment inflamed her cheeks. Had she imagined the whole thing? Had she been dreaming? Or had he done this to her? Had he somehow implanted himself in her thoughts, her mind? The thought sent a rash of chills coursing down her arms.

Quickly, Sera sat up. She heard him laughing and sought the source of the sound. He was in the backyard, pushing Aimee on the swing.

He wasn't even in the house.

Sera's stomach turned. She'd dreamed the whole thing, and the worst part was, even in her dream, she'd been left wanting more. Wanting that sweet release. Wanting Trent.

He laughed again, and the sound of it filled her with an overwhelming need to lie in his arms, to rest her head against his chest and feel the warm rumble within.

No. She would not, could not have him. Even by continuing with these thoughts, she was rushing toward a precipice where this time the fall just might break her. She couldn't chance giving herself to that man only to have him rip out her heart and leave her once again. She'd be a fool, worse than a fool.

She stood, moving away from the sound of his laughter, and walked into the kitchen ready to do anything that would take her mind off him. She walked into the room and stopped, her hand rushing to her lips as a small cry escaped her mouth. A small brown leather pouch sat next to a burning white candle on the windowsill.

Sera took several deep breaths and tried to pull her thoughts together. She ignored the pouch and what it might mean and busied herself with making dinner, trying unsuccessfully to keep her mind on the simple task rather than on the restlessness building within her.

Trent always had a way of consuming all her thoughts. Here he'd only been back in her life one day and already her nerves were shredded and nothing was as it should be. Another day of this and she might lose her sanity completely.

With fierce determination, she focused on making pasta and a salad, trying desperately to shut him out of her mind.

Sixty minutes later with the table set, spaghetti on the stove and bread in the oven, she walked back out into the living room to check on Aimee and Trent. Trent had set up an expandable folding pen in the corner and Aimee was lying inside sound asleep with one arm curled around the puppy.

Trent sat on the sofa, watching them. "She's adorable," he said quietly.

Sera tried not to smile, but she couldn't help herself as the puppy started to snore. "They both are."

She approached the pen. "Aimee," she said softly as she pulled open the side of the pen and crouched down. She shook her daughter gently. Aimee groaned.

A spike of alarm shot through Sera. Something was wrong. Aimee's skin was too pale, her breathing a little too shallow.

"Aimee, are you hungry?"

Aimee's eyes cracked open. She shook her head, then pulled the puppy closer. Dark purplish smudges tinted the pale skin beneath her eyes. Sera frowned, then placed her hand on Aimee's forehead. She turned to Trent. "She's burning up."

Trent launched to his feet.

Aimee pushed her finger into her mouth, and Sera's eyes widened as she saw the purple-black tinge of her skin. "Aimee, what happened to your hand?"

"I pricked it on the spindle at play rehearsal."

Sera pulled the small bandage off Aimee's finger and she and Trent examined the cut. "That looks more like a slice than a prick. What was Mr. Purdue thinking?"

"Don't be mad at him, Mommy. He felt really bad about it."

"I'm sure he did," Sera muttered. "Did he put the antibiotic cream on it?"

Aimee nodded. "I went to the nurse and she took care of me real good."

Sera turned to Trent. "It looks like she has some kind of infection. I'm taking her to the hospital."

Sera pulled Aimee onto her lap, but before she could stand, Trent lifted Aimee up into his arms. "Grab the puppy and her leash."

Sera nodded, grabbed her purse, the puppy and her leash, made sure the oven and stove were turned off, then ran out of the house, locking the door behind her. Trent rushed to his car and opened the back door. Sera locked the dog in the small dog crate before strapping her and Aimee both into the backseat, then climbed in next to them.

"It's on Market," she said to Trent through a tight throat.

"I remember." The engine roared to life and they rushed toward town.

"Aimee, after you pricked your finger, what did Mr. Purdue do?" Trent asked, trying to sound casual, but Sera could hear the tension in his tone.

"He gave me some napkins, then sent me to the nurse."

"Did he keep the napkins?"

"The ones with the blood on them?" Her voice quivered. "Yes."

"No. Why would he do that?"

"He wouldn't, sweetie," Sera said. She didn't like the fear in Trent's eyes, nor the overwhelming feeling that perhaps this wasn't an accident. But before she could question him, Aimee's small body started trembling as chills rushed through her.

Sera swallowed her tears and put on a brave face for Aimee as they rushed into the small hospital.

"Mrs. Barnhardt, what's the matter with Aimee?" Nurse McKinley asked from behind the front desk.

"I don't know," Sera said, a little breathless. "She has a high fever and chills. And her hand's turning purple."

"Follow me," the nurse said, and they rushed down the hall.

Trent stayed in the lobby, painfully aware of how uncomfortable he felt. He was Aimee's father. He should be back there with her. But Aimee didn't know that. And neither did anyone else.

He sat in an empty row of chairs. Luckily they were in a small town where everyone knew everybody. Had they been in New Orleans, they could have sat in the hospital lobby without being seen for hours.

There's something to be said for small-town life.

Still, he couldn't stand sitting there by himself, waiting, wondering. Was she okay? He'd just found his daughter again, he wasn't ready to lose her. He got up and wandered back the way Sera and Aimee had gone, but a nurse told him to return to the waiting room. He couldn't tell them the truth, not until he'd told Aimee.

If he told Aimee.

He left the hospital and went out front to call his contacts back home. Perhaps they could give him more information as to what this demon was up to.

After an hour or so, Sera came to get him. He stood as she walked toward him, her face ashen. A fist of fear unlike anything he'd ever felt clutched his gut. "What is it? How is she?"

"Lucky we got her here so quickly. She has something called bacteremia. She's on intravenous antibiotics now."

"What is that? Exactly."

"Blood poisoning. There must have been some nasty bacteria on that spindle at school."

That or something else. "Have you met this Mr. Purdue?"

"Once or twice. He's new in town. Seems like a nice man."

"They always do."

Her eyes widened as she stared at him. "You're not saying…"

"That's exactly what I'm saying."

"But why?"

"In my opinion, he's decided to perform the ritual that will bind him to her."

"What does that mean?" she hissed under her breath, then quickly glanced around them. "Explain."

"It means I could have been wrong. He might not want to kill Aimee. He might want her body as a host."

"A what?"

"To live inside her."

Sera's eyes widened and she shuddered. "For what purpose?"

"Any number of reasons. Demons can live inside hosts for years. You'd never suspect. Never know."

"And Aimee?"

"She wouldn't know, either, not until he decided to take over."

"But you'd know."

"I would know."

"Is that what he's done to Mr. Purdue? Is Mr. Purdue a host? And if he is, why then would the demon want Amy? He already has a host." Her voice rose an octave, sounding shrill.

"Honestly, at this point I don't know what the demon is after."

"They just walk around taking over people's bodies and no one ever knows?"

"He won't succeed, Sera. I won't let anything happen to either one of you." His eyes met and held hers, and for a short moment he felt her trust him. He felt her giving in and allowing herself to believe him. Then the gates came crashing down once more.

"I'm going back to check on Aimee."

"Can I...can I see her?"

She hesitated a moment, her eyes searching his. Then she nodded. Relief stronger than he'd expected filled him as he followed her down the cold white hall. As he entered Aimee's room and saw her small form lying on the bed, an IV inserted into her hand, her pale skin marked by purplish shadows beneath her eyes, he was overcome with heart-wrenching anxiety. In that moment, he knew he wouldn't be able to leave her again.

"I need to be with her," he said. "To keep her safe. No matter what it takes. No matter who stands in my way."

Sera didn't say anything, but he could see the doubt in her eyes before she turned and brushed the hair back off Aimee's forehead. Sera kissed her gently. He didn't want to live without either of them again. He'd make Sera see that. Something had to change.

He had to change.

In the dead of the night they brought Aimee home. It felt good to have her safe in his car and out of that hospital where so many people were coming and going. As Trent picked up Aimee and carried her into the house, she wound her arms around his neck, and broke his heart. How could he have missed this all these years?

He carried her into her pink, frilly room and tucked her into her bed. He and Sera both stood in the doorway watching the steady rise and fall of Aimee's chest. "She needs her rest. Then we need to get going. We can't chance staying here any longer."

"She'll be devastated about the play, about leaving all her friends. Why did this have to happen to her?"

"Shh. Come on." He left Aimee's door cracked as they walked back into the living room and sat on the sofa. "You should get some sleep, too."

"Like I could sleep. What are we going to do now?"

"This was too close a call. We can't take any more chances. We have to go to my house. I have people there who can help us."

Sera sat silent for a long moment, then turned to him, her eyes bright with unshed tears. "I should have believed you. Maybe if I'd listened…"

"It wouldn't have made any difference. He got to her before I got here. I was too late. I should have come sooner."

"Trent." She placed a hand on his arm. She was about to say something, and he knew what the damning words would be. *He never should have left them.*

With a great deal of effort, she composed herself. "How long will we need to stay away?" she finally said.

"I'm not sure." Fatigue washed over him, and he leaned back into the sofa. "Until the threat is gone. We might not be able to come back here again. Ever."

Sera closed her eyes and took a deep breath.

"Why don't you sleep? We can discuss it after you've rested."

"You'll be right here?"

"I'm not going anywhere."

"I…" She looked away. "I don't want to be alone."

"You don't have to. Not anymore."

Her surprised gaze met his and held it.

"Sera, I know I don't deserve it, but if you'll have me, I'd like to get to know you again and to get to know my daughter."

"But I thought…"

"If she wears her amulet at all times, it would probably block her presence from them for another five years, by then she'd be old enough to know what to expect, to be able to fight them. I know it's selfish but I don't want to lose another five years. I can protect you both, and teach her what she needs to know."

Sera's expression froze. "Are you saying that this one just might be the first? Of how many?"

"I don't mean to scare you. But yes. That's why she needs to know who she is, and what she can do to protect herself."

Sera dropped her head into her hands.

He placed a hand on her shoulder. "And you need to know, too. What to look for and how to protect our daughter."

She shook her head. "It's too much."

"I know." And he did know. He wouldn't wish this life on anyone, and now his precious baby girl was going to have to come face-to-face with her worst nightmares. He pulled Sera into his arms and held her tight. Not just to comfort her, but to comfort himself. They'd come close to losing their daughter tonight. Too close. And that was something he couldn't live with. Maybe together they'd have a chance of making something good out of all this.

Just then the phone rang. "Who on earth could be calling at this hour?" Sera said. Trent tensed, knowing it couldn't be good. She picked up the handset from the receiver next to them and held the phone so he could hear. "Hello."

"Sera? This is Nurse McKinley. I'm sorry to bother you, but I was hoping to catch you before you went to bed."

"You did. Is something wrong?" Sera's voice wavered with fear.

"No, not at all. It's just Dr. Gibbons had some questions about Aimee's blood work. Would it be all right if she came back in later today to give us another sample?"

"Well, yes. Of course. Are you sure everything is all right?"

"Absolutely. Don't you worry yourself. She'll be fine."

Sera sighed with relief. "All right. We'll see you in a few hours. I'd like Aimee to get some sleep first."

"No problem. Thanks, Sera."

Sera replaced the handset in the base and turned to him. "What do you think that's all about?"

"I'm not sure, but something doesn't feel right about it."

"Dr. Gibbons has been my doctor for my entire life. And Aimee's, too. I trust him completely."

"Still, I'd feel better about this if we went to see my doctor in Tennessee."

"You said her blood…your blood was different. Any chance those differences show up on blood tests?"

"None."

Sera shrugged and stood. "Well, I think it's best we find out what the problem is sooner rather than waiting until we get to Tennessee. Who knows when that will be? Are we driving or flying?"

"Driving."

She sighed. "Great."

"It would be better to wait, Sera. For all we know this doctor could be the demon."

"No. Not Dr. Gibbons. Besides, I thought you can…smell them." Her lips twisted in revulsion as she said the word.

"What, you mean like some demonic bloodhound?"

"Well, yes, since you put it that way."

"Unfortunately, I wasn't allowed back to see Dr. Gibbons or maybe I would have."

"Well, I can assure you, he is the same sweet doctor he has always been."

He could see her grasping, trying to hold on to what she'd always believed was true. But the point was, she couldn't know who was and who wasn't a threat. And from this point forward, she never would be able to again.

"Sera, you need to trust me."

Her lips thinned. "Sorry, but I don't take chances where my daughter is concerned."

"And neither can I. You're going to have to trust my judgment, and believe in what I do. She needs me. You both do."

"Really." Sera stiffened, her back going ramrod straight. "There are things about parenting you are just going to have to trust my judgment about. And, yes, I needed you once. But I had to learn to get by on my own. You taught me that." She turned to walk out of the room.

He had to make her see reason. In two quick strides he was standing in front of her, pushing her up against the wall. His body pressed against hers. His head dipping, his lips inches from her lips. His hot breath on her cheek.

"I'm sorry I hurt you. I know you think you can, but you can't manage this on your own. You need me to help you."

Sera gasped, then tried to shake her head, to deny him, to stop this before it went too far, but then his lips crushed hers. His tongue swept inside her mouth. And it was as if he'd never left. As if the past eight years had never happened.

She whimpered, melting, as his taste filled her. She swayed. Reaching up, she gripped his shoulders to keep from falling. Only she was too late.

There was no turning back from this free fall.

"Trent, no... I—"

"You want me as much as I want you."

"No," she denied, even as the hard ridge of his desire pressed against her stomach. "I don't." But she did, and she couldn't stop herself from pressing up against him.

He gasped a breath, pulling her close, his eyes hooded with longing.

Her body trembled.

Heat coiled inside her.

His lips trailed down the column of her throat.

She moaned, then pulled away. "This has to be about more

than sex. *We* have to be about more than sex. Aimee deserves more than that from us, Trent."

"We can be," he breathed. "We will be." His lips fell over hers once more.

She pushed her hands up under his shirt, pulling it over his head. Instantly, her hands went to his chest, her fingers soothing the hard muscles and seeking the peaks of his nipples. They hardened beneath her touch.

Trent let loose a throaty moan. He pulled her T-shirt over her head and expertly unclasped her bra, then dipped his head, taking her breast into his mouth.

Unrelenting heat swept through her and she swayed on her feet. She grabbed his shoulders for balance and tilted her head back to grasp at a desire-filled breath.

This was Trent, who could touch her like no other. But no matter what he said, what he promised, he wouldn't stay for long, and she wouldn't be able to count on him to care about how she felt. But this time she knew that going in. She wouldn't let herself care about him, and she wouldn't expect him to stay.

But right now he was the only one there for her, the only one who could help them, and he was right, she had to trust him when it came to Aimee, even if she knew he'd break both their hearts.

But maybe this time he would stay?

No. She wouldn't think that, wouldn't let herself believe it, not even for a moment. Right now there was only one thing she wanted from Trent Droulliard and it was within her grasp. And even though she knew she shouldn't, she unzipped his pants and reached inside.

God, but he was irresistible to her. The fire. The ache. The need sweeping through her body overrode her mind in a heated tidal wave of desire. And then all thoughts went away, and all she could do was feel, and surrender to his touch.

Chapter 4

Sera stirred in Trent's arms on the sofa. She lay there, burning this moment into her memory—what it felt like to lie nestled up against him, her head resting on his warm chest, the steady sound of his heart beating in her ear. She inhaled his spicy male scent and knew she'd miss that most of all.

Now that she had a taste of him, it would be even harder to live without him this time. To go back to her lonely—

Shirley growled from her pen in the corner. Sera lifted her head, trying to make out the dog in the gloom. Furious barking filled the room. Trent bolted upright. The pen crashed to the floor as Shirley jumped over the top of it. Aimee screamed from the other room.

"Aimee," Sera choked out as fear squeezed her throat.

Shirley jumped up onto the coffee table, sending Sera's mother's porcelain tea set shattering across the floor before bolting out of the room and down the hall.

Sera ran after Trent into Aimee's room. Trent flipped on

the light as Shirley jumped out Aimee's open window, barking furiously as she disappeared out of sight. Sera's shocked gaze swung to the rumpled covers on the empty bed and the juju dog lying on the floor.

Aimee wasn't there.

A cold fist of fear numbed her heart, then spread through the rest of her body, her arms, down her legs, muddling her mind.

"Damn!" Trent exploded. He rushed past her, back into the living room.

"What's happening?" she screamed, following him.

Trent stepped into his jeans and pulled his shirt over his head. "Don't worry. I'll find her." Determination filled his voice while desperation hardened his jaw.

I'll find her.

Tears rushed to Sera's eyes as the knowledge broke through the numbness and slammed into her chest. "Where is she?"

Trent scooped her clothes up off the floor and pushed them at her. "Get dressed. We've got to go."

She pulled on her jeans and shoved her arms into her shirt. How could this have happened? How could her baby be gone? It wasn't real. Couldn't be real.

Pain sliced through her chest, searing her heart, making her fold into herself. *Her fault.* She didn't believe in demons. Not really.

"Come on!" Trent grabbed her hand and pulled her through the house.

"What about the juju? The candles?" she asked, trying desperately to understand something she'd never be able to comprehend.

"I thought they would stop him. I can't believe he could grab her with her wearing the amulet."

"Oh, God. She wasn't." Sera pulled the amulet still sealed

in a plastic bag out of her purse. "They took it off her at the hospital."

His lips thinned, and she could sense the rage rippling through him.

"Can you sense him?" she asked.

"Faintly."

She could hear the fear in his voice, and it made her that much more terrified. He was all she had to believe in; if she lost her faith in him, then she truly was lost.

"Look!" She pointed far down the street. Shirley was running as fast as her little legs would carry her, chasing something she couldn't see.

"That's my girl," he said. They jumped into the car and sped up to catch the dog. "She can smell the beast even better than I can."

Sera turned to him. "Seriously? How would she even know to go after them?"

"That's what she's been bred for. Her mom is a master."

Sera stared at him wide-eyed. And here she thought he had brought the dog to worm his way into Aimee's heart. Embarrassment warmed her cheeks. "But Shirley's so young," she said in astonishment.

"And good."

Hope filled Sera, though she knew it was crazy. Putting her hope in a little bundle of fur that would most likely tire of the chase at any moment and drop was stupid. But at this point, what choice did she have?

The nightmare that Trent and Mary had warned her about was true. There really were monsters, and one had taken her baby. She swiped at the tears in her eyes. She couldn't go on without Aimee. She couldn't do it.

Trent reached over and grabbed her hand. "We'll get her back, I promise."

She grasped on to the hope he offered, even though she realized he couldn't offer her any guarantees. Not really.

"I shouldn't have left you." Trent's voice was full of anguish. "This was exactly what I was hoping to avoid, and instead I've made things worse. Now she has no idea who she is and how to protect herself. All she knows is some evil son of a bitch has taken her. And that she's all alone."

"No, she's not! She's not alone. She knows we're coming for her. She must."

"You. She knows you're coming for her. She doesn't know anything about me. She doesn't even know—" His voice broke, and he swallowed hard.

Sera squeezed his hand tight. "She will. We'll tell her everything as soon as we find her. And we will find her." Now she was the one offering empty guarantees. But she didn't care. They would make them true. They had to.

He turned to her and the suffering in his eyes broke her heart.

"Stop it," she demanded. "If you don't believe we can save Aimee, then we won't. You have to believe because I have to believe in you. Do you understand? I need to trust you. I need to know you won't let us down."

He stared at her for a moment, then nodded, and was about to say more, but up ahead, the puppy turned down a dirt road Sera had never been down before. They moved at a crawl, pacing the tiny dog, but Sera's heart pounded in her chest as if she was running for her life.

Soon they came to a shack at the end of the road. The old structure was built on stilts that jutted out over the water. Trent stopped the car as Shirley bolted toward the open door.

"Do you sense anything?" Sera asked.

Trent shook his head. "Something doesn't feel right."

They hurried forward, moving toward the shack as Shirley rushed inside. Something crashed. Wood splintered. A high-pitched yelp broke the stillness of the early-morning air.

"Oh, my God, Aimee!" Sera bolted after the dog. Trent yelled a warning, but it was too late. She burst into the shack, then grabbed hold of the doorway, teetering on the edge of a gaping hole in the wooden floor.

Just below her, Shirley treaded water furiously, as the murky swamp lapped at the stilts beneath the house. The puppy's little paws paddled desperately. Her snout crinkled as a growl rumbled through her.

"Trent, something is in the water with her!" Sera called.

Trent dropped to his belly and stretched over the jagged edge of the broken floor. His hand shot out and he grabbed the dog, launching her through the air just as the snapping jaws of an alligator broke the surface.

Sera caught her, instinctively pulling the pup against her chest. Her shirt immediately soaked through with foul swamp water and blood.

"She's bleeding, Trent."

The puppy's side had been split by a shallow slice. Either from the fall, or from sharp, gnashing teeth, she couldn't be sure.

Trent carefully got to his feet and looked at the puppy's wound. "She will be fine as soon as we get her stitched up."

"Where's Aimee?" Sera stared down into the water, as terror rushed through her.

"This was a trap. For me."

He pointed to the shirt floating in the water. "He left that there, hoping I'd follow his scent. He must have sabotaged the floor."

A lump filled Sera's throat. What were they dealing with?

"We have to find her."

They hurried out of the shack and back onto the road. Sera

held the puppy in her arms. Trent stood still, his head cocked to one side. Shirley whimpered.

"Do you sense anything?"

"Not from the demon, but I'm getting something from Aimee."

Hope surged through Sera. "What?"

"Fear."

Sera's stomach lurched.

"She's close and she's still alive. Let's focus on that."

He gestured down a path that led along the water's edge. "She's down that way."

Sera followed his gaze down a small path leading through the woods. "If you can sense her, can Aimee sense you?"

"I doubt it. She doesn't know what to focus on. But he can. That's what worries me."

"Then, stay here," Sera insisted. "Let me go first. We can't afford to walk into another trap. If he can feel you coming, then he has the upper hand. I'll find out where he has her and what he's doing, then I'll come back for you."

Doubt filled Trent's eyes.

"Come on, Trent. You know I'm right."

"I know it's dangerous. You don't know the first thing about how to protect yourself from a demon."

"I'm a mom. I'll face anything to protect my daughter."

She followed close behind as he hurried to the trunk of his car and opened it. She locked the puppy in her cage, then took the walkie-talkie he handed her. "Take this and tell me everything you see. And if he finds you—" He handed her a wicked-looking knife. "Use this. Don't be squeamish. He may look like someone you trust. But he isn't. Remember that."

Sera stared at the heavy serrated blade in her hand, and felt the first doubts trickle through her.

"Don't let him see you. Promise me, Sera."

"I promise."

"You've got five minutes, then I'm coming after you. Now, let's go save our daughter."

Sera ran down the path though the woods without looking back. Within moments, she saw another hunting shack on the banks of the swamp. As quietly as she could, she stepped up onto the dock that ran alongside the shack and extended out into the water. She peered through the window and smothered a gasp. Aimee was inside with tears streaming down her cheeks. Her hands and feet were bound and a gag covered her mouth.

She couldn't let Aimee see her. She ducked down and gasped a deep breath. She took another quick peek and saw Dr. Gibbons move in front of the window. He stopped next to Aimee and drew his thumb across her forehead, leaving it streaked with blood.

Sera crouched down as bile rose up in her throat. She shoved her fist against her mouth to stop from crying out. Not him. It couldn't be. Had he been lying to her at the hospital the whole time?

She stiffened as anger surged through her, and she fought down the urge to run into the shack and attack the bastard. She trusted him and he'd stolen her daughter. Adrenaline pumped through her. She could take him. She would take him.

If he were human.

She took another steadying breath and crept away from the shack, careful not to make a sound. When she was a safe distance away, she called Trent on the walkie-talkie and told him what she'd seen.

"Stay there, Sera. Wait for me. I'll be there in a second," he said, his voice crackling over the radio.

"All right," she whispered. But she couldn't get the image of her daughter's tear-streaked face out of her mind. What if he was hurting her right now? She had to know what was happening. She hurried back to the shack, back to the window.

But Aimee was gone.

Sera ran around to the front of the shack and skidded to a stop.

"Hello, Sera," Dr. Gibbons said, and smiled. He was standing in dirty brackish water up to his thighs, holding a frightened Aimee in his arms.

"What do you want with my daughter?" she asked, still unable to believe what she was seeing. This man delivered Aimee. He brought her into the world and had taken care of the two of them their whole lives. Surely Trent was wrong. Please let him be wrong.

But as she saw coal-black eyes shining in the predawn light, she knew the ugly truth. Dr. Gibbons was gone and a demon was about to kill her baby. She'd seen this moment, seen it in her mind the day Trent had kissed her back in Mary's shop.

The demon started chanting in Latin and lowering Aimee into the swamp water, as if Sera weren't even standing there. As if she was powerless to stop him.

But she wasn't.

She felt the weight of the demon dagger in her pocket. From a distance, she heard Trent calling to her. Aimee screamed behind her gag, her eyes pleading for help. Sera looked for Trent but couldn't see him. She couldn't wait any longer.

She pulled the knife and jumped, throwing herself off the dock and onto the demon. She knocked him off balance, the knife grazing his shoulder. He dropped Aimee and she sank beneath the surface.

Sera frantically reached for her, pushing through the water. Fingers grasping, she touched Aimee, but before she could grab hold, the demon backhanded her with a dizzying blow that sent her flying back toward the dock. Brackish water filled her mouth and burned her eyes. She pushed to the surface, struggling once more to find her footing.

The demon yanked Aimee back out of the water and raised a knife high above her head, all the while whispering…chanting.

He was going to kill her. Sera hadn't been fast enough or strong enough to stop him. Anguish rose in her throat and choked her.

In stunned horror Trent saw Sera fall below the surface. The demon raised the knife high above Aimee's head, and Trent knew he had mere seconds. He dove off the dock. A wide smile cut across the demon's face as he dropped Aimee and turned, pointing the knife toward Trent.

Trent twisted in midair, trying to avoid the blade. As he hit the demon, the knife slid easily into his skin. A burning sensation spread through him as he and the demon rolled beneath the water.

Trent grasped hold of the demon's neck and squeezed. They struggled until the pressure in Trent's chest was too much to bear. He pushed to the surface and gasped a deep breath. The demon thrust the knife at him again. Trent turned, going under once more as the knife sliced though his arm.

Suddenly, Sera was there, thrusting the demon dagger into his hand. Trent crouched under the water, holding his breath until he thought his lungs would explode, then, as the demon drew near, he launched himself upward, slicing the dagger across the demon's neck. The demon threw his head back and let out a roar. Black smoke poured from the wound and filled the air, as the body crumpled into the swamp.

Trent turned and saw Sera struggling to get Aimee up onto the dock. He rushed toward them. Sera pushed the water out of Aimee's chest, then breathed into her mouth.

"She's not breathing," Sera cried as he reached them.

A deep well of agony surged through him. He took over, giving Aimee CPR while Sera struggled to catch her breath. Aimee jerked, then water spilled from her lips as she coughed and started to cry.

"It's okay, baby. We're both here. Nothing or no one can hurt you now," Sera crooned, tears rolling down her cheeks as she held Aimee in her arms and rocked her gently.

"You really should get some rest. The demon is dead," Trent said.

Sera smiled as giddy relief filled her once more. "I know. I just can't seem to take my eyes off her."

They were lying in Sera's bed with Aimee tucked between them. Neither one of them would be leaving her side for the rest of the day.

"I had the nurse double-check Aimee's tests. There was nothing wrong with them, the demon just wanted to make sure we weren't going anywhere." Trent pulled a strand of Aimee's hair through his fingers, touching it as if he'd never felt anything like it before.

So much warmth filled Sera's chest, she ached with it. "And the pinprick on her finger was really just an accident?"

"Looks like it."

"I never would have believed it was Dr. Gibbons."

"Like I said, demons can be dormant in their hosts for years and no one ever suspects."

"Until they have a reason to surface?"

"Exactly."

"So there is no more threat, then?"

"Not right now."

Sera bit her lip. "Then, I guess you'll be leaving soon?" She cringed as she heard the tremor in her voice.

"From what I hear there's something big going down with the demon Kafu."

"I don't like the sound of that."

"No, he's a nasty one. What's worse, the priestess and her cult who we suspect of trying to raise him don't live too far from here."

"A voodoo priestess?" Fear skittered down Sera's back. "Aimee and I will leave. Move across country. Anywhere."

"I was hoping you and Aimee might like to come home with me."

Sera grew very still; she was afraid even to breathe, as if breathing or moving would somehow take his words away. She wanted to go, wanted to be with him. Her heart ached with the hope of it, but if she did, and he left them all over again…

"It's different from here," Trent continued. "We don't have swamps, we have horse farms. Aimee would like it."

She brushed her hand across her daughter's. Aimee would love it. They both would. Which would make it even more horrible if they had to leave. "I think she took the news about who she is, and who you are, really well, don't you?"

"She's tough. She's going to be okay, Sera." Trent carefully pushed himself up until he leaned against the headboard. "Sera, I don't want to do this alone anymore. I almost died today, would have died, if not for you."

"You mean you would have died if I hadn't made you go to the hospital and get stitches."

"Who knows how many more demons could be in this town."

Sera laughed. "Oh, yeah, our little neck of the swamp is just a hotbed of demon activity."

"Well, it is kind of dark, dank and moldy. Prime demon-breeding territory. Not to mention that voodoo priestess and her cult. All the more reason you should come with me."

Sera sighed. "I don't know, Trent."

He took her hand and held it across Aimee, who was still

sleeping peacefully. "I don't want to waste another minute wondering what if things had been different. Alone we are vulnerable, but together we're a family, we're invincible."

He slid off the bed beside her, then took her hand once more and dropped to one knee. "I love you. And I love Aimee. I always have. I never should have left, Sera. Will you marry me?"

Sera's throat tightened as tears brimmed in her eyes.

"Say yes, Mom," Aimee said, her eyes wide open and a huge grin splitting her face.

Surprised, Sera laughed. She certainly couldn't say no to both of them.

"Yes, Trent, I'll marry you."

* * * * *

nocturne™

COMING NEXT MONTH

Available OCTOBER 25, 2011

#123 LORD OF THE WOLFYN
Royal House of Shadows
Jessica Andersen

#124 DARK SINS AND DESERT SANDS
Mythica
Stephanie Draven

You can find more information on upcoming
Harlequin® titles, free excerpts and more at
www.HarlequinInsideRomance.com.

REQUEST YOUR FREE BOOKS!

2 FREE NOVELS FROM THE PARANORMAL ROMANCE COLLECTION PLUS 2 FREE GIFTS!

YES! Please send me 2 FREE novels from the Paranormal Romance Collection and my 2 FREE gifts (gifts are worth about $10). After receiving them, if I don't wish to receive any more books, I can return the shipping statement marked "cancel." If I don't cancel, I will receive 4 brand-new novels every month and be billed just $21.42 in the U.S. or $23.46 in Canada. That's a saving of at least 21% off the cover price of all 4 books. It's quite a bargain! Shipping and handling is just 50¢ per book in the U.S. and 75¢ per book in Canada.* I understand that accepting the 2 free books and gifts places me under no obligation to buy anything. I can always return a shipment and cancel at any time. Even if I never buy another book, the two free books and gifts are mine to keep forever.

237/337 HDN FEL2

Name	(PLEASE PRINT)

Address		Apt. #

City	State/Prov.	Zip/Postal Code

Signature (if under 18, a parent or guardian must sign)

Mail to the Reader Service:
IN U.S.A.: P.O. Box 1867, Buffalo, NY 14240-1867
IN CANADA: P.O. Box 609, Fort Erie, Ontario L2A 5X3

Not valid for current subscribers to the Paranormal Romance Collection or Harlequin® Nocturne™ books.

Want to try two free books from another line?
Call 1-800-873-8635 or visit www.ReaderService.com.

* Terms and prices subject to change without notice. Prices do not include applicable taxes. Sales tax applicable in N.Y. Canadian residents will be charged applicable taxes. Offer not valid in Quebec. This offer is limited to one order per household. All orders subject to credit approval. Credit or debit balances in a customer's account(s) may be offset by any other outstanding balance owed by or to the customer. Please allow 4 to 6 weeks for delivery. Offer available while quantities last.

Your Privacy—The Reader Service is committed to protecting your privacy. Our Privacy Policy is available online at www.ReaderService.com or upon request from the Reader Service.

We make a portion of our mailing list available to reputable third parties that offer products we believe may interest you. If you prefer that we not exchange your name with third parties, or if you wish to clarify or modify your communication preferences, please visit us at www.ReaderService.com/consumerschoice or write to us at Reader Service Preference Service, P.O. Box 9062, Buffalo, NY 14269. Include your complete name and address.

PARA11

Harlequin® Special Edition® is thrilled to present a new installment in USA TODAY *bestselling author RaeAnne Thayne's reader-favorite miniseries,* THE COWBOYS OF COLD CREEK.

Join the excitement as we meet the Bowmans—four siblings who lost their parents but keep family ties alive in Pine Gulch. First up is Trace. Only two things get under this rugged lawman's skin: beautiful women and secrets. And in Rebecca Parsons, he finds both!

Read on for a sneak peek of
CHRISTMAS IN COLD CREEK.
Available November 2011 from Harlequin® Special Edition®.

On impulse, he unfolded himself from the bar stool. "Need a hand?"

"Thank you! I…" She lifted her gaze from the floor to his jeans and then raised her eyes. When she identified him her hazel eyes turned from grateful to unfriendly and cold, as if he'd somehow thrown the broken glasses at her head.

He also thought he saw a glimmer of panic in those interesting depths, which instantly stirred his curiosity like cream swirling through coffee.

"I've got it, Officer. Thank you." Her voice was several degrees colder than the whirl of sleet outside the windows.

Despite her protests, he knelt down beside her and began to pick up shards of broken glass. "No problem. Those trays can be slippery."

This close, he picked up the scent of her, something fresh and flowery that made him think of a mountain meadow on a July afternoon. She had a soft, lush mouth and for one brief, insane moment, he wanted to push aside that stray lock of hair slipping from her ponytail and taste her. Apparently he needed to spend a lot less time working and a great deal *more* time recreating with the opposite sex if he could have sudden random fantasies about a woman he wasn't even inclined to like, pretty or not.

"I'm Trace Bowman. You must be new in town."

She didn't answer immediately and he could almost see the wheels turning in her head. Why the hesitancy? And why that little hint of unease he could see clouding the edge of her gaze? His presence was obviously making her uncomfortable and Trace couldn't help wondering why.

"Yes. We've been here a few weeks."

"Well, I'm just up the road about four lots, in the white house with the cedar shake roof, if you or your daughter need anything." He smiled at her as he picked up the last shard of glass and set it on her tray.

Definitely a story there, he thought as she hurried away. He just might need to dig a little into her background to find out why someone with fine clothes and nice jewelry, and who so obviously didn't have experience as a waitress, would be here slinging hash at The Gulch. Was she running away from someone? A bad marriage?

So…Rebecca Parsons. Not Becky. An intriguing woman. It had been a long time since one of those had crossed his path here in Pine Gulch.

Trace won't rest until he finds out Rebecca's secret, but will he still have that same attraction to her once he does? Find out in CHRISTMAS IN COLD CREEK. Available November 2011 from Harlequin® Special Edition®.

ROMANTIC
SUSPENSE

CARLA CASSIDY
Cowboy's Triplet Trouble

Jake Johnson, the eldest of his triplet brothers, is stunned
when Grace Sinclair turns up on his family's ranch declaring
Jake's younger and irresponsible brother as the father of her
triplets. When Grace's life is threatened, Jake finds himself
fighting a powerful attraction and a need to protect. But as
the threats hit closer to home, Jake begins to wonder
if someone on the ranch is out to kill Grace....

A brand-new Top Secret Deliveries story!

Available in November wherever books are sold!

Harlequin *Desire*

ALWAYS POWERFUL, PASSIONATE AND PROVOCATIVE.

**NEW YORK TIMES AND USA TODAY
BESTSELLING AUTHOR**

BRENDA JACKSON

**PRESENTS A BRAND-NEW TALE
OF SEDUCTION**

TEMPTATION

TEXAS CATTLEMAN'S CLUB: THE SHOWDOWN

Millionaire security expert and rancher Zeke Travers always separates emotion from work. Until a case leads him to Sheila Hopkins—and the immediate, scorching heat that leaped between them. Suddenly, Zeke is tempted to break the rules. And it's only a matter of time before he gives in....

Available November wherever books are sold.

Harlequin Presents®

brings you

USA TODAY Bestselling Author

Penny Jordan

Part of the new miniseries

RUSSIAN RIVALS

Demidov vs. Androvonov—let the most merciless of men win...

Kiryl Androvonov

The Russian oligarch has one rival: billionaire Vasilii Demidov. Luckily, Vasilii has an Achilles' heel—his younger, overprotected, beautiful half sister, Alena...

Vasilii Demidov

After losing his sister to his bitter rival, Vasilii is far too cynical to ever trust a woman, not even his secretary Laura. Never did she expect to be at the ruthless Russian's mercy....

The rivalry begins in...

THE MOST COVETED PRIZE—November
THE POWER OF VASILII—December

Available wherever
Harlequin Presents® books are sold.

www.Harlequin.com

HPI3023